Catherine Tinley has loved reading and writing since childhood, and has a particular fondness for love, romance and happy endings. She lives in Ireland with her husband, children, dog and kitten, and can be reached at catherinetinley.com, as well as through Facebook and @CatherineTinley on Twitter.

Also by Catherine Tinley

The Chadcombe Marriages miniseries

Waltzing with the Earl
The Captain's Disgraced Lady

Discover more at millsandboon.co.uk.

THE CAPTAIN'S DISGRACED LADY

Catherine Tinley

MILLS & BOON

First published in Great Britain 2017
by Mills & Boon, an imprint of HarperCollins*Publishers*
1 London Bridge Street, London, SE1 9GF

Large Print edition 2018

© 2017 Catherine Tinley

ISBN: 978-0-263-07474-1

MIX
Paper from
responsible sources
FSC
www.fsc.org   FSC™ C007454

This book is produced from independently certified FSC™ paper to ensure responsible forest management. For more information visit www.harpercollins.co.uk/green.

Printed and bound in Great Britain
by CPI Group (UK) Ltd, Croydon, CR0 4YY

For my family—
Andrew, Danny, Aoife and Maeve—
with love.

And for my friends Bryan and Beryl, for
loyalty and love through good times and bad.

Chapter One

Dover—March 1815

'Come along, Mama—it's this way.'

Juliana moved confidently along the wharf, ignoring the rain, the sailors, dockworkers and passengers. She wore a fashionable travelling gown of dark-green merino, which clung to her form, and a fetching hat with a small feather stuck in it at a jaunty angle.

'You there!' Her voice was strong, clear and assured.

'Yes, miss?' The docker doffed his hat, despite the rain.

'We require a carriage—a *good* carriage. It will take us to Ashford tonight, then on towards Surrey.'

'Yes, miss. Right away, miss.'

'The porter will bring our luggage. We shall require a place to wait, out of the rain, while our luggage is brought from the ship.'

'Er, yes, miss. You won't want to go to the Swan—it's not for the likes of you. You'd be better suited to the King's Head.' As he spoke, the docker indicated the King's Head, failing to conceal his horror at the thought of two gently bred ladies wandering into the Swan in broad daylight. Juliana tried not to smile.

'Thank you.' Her voice gentled. 'See, Mama? Did I not tell you all would be well?'

Her mama did not look convinced. She glanced around fearfully, clinging to her reticule as if convinced it would be stolen from her at any moment. Juliana sighed inwardly. Her mama's anxiety was even worse than she had anticipated. She needed to get her indoors and offer her reassurance. Ignoring the spring rain, which was getting heavier by the minute, Juliana marched purposefully to the inn, her mama following in her wake.

The King's Head had seen better days. The sign over the door was a little faded, as was the wool rug on the floor of the taproom. The wooden panelling and gloomy portraits on the walls gave an air of an age gone by, but the stone floor was clean and the brass taps shone.

The landlord, assessing their quality at a glance, bustled forward to welcome the two ladies. Inviting them to follow him out of the common taproom to the cosy parlour, he asked for their requirements—

tea, cakes, and the fire to be built up. As usual, Juliana took charge, making her requests politely but firmly. They were to have sole use of the parlour. The tea should be served very hot, with an additional pot of hot water.

Mama sank into the nearest chair with an attitude of great relief.

Juliana immediately went to her. 'Oh, Mama! You look fagged to death. And I have dragged you across the sea when you never wanted to come. You know I could have travelled to visit Charlotte with just a maid to accompany me. You did not have to come! Here, let me put this cushion behind you. Your tea will be here directly.' She threw an imperious glance at the landlord, who quickly absented himself in pursuit of the hottest tea he could procure. *Good!* Now she could spend the next hour or so seeing to her mama's comfort, soothing her and ensuring she was relaxed enough to cope with the next part of the journey.

Juliana knew exactly what her mama required, for had she not done this many times before? Mama needed solitude—the parlour door closed against strangers, along with hot tea and reassuring words.

Mama waited until the door had closed behind the landlord, before declaring tremulously, 'I do not mind, Juliana. Well, that is to say… I cannot claim

I *wanted* to come, but I could not let you travel by yourself, all the way across the sea. Why, you have never been to England before!'

Juliana sighed, remembering the many hours of agonised debating. Mama had wanted to accompany her, yet had also *not* wanted to. Juliana had bitten her lip, not having wanted to influence her mother, content to travel with her or without her. It had been months before Mama had made a final decision.

'And I have told you before, I can look after myself, Mama. Why, I have travelled from Brussels to school in Vienna with just a chambermaid for company, many times!'

'That is different.'

'How is it different? I—but, no, let us not go over this again. You are here and you are weary, and I should make you comfortable. Should you like to lie down for a while?'

'I confess I still feel as though the ground is rolling under my feet, as it was on that awful boat! I declare I thought we would all end up in the sea, it was so stormy! I should like to sit here for a little while, before we continue on.'

Juliana looked at her mother doubtfully. The crossing had been an easy one, the sea smooth. The rain had only started as they approached Dover. Mama had stayed in the cabin the whole time, not actually being sick, but expressing strong disapproval of the sea and everything associated with it. Juliana had paced the deck, exhilarating in her first sea voyage, inhaling the sea, immersing herself in the experience.

Perhaps this was why they had never travelled home to England before. Although Juliana was used to her mama's nerves, she did seem to be reacting particularly badly to her sea journey. Mama rarely left their home city of Brussels, but had made the long journey to visit Juliana in Vienna the previous year, accompanied by her devoted maid, Sandrine. Strange to think Mama had grown up here, in England, yet Juliana had never even visited.

Until now. Juliana's dear friend Charlotte—her best friend from the school for young ladies—had moved to England and was now married, and Juliana had not seen her for more than a year.

Tea was the solution, Juliana decided. Mama would rest here awhile, in solitude, then they could continue their journey.

Captain Harry Fanton, darling of the Thirtieth Foot Regiment, strode into the King's Head, glad to get out of the rain. The sea crossing had been smooth enough, but he was frustrated at having to return to England when his fellow officers were busy preparing to take on Napoleon again. His colleague Evans followed diffidently. Harry was rarely seen without a smile or a light-hearted remark, but today, his usual good humour seemed to have left him. Harry drummed his fingers impatiently on the high bar. 'Landlord!'

Harry had lodged many times in the King's Head and the landlord recognised him and his colleague immediately.

Ignoring the landlord's effusive greeting, Harry informed him, curtly, that they required overnight rooms, as well as the use of the parlour.

Wringing the corner of his apron, the landlord explained haltingly that the parlour was in use, that two ladies—a mother and daughter just off the packet from Calais—had need of the parlour for an hour while they awaited their carriage and—

'Tosh!' said Harry. 'Why, we have shared the parlour before, with many fellow travellers! We shall speak to these ladies and all will be well! Come, Evans...' he nudged his portly, sandy-haired friend '...follow me!'

Knowing his way about, Harry led the way unerringly to the parlour. The landlord stayed at the end of the hallway, still clutching his apron for comfort. Ignoring him, Harry scratched on the parlour door. His friend, experiencing sudden qualms, baulked.

'Dash it, Harry, we need not intrude. Perhaps we should have stayed in the taproom. The beer is the same there!'

Harry brushed off his concerns. 'Nonsense, Evans! I have a fancy for the parlour and its fire. I will handle this—trust me.'

On hearing the command to enter, Harry opened the door. He paused to survey the scene. On a chair beside the fire sat a faded, middle-aged lady with fair hair and gentle blue eyes in a pale face. Standing beside her chair was a young woman, who—

Lord!

She was strikingly beautiful. Her height was average, but she seemed taller—something to do with the air of suppressed energy about her. She was as dark as her mother was fair, with glossy brown curls, a stubborn chin and expressive chocolate eyes, framed by thick black lashes. His own eyes swept over her, noting the confident stance, white neck and shapely figure. A vision!

He smiled—a smile his friends would recognise. They called it the Dazzler, for the effect it had on young ladies.

He made an elegant bow. 'Ladies! Allow me to present myself! I—'

'You have made a mistake. This is the wrong room.'

'Pardon me?' He blinked.

'I said…' the young lady spoke slowly, as if he had trouble understanding '…this is the wrong room. You should not be here. This room is taken.'

Beside him, Evans gave a snort of laughter, quickly suppressed. Harry's spine stiffened. He would not be made to look a fool in front of one of his lieutenants!

'This room,' he returned, speaking equally patiently, 'is a public room. It is not a private parlour. Therefore—' he stepped forward '—we will join you.'

'You must know,' she insisted, through gritted teeth, 'I cannot physically remove you. Hence I must ask you, if you are a gentleman, to allow my mother and me the private use of this room.'

'An interesting dilemma. For you cannot know if I am a gentleman or not, as we have not even been introduced. I am—'

'I do not wish to know who you are! I wish only that you leave this instant!' Incensed, she stamped a little foot. Her mother, who had been becoming increasingly agitated, chose this moment to intervene.

'My dear Juliana, they are doing no harm. They have been out in the rain, like us, and perhaps also need the warmth of the fire.'

Two points of high colour appeared in Juliana's cheeks, as she heard her mother's words. They were gently uttered, but delivered a public rebuke, nevertheless. Harry almost felt sorry for her. Almost.

She was not to be defeated. 'Very well, you may remain. We shall remove ourselves to the taproom!' She swept towards them, all grace and haughtiness. 'Mama, we shall allow these men to have the parlour.' She clearly expected her mother to follow.

'Oh, no! My dear, please!' Juliana's mama shot a look of entreaty at the soldiers.

Harry knew himself to be defeated. He spoke coldly. 'There is no need for you to leave. We shall retire to the taproom.' He bowed politely to the older lady. 'I shall cause you no further distress, ma'am.'

He turned to Juliana. 'Miss.' It was the shallowest of bows, designed to show his disdain.

She responded with the slightest nod of her head, mirroring his iciness, but her eyes blazed.

Evans, who had been squirming in agitated silence, made his bow to the two ladies, then followed his friend out of the room. They closed the door behind them.

'Well!' Juliana exploded in a flurry of movement, pacing up and down the parlour. 'What an insufferable man!'

'Now, Juliana—'

'So rude! So arrogant! Thinking he could just burst in here, uninvited—'

'They did knock, my dear. You bade them enter.'

'No, but—well, yes, I bade them enter, but only because he knocked. I did not bid him to *stay*!'

'It is not seemly to draw attention to yourself in such a way.'

'Oh, stuff, Mama! What should I do? Allow people to dominate me? Never!'

'We could have shared the parlour with them, you know.'

'Mama, you know you could not have rested properly with strangers in the room!'

'But you must not appear *hoydenish*, Juliana. We are in England now and it is important you are not *noticed*.'

'I care not if I am noticed or not. But I will not stand by and have your comfort disturbed by some boorish soldiers!'

Mama sighed. 'I do not mind, Juliana.'

Juliana put her hands to her head in exasperation. 'You know I am right, Mama. Why do you say you do not mind, when we both know that you mind very much?'

Mama had no answer to this. Looking at her confused face, Juliana relented. Taking Mama's limp hand, she spoke kindly to her. 'Mama, you cannot always please everyone. Sometimes you must think of yourself. Why, you are so kind, so yielding, that you would be insulted by every *demi-beau* and dunned by every tradesman in Brussels! How I used to hate it, when I was younger, watching them be rude to you or try to cheat you with false accounting. If I were a boy I'd have called them out over it! But you are so *good*, Mama. They sense your weakness.'

'I do not believe those young men offered us any insult or inconvenience, Juliana. Oh, how I wish you would think before you act!'

Juliana was only half-listening. She moved to the window and stared out, lost in thought. 'I swore when I was twelve I would grow up and take care of you.'

She would never forget the day she had made that vow. She had entered their little sitting room in the rented house in Brussels, to find her mama crying, sheets of paper with numbers on them scattered across the table. Twelve-year-old Juliana had been shocked. 'What is wrong, Mama?'

'Oh, Julie-Annie,' her mama had said. 'It is just these bills—tiresome grown-up things. I think the butcher has made a mistake with his reckoning again, but this time I have not the funds to pay the difference.'

'What difference, Mama? What do you mean?' Juliana had never been interested in the accounts before. Mama meticulously counted out the money every month and gave some of it to the landlord, some to the butcher, some to the other tradesmen. It had always been that way. Juliana's father, a soldier, had died of a fever when Juliana was just a baby, so there had only ever been the two of them.

'It says here that we had a haunch of venison, which I know we did not, for I would surely remember if we ate anything so extravagant. Well, I know we had only the bacon and the squabs this week, and the mutton for stew.'

Juliana was shocked. 'You mean the butcher has added something to the list that we did not have?'

She took the bill from her mother's trembling hand. There it was. Venison. They hadn't eaten venison since April, when they had been invited to the Vicar's house for dinner.

'It must be a mistake,' said Mama. 'He does make mistakes, sometimes.'

But it wasn't a mistake. Standing there, in that little parlour, with its faded French rug and damson-coloured curtains, Juliana suddenly understood something for the first time. The butcher was cheating her mother. Cheating both of them.

In an instant, Juliana suddenly made sense of things she had seen and heard before. Some people—unscrupulous people—would see her mother's gentle nature as an opportunity to cheat her. Mama was so good, so giving, so pliant. But where she saw goodness, others would see opportunity.

'He is cheating you, Mama! Why should you allow him to do such a thing?'

'Oh, no, Juliana! It is an honest mistake, that is all. I shall not even mention it.'

Looking into her mother's angelic, trusting blue eyes, Juliana knew there was no point in trying to persuade her mother of the butcher's deceit. She would simply not believe it.

In that moment, Juliana understood something else. She and Mama were different. Her twelve-year-old self could not have explained how, or why. But she, Juliana, was different. She saw what Mama could not, *would* not see. And she could act.

'I will go with you to the butcher's tomorrow, Mama.'

This time, when Mrs Milford went to settle her reckoning with the butcher, her daughter was with her. The child calmly explained there had been a mistake with the bill. She made the point in full ear-shot of three other customers, who tutted in shock that such a thing should happen. The butcher looked into the girl's resolute, angry gaze and immediately realised he had met his match. He apologised pro-fusely to Mrs Milford, thanked her daughter through gritted teeth for pointing out the error, and assured them it would not happen again.

It hadn't. And Juliana had been her mother's guardian ever since.

She turned back, returning to the present and the parlour in Dover. Her mother was pressing her hands to her temples. 'Mama, are you unwell?'

'Just a little headache, my dear.'

'Oh, no! What shall I do? Would you like a tisane? Some tea? Where is that tea?' She moved to the door. 'Landlord!'

He bustled towards the parlour, followed by a sullen serving girl carrying a tray.

'At last! Please set it on the table. Thank you.'

'Your carriage is prepared, miss, and ready to leave at your convenience.'

Juliana gave him a grateful smile. 'Thank you.' Now Mama, finally, could begin to settle.

Chapter Two

An hour later, the ladies left the parlour, Mama, thankfully, now easy and calm. Juliana rang the landlord's bell in the taproom. She pointedly ignored the two soldiers, who sat at a table opposite the door, enjoying tankards of foaming beer. The one who had spoken to her—the tall one with the dark hair and piercing blue eyes—lifted his head and watched her. She could *feel* the intensity of his gaze.

The landlord appeared from the back room, all bustle and busyness. 'I am sorry to keep you waiting, miss.'

'I should like to pay the reckoning.'

'Yes, Miss.' The landlord glanced at Juliana's mother and his expression changed. 'Ma'am, you are unwell! May I be of assistance?'

Juliana turned quickly. 'Mama!' Her mother looked dreadful. Her normally pale skin was ashen and she was gasping for breath. She seemed to be staring fixedly at a painting on the facing wall—a portrait of a stern-looking army general.

Juliana took Mama's arm and gently led her to a nearby settle. The two soldiers, who had leapt to their feet, approached with concerned expressions.

'Oh, dear! I am sorry! I do not wish to make a fuss!' Mama's voice was faint and trembled slightly.

'It is nothing, Mama. You see, you can sit here, until you feel better.' Juliana was pleased to note that her own voice remained steady, though inside she was distressed. What on earth was wrong with her? And what was she to do?

'How may I be of assistance?' The dark-haired soldier spoke softly.

'We do not need your assistance!' Juliana hissed. Gathering herself, she added a reluctant, 'Thank you.'

'I think you do. Unless—' his blue eyes pierced hers '—you wish to fetch the doctor yourself?'

'The landlord will do it.' Mama probably did need a doctor.

'The landlord cannot leave his inn. And we saw his manservant riding off as we arrived.'

'Gone to the market,' confirmed the landlord gloomily. 'Won't be back 'til nearly sundown.'

Her mother had closed her eyes and seemed to be

concentrating on breathing slowly. Juliana bit her lip. She knew herself to be at a standstill.

'Quite.' There was satisfaction in the soldier's tone. Juliana looked at him. Was that a gleam of enjoyment in his eyes? She stood straighter, then addressed the other soldier, the sandy-haired one.

'Sir, might I request your assistance?' She ignored the arrogant soldier completely. 'I would be grateful if you could fetch the doctor to assist my mother.'

His eyes bulged. 'Anything! I am at your service!' He bowed. 'Lieutenant Roderick Evans, of the Thirtieth Foot.'

Juliana inclined her head. 'I am Miss Milford. My mother, Mrs Milford.'

He gestured towards his friend, as protocol demanded. 'Captain Harry Fanton, also of the Thirtieth.'

Captain Fanton bowed ironically. She wasn't sure how he managed it, but the bow was definitely ironic. *Stop!* She should be concentrating on Mama. She rubbed her mother's white hands, speaking softly to her.

'Mama, this gentleman will fetch the doctor. All will be well.'

'No! I do not need to see a doctor. I am well.'

Juliana looked at her closely. In truth, her mother did look a little better. She bade Lieutenant Evans wait, then sat by Mama's side for a few minutes. She closed her eyes. Slowly, the colour began to return to her cheeks. Juliana's own heart also began to calm a little.

Her mother opened her eyes, a frown appearing as she realised she was being watched by the two soldiers and the landlord. All bore similar expressions of concern, but Juliana was conscious that Mama would hate to be the focus of attention. She turned to Juliana, her eyes pleading. 'I am ready, Juliana. I wish to travel on. Let us go to the coach.'

'If you are certain, Mama, then we will go.' At least in the carriage, her mother would be safe from the kind eyes of strangers. But what if she were truly ill? Oh, how Juliana wished she knew what to do!

Mrs Milford stood, though slowly and carefully. Seeing it, Juliana frowned.

Captain Fanton still looked concerned. 'Mrs Milford, may I enquire—were you ill during the crossing?'

'Indeed I was, Captain. The crossing was very rough, you see.'

'Then let me advise you. Stay in Dover tonight. The worst thing you can do is to travel onwards by carriage. It will remind you too much of the movement of the sea.'

'Oh, but Juliana says we need to travel on tonight. Our rooms are booked in an inn twenty miles from here.'

'Twenty miles!' His jaw set. 'I am concerned you are not well enough to travel.'

Juliana felt her anger rise. How dare he interfere? What did he know of her mother or their needs? She was having trouble enough trying to decide what was best, without an interfering stranger trying to influence Mama!

'I thank you, sir...' her voice dripped with contempt '...but we have no need of your advice. Or your concern.'

He sent her a cold look. 'I intended no insult. I meant only to help.'

Mrs Milford spoke, shakily. 'Thank you for your kindness, Captain Fanton, but I am quite well.'

Juliana bit her lip. Mama was not recovered, it was clear, and that insufferable man might be right. Her mother would surely benefit from a quiet evening in the inn, rather than a long coach journey, but how was she to back down now?

'Landlord, we shall retire once more to your parlour. You may tell the coachman to wait. Lieutenant, I should be grateful if you would fetch the doctor.'

'Oh, no, Juliana, but we must travel on. Our room

is reserved and if we do not leave soon we shall be too late.'

'We shall discuss it in private, Mama.'

'Landlord! Do you have another chamber free—one suitable for these ladies?' Captain Fanton took it upon himself to question their host. Juliana's fury increased. *Really!*

The landlord confirmed it.

Captain Fanton addressed Mrs Milford. 'We can vouch for the rooms here in the King's Head, for we have stayed here many times.' He glanced at Lieutenant Evans, who shuffled in discomfort, clearly unwilling to be drawn into the battle of wills between his commanding officer and a young lady they had never met before.

Juliana was now fuming. This was intolerable interference! What business was it of his what they did?

'If I wish for your opinion, on inns, or any other matter, then I shall ask for it!' She sent him a daggered glance, then turned back to her mother. 'Mama, come with me to the parlour.'

Mrs Milford, always polite, thanked the two men before allowing Juliana to take her arm and lead her from the taproom. Juliana ignored them.

The landlord followed them back to the parlour, where Juliana immediately saw Mama settled again in the chair beside the fire. She then quizzed the landlord on all the possible inns in the area. None, it seemed, would suit their purposes, either being full, as far as he knew, or unsuitable for the Quality.

'Then we have no choice. We must stay here.'

The landlord, who had clearly been troubled by the altercations between the fiery young lady and Captain Fanton, confirmed this with an air of resignation.

'You may tell the coachman to return in the morning. We require a chamber with two beds, and I shall inspect the sheets.' He nodded resignedly and left, in his haste omitting to close the door behind him.

Juliana turned to her mother. 'How are you feeling now, Mama?'

'Much, much better. Juliana, I do wish we had travelled on.'

'Captain Fanton did not advise it.' There was a hard edge to Juliana's voice.

'Did you dislike the Captain? I thought him a charming young gentleman. So obliging!'

'I did not find him charming in the least! In fact, I found him conceited, rude and arrogant! He had no business interfering in—'

She broke off, as the object of her tirade appeared in the doorway, her mother's reticule in his hand.

'Mrs Milford, I believe you dropped this.' Captain Fanton's voice dripped with ice, his jaw set into a hard line. His eyes, connecting with Juliana's, flashed fury.

He marched smartly across to her mother's chair, handed her the reticule, bowed and left.

Juliana stood stock still for a moment, as the realisation of her own rudeness washed over her. Her face flushed. She put both hands up to cover her embarrassment.

'Juliana! How could you?' Her mother's voice signalled her shock.

'Oh, I know, I know,' Juliana groaned. 'But how was I to know he would come sneaking up on me, eavesdropping at the door?'

'He was not eavesdropping! Juliana, I do not understand what has come over you. Indeed, I am most disappointed in you today and now you have insulted that young man. How many times have I told you that your behaviour must be beyond reproach? I knew no good would come of going to England. I just *knew* it!' Mama began to cry.

Juliana rushed to her mother and knelt by her side.

'Oh, Mama, indeed I am sorry! My dashed temper got the better of me—and it has not done so in years! I can only blame the long journey and his rudeness earlier. Perhaps I, too, am more tired than I knew. I do not normally behave so, you know this!'

Her mother's eyes were sorrowful. 'I am surprised, Daughter. If there is one thing I wished, it was to raise you to be a lady, not a termagant! You know how hard it was for me as a widow, raising you by myself. And you know that you *must* give no reason for anyone to question your behaviour!' Her mother began to sob gently into a lace-edged handkerchief.

Shaken by the knowledge that she was the cause of her mother's distress, Juliana just managed to hold back her own tears. Over the years Mama had drummed it into her that she must be ladylike, circumspect, and wary at all times. She must not draw attention to herself. Her reputation was a fragile thing. The consequences of attracting gossip could be fatal to her place in good company.

There were reasons, her mother always said, that she couldn't divulge, why Juliana must be even *more* careful than other young ladies. *What reasons?* Juliana had asked, many times. Her mother had resolutely refused to answer.

Conscious of her mother's frailty, Juliana had complied—though it had frequently cost her to hold her tongue and behave properly. Today's lapse was inexcusable. She spent so much of her energies devoting herself to protecting her mother, yet now she had troubled her. 'I am sorry, Mama. I truly am.'

Her mother, unable to withstand her daughter's remorse, stroked Juliana's dark curls.

'I know, Julie-Annie.'

'I hate it when you are disappointed in me.'

'You should apologise to him.' Mama held her gaze evenly.

Juliana swallowed hard. 'I know.'

'Invite them to join us in the parlour. They can dine with us later.'

'Must I?' Her mother's stern look was enough. 'Very well. But you cannot force me to like him.'

Steeling herself to face him, Juliana moved swiftly along the narrow hallway to the taproom. There he was, glowering into his beer. Lieutenant Evans had gone—presumably to fetch the doctor.

Juliana lifted her chin. 'Captain Fanton, I must speak with you.'

He looked at her. His eyes narrowed. 'Well?'

Such insolence! She clenched her fists by her side, managing to hold back the angry retort on her lips.

Deliberately, he leaned back in his chair, stretching out his legs. Long, sturdy legs, she noted absentmindedly. The thin breeches hugged his long limbs, revealing the curve and sweep of well-developed, powerful muscles. She had heard that some men filled their stockings with sawdust, to falsify muscular calves. Not this man! She felt herself flushing, unaccountably.

Ignoring his attempt to disconcert her, she pressed on. 'I wish to apologise. You should not have had to hear my angry words.'

A gleam of surprise lit his dark-blue eyes. 'Are you apologising for saying what you said, or only for allowing me to *hear* your opinion?'

Oh, he was sharp-witted, this one.

'I would have preferred you hadn't heard me, but...' she sighed ruefully '... I should not have said those things. My anger got the better of me.'

'A frank apology, then. I admire plain speaking and will accept it.' He offered his hand. Reluctantly, she took it.

His hand was warm, his grip firm without being crushing. She pulled her hand away as soon as she could and noticed a wolf-like smile lurking in the corner of his eyes. Her hackles rose again. A lifetime of protecting herself and Mama had made her wary.

'My mother bids me invite you and Lieutenant Evans to join us in the parlour for dinner in one hour,' she informed him.

'And what would you bid me do?' His voice was soft, warm, confusing.

'I would prefer to dine in private, with only my

mother. I do not wish to prolong my acquaintance with you!'

He looked surprised for an instant, then threw his head back and laughed. Despite her frustration, she could not help but notice, in that moment, that he was actually very handsome. Acknowledging it— though she had realised it from the first moment she had laid eyes on him—caused her a great deal of annoyance. Why couldn't his face match his character?

'You are refreshingly honest, Miss Milford. But, I must point out, it seems your mother holds a different view.'

'My mother is unwell. She would be better resting quietly in the parlour than conversing with strangers, which will tire her out! But then, your aim from the start has been to gain access to the parlour!'

His eyes flashed. She had scored a hit then? *Good.*

'Indeed?' he said coolly. 'I did not think you cared so much for your mother's comfort earlier, when you were bustling her towards the carriage when she was clearly unwell! Or when you wanted to take her away from the warmth, to the taproom, rather than share the parlour!'

Juliana gasped. 'And what business is it of yours, may I ask?'

'In a sense, none. But I am used to considering the needs of those around me and I saw how ill she looked in this very room!'

'Are you suggesting I fail to consider my mother's needs?' She was livid. No one had ever dared suggest such a thing. Why, she had devoted all her energies to looking after her mother!

'That isn't what I said.'

No, but he had certainly implied it! *How dared he?*

'I shall thank you to keep your opinions to yourself! I do not wish to discuss my own personal business with you!'

He threw her a look filled with challenge. 'And yet you just have.'

'That was a mistake. It will not happen again.'

Juliana had had enough. Without a word of goodbye, she turned and strode away. She swept regally across the taproom, head held high, then collided inelegantly with the serving girl, who almost dropped her basket. Juliana rocked on her heels and put a hand out to touch the table in order to prevent herself from falling. Lord, what a time to be clumsy!

She could feel his eyes on her and knew he was laughing. This was fast turning into one of the worst days of her life. She mumbled an apology to the girl and scuttled out of the room as fast as she could.

Harry stood, filled with agitation. Absent-mindedly informing the serving girl that, no, he did not require another beer, he began to pace around the taproom. *Damn Miss Milford!* She had made him lose his temper and he had spoken hastily. He, who prided himself on his self-control.

It had been hard-earned, this ability to detach himself from situations so he could always act coolly and rationally. It had taken years of relentless practice and self-discipline. Anger—like fear—was simply not permitted in his gut. He knew the risks of too much emotion. These days, it was almost impossible for an insolent private or an untidy lieutenant to cause him to bristle. He paused. *Until today.*

He had been aware of his own frustration at being forced to return to England. He had not, however, expected his own temper to be so damn short!

Provocation. That was his defence. The fiery Miss Milford was altogether too insolent and fearless with her words and manner. The disdain in her eyes still irked him now. Such insubordination would not be tolerated for a minute in the army. Men had been flogged for less! And for more…

He checked himself. *Insubordination?* Had he somehow expected her to obey him, to take his commands as though he were her senior officer? He sighed ruefully. Yes, he had. Because he was a man and she was a young woman, he had expected her to defer to him and had been shocked when she hadn't. He also, he realised, felt strangely protective of her. His instincts told him Mrs Milford was heavily reliant on her daughter and that, at times, this was something of a heavy burden for the young woman to bear. Not that she was helpless! Along with foolish amounts of courage, her evident wit and intelligence had been clearly displayed.

He thought he'd had her at a standstill when she realised she would need someone to fetch the doctor, but she had outwitted him by asking Evans. Strangely, the thought gave him a sense of satisfaction, not dissimilar to finding an opponent who could genuinely challenge him in chess. A worthy foe, then.

The fact that she also happened to be one of the most stunning women he'd ever met had not escaped his attention, either. Even now, he could picture her perfectly clearly in his mind's eye. A beautiful opponent, and one who had stirred his emotions, and his body, as much as his mind.

She had challenged him and bested him, but he was not without small victories either. She would be forced to dine with them tonight, against her inclination. He wondered if he could charm her.

He reflected again on their battle of wits. *Damn it!* She had made him say unforgivable things. He recalled her face as he had accused her of not caring for her mother's comfort. Beneath the anger, she had looked stricken. Harry squirmed uncomfortably.

How could he possibly understand her motivations for behaving as she did? He should not have accused her so. Now, how was he to atone for it?

Chapter Three

In the hallway, Juliana paused. Leaning against the wall, she closed her eyes and tried to calm her breathing. Never had she been so incensed! She dashed away angry tears with the back of her hand.

The worst thing was, she admitted, Captain Fanton was right in a way. She had been so anxious to travel on tonight, she had failed to notice that her mother was still feeling ill. She had selfishly tried to push forward with her plans, without checking on Mama's health.

Yet, she remembered, her mother had seemed recovered as they left the parlour. She had enjoyed her tea, topped up with hot water, and had eaten two pastries with some enthusiasm. Had Mother really been hiding her illness? Or had she genuinely taken a relapse in the taproom?

Captain Fanton had looked at her with such contempt. He clearly believed her to be insensitive to her mother's needs. The fact that he had overheard her tirade didn't help. But if the man went around interfering in other people's business, then he should expect consequences from time to time.

Anger warred with guilt, both emotions swirling around inside her, making it difficult to think straight. The thought of sharing a dining table with him tonight filled her with dread. Yet Mama had set her heart on it—trying to compensate for Juliana's earlier rudeness. It was, she admitted, entirely her own fault.

The fact that Captain Fanton was one of the most attractive men she'd come across had not gone unnoticed. Something about his handsome features, knowing grin and lithe body was making her heart race and her stomach flip. *Behave!* she told her disobedient body.

Dinner would undoubtedly be difficult. But she was ready for the challenge.

'Are you feeling quite recovered, Mrs Milford?'

'Indeed I am, Captain Fanton, and I confess I am feeling a little silly for making such a fuss. Thank you for your concern, and to you, Lieutenant, for fetching the doctor.'

Evans muttered something about it being no trouble. He was clearly ill at ease and nervous, though had managed to eat four courses with a hearty diligence. 'Not accustomed to making the civil—all bachelors,' he'd mumbled apologetically when Juliana's first attempts to engage him in conversation had fallen flat. By this she'd understood he was uncomfortable in female company. Juliana felt quite sorry for him and set out to put him at ease.

She now knew most of his life story, his likes and dislikes in food and horses, and the fact that he was the only child of a lawyer and a seamstress. He had a perfectly respectable background, but confessed he was still much in awe of the gentry. He adored his commanding officer, Captain Fanton.

This, Juliana put down to Evans's obvious naïveté. Of course he would be in awe of the suave Captain, whose responses to Mama's questions had included Harrow and Cambridge, so he likely had an aristocratic background, like many army officers. Not that she was listening to their conversation. She was perfectly happy to converse with the amiable Lieutenant Evans.

However, for some reason, she did not want Mama to share too many details about herself—about their life. She had heard the Captain ask where they lived and Mama had described some details of their life in Brussels.

'So, what brings you to England?' he asked.

'We are visiting friends,' Juliana intervened quickly. 'We will return to Brussels in the summer.'

'As long as that monster, Napoleon, has been captured by then,' added Mrs Milford. 'When I heard of his escape from Elba, I declare it was the only thing that could have persuaded me to agree to Juliana's scheme of visiting England.'

Captain Fanton raised an eyebrow, looking from one woman to the other. 'Ah! So it is you, Miss Milford, who wanted this trip.'

'It was, though Mama was in agreement.' He threw her a sceptical glance, clearly unconvinced. Again, this cynicism!

'Were you really in agreement, Mrs Milford? Or did your strong-willed daughter force you?' He laughed lightly to take the sting out of his words, but Juliana knew they were sincerely meant. Mama, ever trusting, smiled in response.

Can't she see, thought Juliana, *that it is just empty charm? That he is saying it to attack me?*

'Juliana has always been strong-willed, ever since she could first speak and walk. It is her nature.'

Juliana squirmed. *Speak of another subject!* she thought.

'Indeed.' He threw a glance in Juliana's direction, his eyes dancing. Unexpectedly, her heart skipped a little—she was unsure why. 'I wish I could say you surprise me.'

'But, in this instance, her will did not overpower mine,' said Mrs Milford. 'I agreed to come to England, though I wish to return home to Brussels as soon as we can.'

'You do not think of England as home, then?'

She pondered this. 'In a way. I grew up here, so it is a part of me. But I have lived in Brussels for over twenty years and Brussels is where I am comfortable.'

'So…was your daughter born there?'

Juliana stiffened. Really, he was too inquisitive! She opened her mouth to cut off the direction of his questions, but, luckily, Mama herself changed the subject.

'Yes, she was. But I must tell you, Captain, I am surprised to see you army officers here, when Wellington has made Brussels his headquarters. The army is encamped in the towns and villages around, for we had word of it in Brussels society.'

'Indeed.' His forehead creased. 'We are sent to London on official business. We must, of course, follow orders, though it pains me to leave my friends and colleagues behind. We hope to rejoin them before long.'

'Well, if you return to Brussels, you must call on

us. I declare I should be pleased to see you both again.'

A strangled sound escaped from Juliana. She would certainly *not* be pleased to see him again! As she looked towards him, they locked eyes, an unholy gleam in his. He knew exactly what she was thinking and she was powerless to intervene—oh, how *manipulative* he was!

'Thank you, Mrs Milford. If you give me your direction, I shall be sure to call.'

'Juliana will write it down for you.'

'Will she?' He looked at Juliana, who dropped her gaze. 'Actually, if you tell me now, I shall write it down myself. I would not put Miss Milford to the trouble.'

Juliana bit her lip. He had known she had planned to write the address down incorrectly and had outfoxed her.

She lifted her head to look at him again. His eyes were dancing with glee. Despite herself, she suddenly saw the humour in the situation and the corners of her mouth turned up. He looked startled.

'So you do know how to smile then?' His voice was low, as he leaned forward to talk to her, under cover of Mrs Milford's conversation with the Lieutenant. His deep voice, so close, sent a shiver through her, though the room was warm.

'Well, what a strange question! Of course I know how to smile. I just choose when to smile.'

'That is a pity. Your smile is a powerful one.' Juliana flushed, confused by his words and warm tone. She could not, in that moment, think of anything to say.

The Captain walked to the writing desk near the window, where he lifted paper and a sharpened pen, then wrote as Mrs Milford dictated their address. Juliana took the opportunity to study him.

She had already noted his height, strong figure and ease of movement. She knew him to be handsome—this she had acknowledged even as his arrogance had incensed her. Now, unobserved, she looked at his face in more detail.

A strong profile, straight nose, good jawline. His intense blue eyes were hidden, directed to the page, but she noticed he had surprisingly long lashes, which did not at all reduce the masculinity of his looks.

As if sensing her scrutiny, he suddenly looked up. Juliana glanced away immediately.

'...shall retire. Thank you for a most enjoyable evening.' Juliana, distracted by her observations of the Captain, suddenly focused on her mother again. Mama was standing, saying goodnight.

Belatedly, Juliana also stood. She said all that was

polite, but in truth there was a great deal of confusion in her mind. The Lieutenant lifted her hand politely, thanking her for her company.

Captain Fanton was next and he actually kissed her hand, rather than simply bending over it. His lips were warm on her skin and surprisingly soft. Her heart racing, she mumbled a goodnight and followed her mother out of the room.

Later, listening to her mother's even breathing in the other bed, Juliana's thoughts returned to Captain Fanton. An attractive man, that much was evident. He had arrogance in abundance—she felt anger return as she remembered his confidence, the empty charisma by which he had expected two simpering women to give up their privacy and comfort. And his accusations towards her! Juliana could not remember the last time someone had made her feel so small, so filled with self-doubt. Somehow, he had got under her skin.

Then, the attempts to charm her mother at dinner…and he had even tried his charisma on her, in quite a different way. She shivered at the memory of his lips on her hand. The man was clearly an accomplished flirt! She might have guessed it. Charm had many forms and the bold Captain, it seemed, had acquired them all.

* * *

Harry, meantime, was finding it surprisingly difficult to sleep. Miss Milford was unlike any young lady he had met before. Beautiful, undoubtedly. But it was her manner which intrigued him. She did not flirt, or simper, or hide her feelings. She was as plain-speaking as a soldier and a disturbing contrast to the coy, coquettish ladies he was used to. He was not clear why this had disturbed him so, but was confident he would soon forget her.

Chapter Four

'Oh, it is so good to see you again!' Juliana hugged Charlotte tightly. 'It seems so long since we were at school together.'

'It has only been a year, you know,' laughed Charlotte.

'But what a year for you! Moving to England and getting married. Is your husband at home?'

'Yes, Adam is here, but out with his steward. You will meet him later.'

The two young women were seated together in the drawing room at Chadcombe, the large estate owned by Charlotte's husband, Adam, Earl of Shalford. Juliana's mother, claiming tiredness, was lying down and being fussed over by Adam's great-aunt Clara, who seemed like a darling. Mama had suffered no relapse of her illness during the remainder of their journey, though had seemed relieved their voyage was ended.

'The house is beautiful, Charlotte—and so large! How on earth are you managing as mistress of it?'

'Oh, it is fine—I enjoy it, actually. There is a lot to do—and an army of servants to manage. I love it!'

'Well,' said Juliana doubtfully, 'I am glad, for I could not imagine coping with the responsibility. It is all I can do to manage myself sometimes!'

Charlotte laughed. 'That is such a Juliana thing to say! Oh, how I've missed you!'

'I've missed you, too, Charlotte. But tell me about your husband. Is it true you are a countess now?'

'Indeed I am, though I confess I always think they are talking about someone else when people mention Lady Shalford.'

'Lady Shalford—just think! Though I must say you look and sound like the old Charlotte!'

'I don't think I have changed very much at all.'

Juliana considered this. 'Something has changed, though, Charlotte. There is something different about you.'

Charlotte looked disconcerted. 'Well, I hope I haven't changed for the worse.'

'Of course not, for I can sense already you are still as lovely—and as calm—as you ever were. Oh, how I've missed your calmness when I get myself in a scrape!'

'And we certainly had plenty of scrapes together!'

Charlotte smiled. 'Remember the time we stole the apple pie that cook had made for Herr Meindl's visit? And we had to eat a full supper as usual so the teachers didn't suspect it was us?'

'Yes! And the time you got the love letter from that Italian Count, and we had to burn it quickly because the head teacher was on her way to our chamber?'

Charlotte sighed. 'He was exceedingly romantic—and terribly tiresome! But I was pleased he actually noticed me. All the young men used to fall in love with you, Juliana.'

Juliana snorted. 'Not *all* the young men, Charlotte. Why, in Dover…' She tailed off and bit her lip.

'Juliana…' Charlotte's tone was suspicious '…you might as well tell me, for I can read you easily. What is your latest scrape?'

Juliana grimaced. 'Well, I am not sure I should tell you, for I feel quite ashamed of myself. But I was provoked beyond measure!'

'No need to give me your fierce look! Tell me the whole—who has provoked you and what did you do that makes you feel ashamed?'

Juliana told the story. She knew as she did so that she wasn't telling it well, or clearly—her emotions were too heightened for logic, though she thought Charlotte eventually understood the essentials.

'And now,' she concluded, 'that horrible man is

likely to visit us in Brussels, for Mama gave him our direction.'

'If he does, many months will have passed and you might not feel the same way.'

'I cannot imagine ever feeling any differently about him! Why, he has followed me everywhere!'

'What?' Charlotte's eyes opened wide. 'He *followed* you? Who is he? What is his name? We can report him to the army…'

'Oh, no! His name does not matter, for of course I do not suggest he *actually* followed me! What I mean is—he *haunts* me! I cannot forget his disdain, or how unjust it was! Twice on the journey I saw dark-haired men and my heart leapt with anger, as I thought it was him. But it was not him.'

'I see,' said Charlotte, though she looked confused.

Juliana had had enough of remembering him. 'Anyway, tell me more about your life here. Who else lives in this huge house, apart from you and Adam and his great-aunt Clara—and your army of servants, of course?'

Charlotte looked as though she was considering persisting with her questions, then let it go. 'Adam has a younger brother and sister. His brother is with the army in France and his sister is visiting friends in Lincolnshire. And Papa lives here, too—though spends much of his time socialising in London.'

'Dear Sir Edward! I was so shocked when you told me how he was attacked in France last year. I do hope he is well.'

'He is and flirting with every widow in London! Though I do believe he has a particular fondness for Adam's godmother, Lady Annesley. But he is quite shocking, you know.'

Juliana giggled. 'I do not doubt it! Are we to visit London?'

'Yes, we will all go in a few weeks, for the Season has begun. But first, I must prepare for a Public Day on Friday.'

'A Public Day? What is that?'

'It's a tradition here, which Adam and I have revived since our marriage last year. We open the house and gardens to all the locals. We provide refreshments and Adam makes a speech. There is entertainment for the children and some sporting competitions—pony races, archery and the like. The night before, some of the local gentry come for dinner and those from further away stay the night. There is no little work in it.'

Juliana gasped. 'And you organise all of this?'

'Not everything, no. Adam and his steward manage the events. I focus on the work the indoor staff do—the food, making sure that bedrooms are all allocated and ready, preventing petty theft, that sort of thing. This will be only our second Public Day.'

Juliana was impressed. 'I could never manage it. But I am happy to be directed. Tell me how I can help, for I would not wish to be a burden on your time.'

'Really? You would not prefer to rest?'

'Now, Charlotte, you know I am not *restful*. I never was. Sometimes I think my poor mama tires more from my company than she does from the journey!'

'Oh, no! For I know she loves you dearly.'

'And I love her. But we have chafed on each other during this journey. My energy tires her out and she needs time alone to revive herself.'

'She will have plenty of rest and solitude here, if that is her wish. Chadcombe is the most peaceful, beautiful place I've ever known. I love it here.'

Juliana frowned. 'I hope I don't cut up your peace, Charlotte.'

'Oh, no, my dear friend! Why, you never tired me out. In fact, you always gave me daring when I needed it. Sometimes when I need to be strong, I think "What would Juliana say?" or "What would Juliana do?" And then I find my courage.'

'Oh, Charlotte! Now I shall have to hug you again, for you are making me cry! And now you are crying, too! I am so glad to be here and so sorry to make you cry!'

'Now then, what's all this? Who is making my wife cry?'

Juliana's heart lurched. The dark-haired man who had just entered the room really looked like— *Stop it!* she told herself. *Stop seeing that arrogant man everywhere! He is not worth your thoughts!*

'Adam!' Charlotte stood and moved to embrace her husband. 'I am crying because I am so happy to see my dear friend again.' He looked down at her, smiling, and kissed her forehead. The warmth between them was evident. Juliana's heart melted. It seemed Charlotte had found a man who truly appreciated her goodness.

Charlotte introduced them, smiling happily. Adam welcomed Juliana and then politely asked about her journey.

'Yes, it was a pleasant journey, thank you.' Charlotte suppressed a giggle. Juliana threw her a quelling look. 'Er…we had to stay in Dover on the first night, which is not what we had planned, but Mama was unwell, so we had no choice.'

Adam's eyes narrowed, but he did not ask any awkward questions, for which Juliana was grateful. She would not wish Charlotte's husband to think ill of her and she still felt the story showed her in a bad light.

The conversation moved on, and Juliana relaxed.

Harry turned towards Horse Guards, the familiar white edifice that housed the War Office. Absent-mindedly, he greeted acquaintances as he walked, for his thoughts were elsewhere. Yet again, the dark beauty he had met in Dover was occupying his mind. Miss Juliana Milford.

Various memories assailed him at different times. Juliana as he had first seen her, standing straight beside her mother's chair, her eyes flashing warnings at him. Juliana, humbled, as she had apologised to him, each word dragged from her against her stubborn will. Her discomfort at the *frisson* of attraction between them when he had kissed her hand. He smiled. He particularly liked that one.

But his favourite memory—the one which intruded most frequently—was the moment he'd made her smile. Of course he knew she would misdirect him, if allowed to write down the details of her direction in Brussels. He had foiled her by asking her mother to dictate it instead and had been unable to resist sending Juliana a crowing look. He had been momentarily stupefied when she had returned it with a reluctant smile, signalling a sense of humour as wicked as his own.

That brief moment of charity between them was causing all manner of disturbing feelings in him. It was a new experience—and a much more complex response than his normal flirtations. He knew he had charm, and enjoyed the game of making ladies like him. He was always careful, of course, to make it clear his intentions were not serious. He would not want to dally with the affections of any lady.

For his *affaires*, he chose either high-born widows or high-class courtesans, and he was able to skilfully separate his basic needs from his flirtations with young ladies. There was no point in lusting after the virgins on the marriage mart, for their goal was marriage, not bed sport.

Confusingly, his thoughts of Juliana were decidedly erotic—something he had always previously guarded against with the young ladies of his acquaintance. He would be better putting her out of his mind, for a gently bred lady would never choose to give up her virginity outside marriage, and he, of course, would never marry.

'Captain Fanton!' It was Evans, using his military title as they were at Headquarters.

Harry greeted his colleague. 'What gives?'

'Major Cooke is waiting for you. I've heard they'll

keep us in England for at least two months. We've been assigned to planning and co-ordinating supplies for the new campaign.'

'Damn!' Harry frowned. He wanted to be back in Brussels, where the real action was happening.

'I know. Perhaps you should have been less clever these past years. This is our punishment for having the most efficient unit in the regiment!'

'I fear you are right, Lieutenant.'

'The only good news is we shall have some time off in England. I'm going home for a few days.'

'Really? That is welcome news, for I have not seen my family in months.'

Harry conversed with Evans for a few moments more, before continuing on to his meeting with the Major. If he must be stuck in England, at least he would have the opportunity to visit home.

He only wished he had sought Miss Milford's direction in England—he had assumed he would be sent directly back to Brussels and that would be his next opportunity to see her. *I wonder*, he thought, *if she will attend any balls or parties in London?*

He grinned at the thought of how chagrined she would be to meet him in some parlour or ballroom, while thinking him safely returned to Brussels. Oh, that would be interesting!

* * *

Juliana watched as her friend graciously welcomed another family to Chadcombe. Charlotte stood with her husband on the steps outside the front door, as carriage after carriage pulled up, as well as farm carts and wagons. Each time, Adam and Charlotte spoke warmly to the arrivals, before directing them towards the public rooms, where they would find refreshments. Juliana stood in the hall behind them, with the list of expected guests, marking each family off as they arrived.

'That's the Beasley family, miss,' said the second footman. He knew everyone in the district and was assisting Juliana in her task. Juliana thanked him and put a mark beside the Beasleys.

As the Beasleys—Mr Beasley, Mrs Beasley and Master Tom Beasley—passed, another carriage was already pulling up. Juliana's eyes widened at the sight of the couple descending from it.

First, a lady. A woman. Possibly a lady. Her ample form was encased in a shocking purple silk and her arms glittered with diamond-encrusted bracelets. At her neck was a garish necklace—also with diamonds and quite inappropriate for day wear. Juliana studied her face. She was in her forties, with pale eyes, a hardness about the mouth and a hint of the rouge pot on her cheeks. Her hair was an improbable shade of blonde, glowing a brassy yellow in the bright daylight.

Juliana closed her mouth, which had been hanging open in shock. The woman's husband was now descending from the carriage, assisted by the groom. He was as lean as his wife was plump, with harsh, angular features and narrow eyes that darted, weasel-like, all around. His clothing was more conservative—a dark-coloured jacket and biscuit-coloured unmentionables, as well as dull black boots. He seemed all bones—elbows, knees and shoulders all poked prominently through his clothes, which hung on him in a most unflattering way. He, too, flaunted his wealth—a diamond pin was stuck in his cravat and he was unconsciously rolling an ostentatious signet ring on the small finger of his left hand.

Juliana consulted her list. This, then, must be Mr and Mrs Wakely, for almost everyone else had arrived. There was a family of five—the Dentons—still to come, but the Wakelys were the only couple. The footman confirmed it and Juliana moved forward, the better to hear the conversation between Lord and Lady Shalford and this strange pair.

'...so sorry for our tardiness, milady,' trilled Mrs Wakely, with a false-sounding titter. 'I said to Mr W. we needed to hurry, but he assured me we would be in good time!'

Her spouse looked less than pleased at having to

shoulder the blame. 'My lord! Lady Shalford!' He made an obsequious bow. 'We are so delighted to finally visit Chadcombe! We thank you for your kind invitation!'

The Earl glowered, but said all that was proper, as did Charlotte.

'Lady Shalford,' said Mrs Wakely, 'you and I must have a comfortable cose! For we ladies know what it is like to run a household, though I confess Glenbrook Hall—our humble home—has nothing on Chadcombe. What pillars! What windows! And look, Mr W.! Peacocks!'

'I had already noted the noble birds, my love,' replied her spouse with a sickly smile. 'We shall have to install some at Glenbrook Hall! Lord Shalford, how much would it cost to buy a pair of peacocks?'

Adam adopted an air of haughty indifference. 'I'm sure I have no idea—my steward, however, may be able to assist you.'

'Of course, of course,' said Mrs Wakely busily, nudging her spouse hard in the ribs. 'Lord Shalford would not concern himself with such things as buying peacocks! And, you know, my lady, we have more than *twenty* servants in Glenbrook Hall—including the grooms and the stable boy—so we can ask one of them to acquire peacocks for us.'

Charlotte seemed unable to speak. On the other

hand, Juliana rather thought Adam was about to say something that he oughtn't. As someone who had frequently found herself at a similar stand, she decided to rescue them. 'Charlotte, if you will introduce me, I will gladly show your guests to the public rooms.'

Charlotte sent her a grateful look. 'Thank you, Juliana.' She turned to the Wakelys. 'May I present my friend Miss Milford, who is staying with us at present. This is Mr Wakely, and Mrs Wakely.'

'I'm pleased to make your acquaintance,' said Mrs Wakely, with an insincere smile. 'Any friend of Lady S....'

Mr Wakely took Juliana's hand. His eyes swept over her body in a most disturbing way. 'Charmed!' he said, planting a wet kiss on her hand. Juliana shuddered slightly. He saw it and a hint of a cold smile gleamed momentarily in his tiny eyes.

Juliana swallowed hard. Then, squaring her shoulders, she indicated the hallway. 'Please come this way. I am certain you are in need of refreshments after your journey.'

'Oh, no,' said Mrs Wakely, as if affronted by Juliana's suggestion. 'For we travelled only four miles to get here and we ate well before we left. We keep a good table at Glenbrook Hall, if I do say so myself. Why, at breakfast today, we had pork *and* beef!'

Juliana was at a loss as to how to respond to this. Mrs Wakely, though, continued without a pause, admiring every detail of the house and its contents— the ceilings, doors, door handles and patterned stone floors all came in for praise. She constantly advised her husband to look and he, too, exclaimed at every detail.

'So, Miss Milford,' said Mr Wakely, who was walking *much* too close to her, 'is your family from this area?'

'No,' said Juliana shortly. 'We are simply visiting Lord and Lady Shalford.'

He nodded as if satisfied. 'I see.'

After leading them to the parlour set aside for refreshments, Juliana waited while they loaded their plates—Mr Wakely with a single cake and a peach, and Mrs Wakely with a generous selection of pastries, fruit and cheese. With some relief, Juliana made her apologies and returned to the hall to find Charlotte.

'Juliana!' Charlotte hurried towards her, taking both her hands. 'Thank you so much for rescuing us!' She glanced around to make sure no one was listening, then added, 'What awful people!' She bit her lip. 'I know I should not say such a thing about my guests, but…'

'They are awful and you're perfectly right to say

it to me,' said Juliana reassuringly. 'Who on earth are they?'

'They've recently moved into Glenbrook Hall, a house and grounds not five miles from here. I had heard they are not at all the thing and have not been accepted into local society.'

'I can understand it, having seen them,' said Juliana with a grimace. 'Will they be here for long—are they leasing Glenbrook Hall, or do they own it?'

'I can't remember.' Charlotte frowned. 'There is some story there that I cannot quite recall. I shall ask Adam later. For now, I must help with the events.' She had a quick word with the footman, reminding him to be on the alert for any intruders who might stray beyond the public rooms or pilfer small items. She then linked her arm with Juliana's and together they stepped out into the sunshine.

Five hours later, Juliana sank down on to a wooden chair with some relief. She had finally located her mother, who was sitting drinking tea with Adam's great-aunt Clara, Miss Langley, outside the Orangery.

'Juliana!' Her mother reached out and took her hand. 'You look exhausted! Would you like some tea?'

'I should love some, for I have had nothing to eat

or drink since breakfast. I had no idea how much work there would be on this Public Day.'

Miss Langley poured her a cup, her wrinkled face a study in concentration as she carefully poured the warm liquid into a delicate china cup. 'Oh, my dear Miss Milford! Here, have some cake!'

Juliana thanked her, and bit gratefully into the sweet sponge. 'Charlotte has not eaten either, I know, for we have been constantly moving around, from competitions to the parlour and back again. Thankfully some of the guests are beginning to leave. It has been a long afternoon.'

'Well, if you are tired, Juliana, it must have been busy, indeed, for you are rarely tired.'

Juliana was not listening. Out of the corner of her eye she had seen a dark figure moving furtively through the bushes and trees on the edge of the garden. Moving towards the house!

The manner of his movement was so suspicious that Juliana's sense of danger was aroused. She remembered Charlotte's warning to the footman and had asked her about it afterwards. Charlotte had said that in years past, there had been reports of thefts during Public Days, with thieves seeing it as the perfect opportunity to sneak in and purloin some small, expensive items while everyone was distracted with the guests and events.

She thought quickly. The footmen had been charged with keeping an eye on the corridors and entrances nearest the guest areas. No one had anticipated someone might try to sneak in through the Orangery!

'Excuse me, Mama, Miss Langley, I have just remembered something.' Acting nonchalantly, Juliana stood and walked casually to the Orangery door, just behind the terrace where the ladies were seated. Once inside, she moved quickly among the fruit trees and exotic plants towards the other external door—the one on the west side. She peered through the glass, scanning for any sign of the intruder. There he was—much closer and still moving stealthily through the shrubbery.

What could she do? There was no time to get help—everyone, apart from Mama and Miss Langley, was at the far side of the building. She looked around quickly, then spotted some tools resting in the corner. Choosing a short spade with a stout wooden handle, she positioned herself behind an enormous fern and waited.

She did not have long to tarry. She heard the door open, creaking slightly as it did so. It was closed again, slowly, then she distinctly heard a sigh, as if the intruder was relieved to have gained entrance, and now believed himself to be safe. *Well!* She gripped the spade more tightly. How dared he intrude into her friend's home?

She held herself completely still, breathing as quietly as she could. She need not have worried. As he moved towards where she was hiding, she heard him whistle. What an arrogant thief! She felt the moment he passed her fern—its leaves moved as he walked along. Stepping out at exactly the right moment, she raised her spade and brought it down smartly on the back of his head.

'Ow! What the deuce—?' He wheeled around and grabbed her, at the same time hooking his right foot behind her calf and knocking her off balance. The spade flew out of her hand and clanged to the ground. She fell heavily, banging her left shoulder hard against the floor. He fell with her, his weight crushing all the breath out of her.

Uh-oh! Once again she had acted before thinking something through, and now she had left herself in danger. She had envisaged him falling, knocked out by her blow, which would have allowed her to run for help before he came to. She hadn't thought that he would attack her! Her mind raced as she searched for a way out. She gasped for air, unable to scream, or even make a sound. His body pinned hers from shoulder to hip and all she could see was his shoulder, encased in a fine wool jacket.

He lifted his head. As his eyes met hers, Juliana's widened in shock.

It was *him*—the man from the inn! Captain Fanton!

Chapter Five

Juliana was all confusion. What was going on here? Had the arrogant Captain indeed followed her?

No. He looked just as shocked as she felt.

His eyes narrowed. 'Well, well,' he said. 'Miss Juliana Milford! What the devil are you doing here? And what possessed you to hit me?'

'Get off me!' she said, finally finding her voice. She gave him her fiercest look, no longer afraid. Now that she knew it was him, her heart was racing in a very different way. This was not fear, but a novel *excitement*. She could feel the length of him with every part of her chest, stomach and hips. He was warm and solid, and heavy. She had never experienced anything like it.

'This is an interesting dilemma,' he said smoothly. 'You have attacked me and I have disarmed you. I think I should get some answers before releasing you.' He shifted his weight slightly, but did not get

up. His slight movement was excruciatingly plea-
surable. Juliana resisted the unexpected impulse to
move a little herself, just to feel it again.

'I have asked you to release me! People may come
in at any second—my mother and Miss Langley are
taking tea just outside—and if they came in and saw
us like this, they might think—they might not understand—' Her voice tailed away.

'Why, what might they think, beautiful Juliana?'
He was looking intently at her mouth.

A new, disturbing feeling swamped Juliana. It was
altogether confusing. Was he going to kiss her? Her
heart, deaf to all sense, leaped in anticipation. Rejecting it, she hissed at him, 'Let me go, if there is
anything of the gentleman in you!'

His jaw clenched. 'I am the one who was attacked
without reason!' As he said it, thankfully he rolled
off to sit beside her, his hand going to the back of his
head. 'Ouch! A lump as big as an egg!' He glared at
her. 'What did you mean by it?'

She sat up. 'You were skulking. I saw you, sneaking through the shrubbery, trying to find a way in. I
know they have been bothered by thieves before on
Public Days. I thought—' She broke off. It seemed
unlikely, now she had time to reflect, that he was
a thief.

'You thought I was a thief, trying to steal from Chadcombe?'

She looked at him, then bit her lip. She nodded.

'That has to be one of the greatest insults I have ever received.' He reflected. 'No, I think it is truly the greatest.' He stood and offered her his hand.

She thought about rejecting it, then, realising how ungainly she would look if she tried to scramble to her feet without his assistance, she placed her hand in his.

He pulled her up—and into his arms! Her hands came up to his chest and for some reason she didn't push him away. Her heart was pounding loudly and she had the strangest feeling in the pit of her stomach. His deep-blue gaze pinned hers and she knew—just *knew*—something was about to happen. She held her breath.

He gazed down at her, then his expression changed. 'What did you hit me with?'

'Er—what?' Her brows knitted in confusion.

'Your weapon. What was it?'

'Oh—a spade.' Why was he asking about that?

'A spade! You are jesting, surely?' He released her and looked around. 'This spade?'

She crossed her arms around herself, suddenly feeling a little cold. 'It was all I could find.'

He picked it up, tested its weight, then looked at

her with a gleam of humour in his eyes. 'Permit me to tell you, Miss Milford, you are an unusual young lady.'

Was he laughing at her? Her chin went up. 'And permit me to say, Captain Fanton, you are the most irritating man I have ever met! And you still haven't explained why you were trying to sneak in!'

'You're right, I haven't,' he said smoothly, setting the spade down again. 'Come with me.'

Eyeing him suspiciously, she accompanied him to the eastern door of the Orangery, the one she had come in by. Outside, they found Mama and Miss Langley, still calmly drinking tea.

He winked at Juliana, then cleared his throat.

Both ladies turned. Mama's face lit up when she saw him. 'Oh! What a pleasant surprise!'

Miss Langley, a little slower to respond, smiled broadly when she saw who it was. 'Harry!' She rose to embrace him. 'What brings you home? And so unexpectedly!'

Home? Had she just said *'home'*? Juliana's jaw dropped in shock.

'Ah, Great-Aunt Clara, I am so happy to see you!' He kissed her wrinkled cheek. 'I am fixed in Horse Guards for at least two months and thought I would come to Chadcombe for a few days to see you all. It was only when I got here I realised you were in the middle of a dashed Public Day. Why Adam had to start them up again I shall never understand!'

'Oh, dear, Harry, I do remember how you always hated Public Days!'

'Well, I hoped to avoid everyone by coming around by the Orangery.'

His great-aunt smiled fondly at him. 'I remember, this was how you avoided your tutor, too, when you wanted to. No one ever could find you when you wanted to hide.'

Juliana snorted. He hadn't been very discreet while skulking through the bushes today! Hearing her reaction, he sent her a sideways glance, his eyes brimming with humour.

Miss Langley turned to Mrs Milford. 'Mrs Milford, may I introduce you to my great-nephew Harry—Adam's brother. Harry, this is Mrs Milford and Miss Milford—dear Charlotte's school friend.'

'But we have met before,' cried Mama, smiling broadly. 'Captain Fanton and his friend were of great assistance to us while we were in Dover.' She offered Harry her hand. 'How wonderful it is we should see you again and that you are Charlotte's new brother! Is it not wonderful, Juliana?'

'Indeed it is, Mama,' said Juliana smoothly, lying without a blink. 'Quite wonderful.'

* * *

Juliana settled into the corner of the carriage with a sigh. She was not looking forward to today. Mama was ill—just a cold, but she had stayed in bed today. Juliana hated to leave her. While she knew her mother was enjoying the best of care and attention from Miss Langley and a flurry of chambermaids, it still felt wrong to abandon her like this. Juliana had been really torn, for Charlotte needed her, too. Her mother had seemed to understand.

'Mama?' Juliana had spoken softly, unsure if her mother was awake or asleep.

'Yes, my love?'

'Do you remember I told you about the Wakelys?'

'That boorish couple from the Public Day?' Mama shuddered. 'What of them?'

'Charlotte plans to visit them today—they live only a few miles away. I do not wish to leave you alone, but I think she would be easier if I accompanied her.'

'Of course you must go with her!' Mama patted her hand. 'If you stay, you will only keep me from sleeping anyway.' Mama smiled to soften her words, but Juliana was unconvinced. 'Go, Juliana! You cannot abandon Charlotte when she needs you. You will be of no use to me today, but a great deal of use to Charlotte!'

Reluctantly, Juliana had agreed—only to discover, just now, that Harry also intended to accompany them. It was much too late to back out, but it galled her to discover she hadn't been needed after all. She wondered if Harry had deliberately ensured she would not discover his plans until she was committed.

Charlotte took her seat beside Juliana, then finally Harry entered, sitting in the centre of the rear-facing seat, opposite them. In the small, confined space, Juliana could not but be intensely aware of him. At a glance, she took in his well-fitted coat, pale breeches and gleaming boots—one of which was threateningly close to her own foot. She moved slightly, further away from him, and resisted the urge to tuck in her dress protectively around her. His nearness disturbed her—though not in the same way that the unctuous Mr Wakely had. No, she felt under no threat from Harry. Rather, she was altogether too aware of him—and was conscious of an incomprehensible urge to enjoy the proximity.

She and Charlotte were both wearing pretty day dresses of sprig muslin, with matching spencers. Charlotte wore a becoming cap, as befitted a married lady, whereas Juliana had opted for a high-poke bonnet with blue satin ribbons. Harry had paid them both extravagant compliments just now. Charlotte had smiled fondly at him, while Juliana had thanked him coolly.

Juliana had managed to keep a polite distance from Harry over the past few days, navigating with outward equanimity the warm welcome and surprise with which his arrival had been greeted. He had suffered no lasting ill effects from being clobbered with a spade, and the bump on his head had been a just reward, Juliana thought, for skulking.

It was clear Harry was well loved at Chadcombe—and not just by his relatives. The staff, Juliana noted, held him in high regard and Charlotte adored him as a brother. Charlotte had squealed with delight when she and Adam had first seen him, outside the Orangery. They had come looking for Great-Aunt Clara and the others when the last guest had gone, and found Harry being plied with cake and questions.

Harry's younger sister, Olivia, had also now returned to Chadcombe and was equally warm towards both her brothers. Juliana was quite envious of the clear bond between them and the fact that Charlotte, it seemed, had been fully welcomed into their family.

While she could only be glad Charlotte had found such a loving home, it had made her consider again her own situation. Growing up as an English child in Brussels, she had never felt she truly belonged there. And the years at school in Vienna had added to her sense of being rootless. It was partly the lack of family, she knew. Growing up without a father had not helped—she felt responsible for Mama and had taken on the obligation for making decisions that would normally fall to one's parents. It had made her wary, old beyond her years and perhaps a little more ready to fight when threatened. Being in England was also unsettling. Though she, of course, had her dear Mama, she had often wondered about her own family background.

Mama rarely talked about her husband. His name, Juliana knew, was John Milford, and he had died while in active service during the Flanders campaign, soon after Juliana's birth. Wounded in a skirmish with French forces, he had succumbed to infection a week later. Mama had said the bitterly cold winter had probably not helped. 'I often wondered,' she had told her daughter, 'if I could have saved him. He was all alone, with no one to properly care for him. The army was in retreat and very few of the wounded survived.'

Juliana had been almost afraid to breathe. Mama so rarely talked about her past. 'Could you not have gone with him?' Juliana had asked tentatively. 'I know many army wives who travel with the campaign—Charlotte's mother did, for a time.'

'Your father insisted I remain in Brussels with you,' Mama had replied. 'I was unwell after the birth, and he said he wanted to know we both were safe.'

Juliana had swallowed hard. 'So it was because of me that he…died?'

Her mother had hugged her fiercely. 'No! Never! He adored you—adored us both. It was simply the timing.'

'Why did you not return to England after Papa's death?'

Her mother's face had crumpled. 'Oh, I could not! To be subject to censure and control from—' She swallowed hard. 'I would have been punished and criticised for going away in the first place—I simply could not have borne it! I am not strong enough, you see.'

Mama had decided to stay in Brussels and focus on raising her daughter. Since then, she said, she had had no reason or desire to return to Kent, where she grew up.

Juliana had had a thousand more questions, but, since that day, almost two years ago, Mama had refused to disclose anything further about her past. She had begged Juliana not to press her, saying even after all these years it remained too painful to talk about. Juliana, conscious of her mother's vulnerability, could not risk pushing too hard for information. She assumed Mama's family had not approved of John Milford—or, perhaps, his decision to take his young bride to Europe to follow the Army. Perhaps there was some scandal there, which had made Mama anxious even all these years later.

Now they were in England, Juliana resolved to try to gently question Mama again about it all. Mama had been an only child, she knew, but surely *someone* remained. Was the estrangement so strong they could not have any contact with them? Could they perhaps visit them? When she was younger, she had often created visions in her head of being welcomed into a warm, loving home and that she would be the one to bridge a reawakening of her mama's relationship with her own family. For who could fail to love Mama?

And what of her papa's family? Was it possible she might have Milford grandparents or cousins? Would her mama be more willing to talk about it, now that they were in England?

'I apologise to both of you that we are making this journey.' Charlotte's voice intruded on Juliana's thoughts. 'I am sure visiting Glenbrook Hall was not how you hoped to spend the afternoon—especially as we are to travel to London in two days.'

'No need to apologise,' said Harry cheerfully. 'I am decidedly looking forward to it. I have heard much of our new neighbours and I confess to a certain curiosity.'

Juliana eyed him balefully. Quite apart from his deceiving her this morning, she still hadn't forgiven him for being so rude and arrogant in Dover, and resented his seeming popularity with the entire family circle. He had been welcomed, fêted and exclaimed over by everyone in Chadcombe, including—the ultimate betrayal—by her own mama.

Everyone had thought him fixed in France and expressed their delight in animated tones at his unexpected arrival. Juliana had held back, a polite smile masking her disdain, until he had made a sly reference to her 'falling over herself to greet him' and how much of a pleasure it had been to meet Mrs Milford and her 'charming daughter' again. Charlotte, who had not been present when Harry had explained himself to Miss Langley, had looked confused.

'But, when did you meet?' she had asked innocently, failing to notice the daggered look Juliana had been sending in Harry's direction.

'In Dover,' explained Mrs Milford, who had then gone on to describe their encounter in the warmest terms. Juliana had clamped her mouth shut and closed her hands into fists, for fear she would tell the truth—or that he would. He had known how she felt, of course, and had looked highly amused by her reaction. Charlotte had seemed astonished, then thoughtful.

'Your curiosity is well warranted, Harry. The Wakelys are an interesting couple.' Charlotte grimaced slightly as she spoke.

'*Interesting?* Come now, Charlotte!' Harry's tone was lightly teasing. 'You may speak plainly with me. And with Miss Milford.' He looked directly at Juliana and she felt the impact of that steady gaze kick somewhere in her middle.

Charlotte shook her head. 'I cannot say what I really think, for I do not wish to speak ill of people whom I barely know.'

'Your discretion does you credit. Perhaps Miss Milford will oblige me. What is your impression of the Wakelys, Miss Milford?'

'They are rude and encroaching, and not the sort of people Lady Shalford should be visiting.' Juliana spoke bluntly, hoping to shock him. He was undaunted, humour glinting in his eyes. She turned to Charlotte. 'Must you visit them?'

'I fear so,' said Charlotte sadly. 'Mrs Wakely caught me unawares when they were leaving Chadcombe and I had agreed to call upon her before I knew what was happening.'

'Did you discover the tale behind their move to Glenbrook Hall?' Juliana hoped the Wakelys would be in the district only temporarily. She did not want anything to spoil Charlotte's happiness and feared Charlotte would be too kind-hearted to repulse the strange duo.

Charlotte nodded. 'Adam has been informed there is a dispute about the inheritance, and the Wakelys have been allowed to live there while the executors establish Mrs Wakely's claim. It is known she has been given a generous allowance, too—the old Baron, Cowlam, was extremely wealthy, I understand. That might account for the diamonds.'

Juliana giggled. 'And the peacocks!'

Charlotte laughed. 'Lord! I wonder if they will have bought some?'

Harry smiled broadly. 'Come now, you must tell me more of this! What peacocks?'

Juliana couldn't resist, for it was too good a tale not to be told. Eyes dancing, she told him of the Wakelys' plan to purchase peacocks. His reaction was gratifying, and for a few moments she actually felt in charity with him. She allowed him to be charming—indeed, she had admitted it from the first. And he was now part of her dear Charlotte's family. Begrudgingly, she admitted he seemed genuinely loved by those at Chadcombe and that he must, therefore, have some good qualities she had not seen. She was sure of one thing, though. She would never wish to be close to him.

Harry watched Juliana as she told her tale, enjoying her animated features and sparkling eyes. He felt an unanticipated thrill as she spoke—this was the most relaxed he had ever seen her in his company.

Since his arrival at Chadcombe, she had tried to keep him at a distance, something which he had taken as a personal challenge. Her coolness was no match for his confidence in his ability to charm young ladies. The only time she had been openly angry and disdainful was during their encounter in the Orangery. Still, he mused, that event had had its compensations. He still remembered how it felt to have her beneath him, for those brief moments. Even the bump on the head now seemed a price worth paying. She was undoubtedly a daring woman!

Finding her installed in his family home had been an unexpected delight. He knew she was determined to dislike him, but somehow, it did not bother him. His instincts told him that, at a deeper level, her feelings towards him were much more mixed. He saw it in her awareness of him—a responsiveness which was entirely mutual. They came alive in each other's company, politely throwing barbed comments, false sentiment and, occasionally, undisguised insults in each other's path. He suspected Juliana was feeling the same exhilaration he was enjoying during these spirited encounters.

This was more than mere flirtation, though flattery was one of the main strategies which Harry was using to irritate her. He had realised quickly she was uncomfortable receiving compliments and that it was the easiest method of getting a response from her. As an accomplished flirt, he had developed the knack, he thought, of persuading young ladies to succumb to his charm—while avoiding, of course, any risk they might fall 'in love' with him. That was a complication he must avoid. With Juliana, he was sure there was no such risk, so his way was clear to see if he could charm her—or outwit her—into warming to him.

He squirmed slightly at the direction of his own musings. He sounded arrogant, even to himself. Deep inside, the monster of his self-loathing began to stir. Sensing the chasm opening up before him, he diverted his thoughts from the depths. Better to focus on the challenge of fencing with Juliana. The last thing he wished was to observe his own soul.

As each day passed, he grew to know her better.

After just a week, he could now read the play of emotions that crossed her features with increasing accuracy, while Juliana was becoming ever more skilful at scoring hits on him.

Their battles—fought with word and gaze—were different to anything he had ever known and he found himself looking forward to each day with greater energy than he had known since—

'And so,' Juliana concluded with a flourish, 'we may discover today whether Lord Cowlam's wealth has been used to purchase peacocks for Glenbrook!'

'Why, this sounds like a high treat!' he declared. 'I thank you both for allowing me to accompany you. There is nothing I enjoy more than absurdity!'

'I know exactly what you mean.' Juliana nodded. 'People can be so humorous—even when they do not mean to be!'

Harry was startled by her straight answer. Honesty—without the hint of a barb—was a rare occurrence between them. He found himself agreeing with her. '*Especially* when they do not mean to be!'

Unthinkingly, they smiled briefly at each other in a moment of mutual understanding, then both broke off eye contact. They stared fixedly at the countryside for the rest of the journey, each lost in their own thoughts. Charlotte, after a keen look at each of them, smiled slightly, but said nothing.

In truth, Harry was a little disturbed by the sudden, unexpected harmony between himself and Juliana. They had each triumphed in various skirmishes, but which of them had won this latest round was unclear.

Chapter Six

'We call this the Blue Drawing Room,' Mrs Wakely tittered. 'As you can understand, for everything is blue, even the rug!'

Juliana suppressed a yawn. How she disliked this ritual, touring people's houses so they could crow about their wealth, furniture and—in Mrs Wakely's case—rugs. She had done it many times around Brussels and Vienna, and knew the behaviour expected of her. She was to exclaim and compliment, and agree with her hostess, all the time understanding that she, who had no property or wealthy relations, was to be grateful even to visit such a wonderful dwelling. This occasion, Juliana recognised, was slightly different, for Mrs Wakely knew Glenbrook Hall was nothing compared to Chadcombe. Juliana was quite enjoying the reflected glory—and Mrs Wakely's feeble attempts to seem humble, yet crow about her fortune.

'As you see, it has blue hangings and the sofas and chairs are all done in blue. The fireplace, you will notice, is white.'

'A most pleasant room, Mrs Wakely.' Charlotte was all politeness. Juliana did not know how she could stand it. Since their arrival, Mrs Wakely had maintained an incessant flow of inconsequential chatter, interspersed with impertinent questions.

Thankfully, after tea, Harry had been taken off by Mr Wakely to inspect the stables, so Juliana did not have to endure the company of either man. Mr Wakely, on their arrival, had raised his quizzing glass to inspect both ladies with uncomfortable intensity, before pronouncing them to be 'fine young ladies', in a voice that made Juliana shiver slightly.

'...you think, Juliana?' Realising belatedly that Charlotte was addressing her, Juliana started.

'Yes, delightful,' she said generally. It seemed to fit, for no one reacted with surprise.

Mrs Wakely rang the bell. 'The portrait gallery is next and I confess I do not know much of the family history, so I have asked our housekeeper, Mrs Campbell, to be ready to explain it to you.'

They stood, listening with seeming interest to Mrs Wakely's description of the pleasant view out of the window, until the housekeeper appeared. Mrs Campbell was a stout, kindly-looking woman in her sixties, with a lined face and iron-grey hair contained in an orderly bun. Her black dress was neat and tidy, and she wore a large bunch of keys at her waist.

'Mrs Campbell,' said Mrs Wakely imperiously, 'please take us to the portrait gallery, and explain everything to my guests. The same way you explained it to me when I first became your mistress.' She turned to Charlotte. 'Lady Shalford, you will know what a trial it is to find good staff and how one must establish dominance over them from the start—especially the "old retainer" types. One would not want to be cheated by dishonest staff!'

Juliana's jaw dropped in shock. What an insulting thing to say, and in front of her own housekeeper! Mrs Campbell's face remained expressionless, but Juliana knew from the brief flash of pain in her eyes that Mrs Wakely's cruel arrow had found its mark.

Charlotte, she saw, was equally taken aback. 'I know how important it is to find—and to keep—good staff,' she said softly. 'I declare I would be lost without my own housekeeper at Chadcombe.' She smiled gently at Mrs Campbell.

Juliana spoke up. 'I would be delighted if you would be so kind as to show us the portrait gallery, Mrs Campbell.' She smiled broadly at the housekeeper, hoping to signal her outrage at Mrs Wakely's rude behaviour.

Mrs Campbell looked at her fully for the first time. Her eyes widened briefly, then she schooled her features into impassivity. 'Thank you, miss.'

Juliana followed as Mrs Campbell led them through two interconnected rooms. Why had the housekeeper looked at her with such surprise? Was she so unused to receiving kindness? Juliana could not imagine how difficult it must be to work for a mistress as coarse and unfeeling as Mrs Wakely.

Unhooking the bunch of keys from her waist, the housekeeper unlocked the door to the portrait gallery, then stood aside while they entered.

It was a beautiful room. Long, narrow and sunlit, with polished wooden floors and plain walls, hung with portraits amassed over three centuries. A single rosewood table stood halfway down and there was another door at the far end of the room. There was an air of peace, tranquillity and quiet tastefulness about the whole house, which did not match Mrs Wakely in the slightest.

Juliana was forced to admit she liked Glenbrook Hall. It was a pretty estate, with farms, mature woodlands, landscaped gardens and a long sweeping drive. The house was a modest building of warm granite and large windows, with high ceilings, ele-

gant fireplaces and tasteful design. It was also im-
maculately maintained—Juliana laid the credit for
this at the feet of Mrs Campbell and the other staff,
for it was clear Mrs Wakely had no knowledge or
understanding of running a country house.

'How long have you lived here, Mrs Wakely?'
she asked, curiosity finally getting the better of her.
Besides, she was unable to resist the temptation to
make her hostess feel a little uncomfortable.

'Almost six months,' replied Mrs Wakely. 'I do
declare it took a while for us to get used to it, rat-
tling around in this big place. I much prefer a com-
pact house, with only the rooms I need—though, of
course, it is gratifying when guests are impressed
by how large the house is.'

Juliana blinked. Mrs Wakely continued, undaunted. 'I have plans to change the house and to
get rid of all this old furniture. We need to moder-
nise it—the family had such old-fashioned taste! I
was thinking of making everything golden. I have
seen beautiful new furniture that has come from
France and Mr W. and I have talked about redeco-
rating. Of course, this war is very inconvenient—
they say it will make importing what we want more
difficult. Lady Shalford, you must come back next
year and see what changes we have made.'

Charlotte made a non-committal answer. Juliana

hoped she would never be back, for she dreaded to think what Mrs Wakely's 'modernising' would do to this lovely house. And to describe the conflict with Napoleon as 'inconvenient' was nothing short of insulting to the soldiers and their families, as well as to the relatives of those who had been lost in war—like Juliana's own father.

It also showed a lack of sensitivity to those who lived near the battlefields. This time, the armies had moved close to Brussels and Juliana dreaded to think of what might happen to her friends and acquaintances who still resided there.

'Mrs Campbell, who are these people?' In an attempt to divert her hostess from pressurising Charlotte, Juliana stopped randomly in front of a family portrait. It looked like a Reynolds, and showed a man, woman and child in an outdoor setting, Glenbrook Hall in the distance.

'Ah, that is my master and mistress, and the young master,' said Mrs Campbell warmly.

'Indeed?' said Charlotte with interest. 'He was a baron, I understand?'

'He was. Lord Cowlam, though the line died out with him.'

Charlotte looked perplexed. 'But, his son...?'

'When Napoleon started attacking all over Europe, nothing would do for the young master but that he must volunteer. Master Jack was always headstrong, especially after his mother died. He was killed in Spain, I believe, or France. The master went into a decline after that.'

'How sad!' Another of the thousands of families affected by war and by Napoleon's thirst for glory. Juliana looked at the portrait carefully. They all looked so happy. The man was smiling broadly, his blue eyes brimming with energy and joy. The woman was beautiful, with soft brown eyes and an air of serenity. Juliana liked to think of them happy together in this house. She looked at the child. He had his mother's brown eyes and was looking innocently at her.

'When did the Baron die?' Charlotte, Juliana saw, was also intrigued by the sad tale.

'Nearly two years ago, milady.' Mrs Campbell spoke with heavy sorrow. 'We never expected him to live on after Master Jack died. In the end, it was twenty years, though he was never the same. We did our best to look after him, and to look after the house and the estate, but we couldn't replace what he had lost.'

Mrs Wakely was frowning at the direction the conversation had taken. 'But, as I always say, good comes out of bad, for if the old Baron's son had lived, then Mr W. and I would not have inherited.'

Juliana frowned, noticing Mrs Campbell's distress at her mistress's words. Really, the woman had no tact or sensitivity!

'Indeed, Mrs Wakely,' Charlotte said coolly. 'And has your inheritance been confirmed?'

'Er...well, you know how these things are... Lawyers will be forever putting obstacles in the way of justice.'

'Obstacles?' queried Juliana, exchanging a wicked glance with Charlotte. This sounded interesting.

'Yes, you know the sort of thing...' Mrs Wakely waved a plump arm vaguely. 'Other claimants that nobody can find. They will turn out not to exist, I am sure of it. And then the lawyers will give me my full inheritance and allow me to redecorate.'

'So it is you, and not your husband, who is related to the Baron?' asked Juliana, though she already knew the answer.

'I am, indeed, and it has been verified. My grandmother and his grandmother were first cousins, you know. And I was never so shocked as on the day I found out that I was gentry! For—this will surprise you to know, milady—' she laid a plump hand on Charlotte's arm '—I was not raised as such. When I got the letter I was so shocked I could barely take it in and I had to ask my dear friend Mr Wakely to explain it to me!'

Charlotte ridded herself of Mrs Wakely's touch by the simple expedient of raising her own hand to touch the plain gold locket around her neck. 'So you and Mr Wakely were not married at that point?'

'We were not—he was a regular customer at the tavern where I worked. The *inn*, I mean, not "tavern"! Tavern sounds altogether too common! A very high-class, select inn, it was, milady. Anyway, I had no idea he was harbouring such warm feelings for me. He had kept his love for me secret, for fear of rejection, you know!' She sighed dramatically. 'But he helped me through all the dealings with the lawyers—and it was with him that I shared my joy at becoming an heiress.'

'Ah,' said Juliana, 'I begin to understand.'

Mrs Wakely beamed. 'It was so gratifying to find myself in such a position—heiress to a fortune and then to discover my dear Mr Wakely wished to marry me. I count it the happiest day of my life.'

Juliana and Charlotte exchanged knowing glances. 'Gratifying to be sure, Mrs Wakely. So you are not long married?'

'Seven months—and at a time in my life when I had finally accepted my fate as a spinster.' She nudged Juliana hard in the ribs. 'So do not give up hope, miss. You may yet find a man who will take you on!'

'Of that, there can be little doubt!' A man's voice rang out behind them. They turned to see Mr Wakely, Harry a step behind him, walking through the long portrait gallery towards them.

Mr Wakely laughed at his own witticism. Bowing to Juliana, he added, 'For one so beautiful to remain unwed and untouched would be a sin.'

'Miss Milford is indeed pretty,' said Mrs Wakely, rather huffily.

Crash! The sound of metal on wood reverberated around the room as the housekeeper's keys fell to the floor, making them all jump. Really, it was surprising just how loud a bunch of iron keys could be.

Mrs Campbell bent to pick them up, apologising profusely as she did so.

'You stupid, clumsy oaf!' barked Mr Wakely, his face white with anger. He turned to Charlotte. 'Lady Shalford, I do apologise! What must you think of us?'

'Oh, dear Lady Shalford, I do hope this does not prevent you from visiting us again,' added his spouse, two spots of bright colour on her cheekbones, 'For as the only notable landowners in the district, I had hoped we could become fast friends!'

Charlotte seemed lost for words. Juliana, her anger building at the rudeness of the Wakelys towards their housekeeper, immediately thought of at least ten things she wished to say. Unfortunately, she realised, none would do. How frustrating it was to be a gently bred lady when one wished to swear like a sailor!

Rescue came from an unexpected source. 'Come now, Mrs Wakely,' said Harry, a glint in his eye, 'you must know there are many estates in our corner of Surrey. Chadcombe, to be sure, is by far the largest, but the Squire's residence and Monkton Park are at least the same size as Glenbrook Hall and quite possibly larger.'

Mrs Wakely opened and closed her mouth, silenced by Harry's smooth intervention. *Bravo, Harry!* thought Juliana gratefully. Hopefully that would divert their attention from the unfortunate housekeeper.

Mr Wakely, with a gesture, invited them to walk with him to the door. 'My dear wife and I,' he pronounced slickly, 'have been to call on the Squire—and he offered a most gratifying welcome! However, we have not yet had the pleasure of visiting Monkton Park. Can you tell me, who lives there?'

They continued to the main staircase—a beautiful, sweeping arc of warm, polished wood leading to the hallway. Charlotte and Mrs Wakely walked first, followed by the gentlemen. Juliana, who had held back a little so as to avoid Mr Wakely, ended up descending the staircase with Mrs Campbell.

Half-listening to Harry's talk of Mr and Mrs Foxley who lived in Monkton Park, she was nevertheless distracted by the housekeeper. Mrs Campbell was pale and seemed distressed, which was hardly unexpected. At one point she looked as if she might speak, then she glanced ahead at her master and mistress and subsided.

Whether she wished to say thank you, or ask a question, Juliana was not to discover. Reaching the hallway, Harry informed the Wakelys apologetically that he and the ladies must leave, for he had an urgent appointment he had quite forgotten about. Despite the protests of Mr and Mrs Wakely, he insisted, so the carriage was called for. Mrs Campbell remained silent, as if hoping not to be noticed.

Charlotte managed, through apologetic talk of engagements, to avoid making a firm commitment to see the Wakelys again, though when she mentioned the family were to visit London—

'London! A capital idea! Mr W., perhaps we, too, should go to London. I should love to go shopping again!'

'Then so you shall, my love!' Mr Wakely smiled insincerely at his wife, who beamed at him with adoration. Juliana shuddered inwardly.

A few moments later, they waved goodbye with some relief and the carriage started up the drive.

'Well!' said Harry. 'I am sorry if I took you away before you wanted to leave, but I could not have remained a moment longer in that house without saying something unforgivably rude!'

Juliana, caught up in the moment, spontaneously reached across the carriage and took his hand. 'Indeed, Captain Fanton, I was feeling exactly the same way myself! Poor Mrs Campbell! How she must suffer under their rule! I was never so grateful as when you diverted the Wakelys' attention from her, for I was biting my tongue. Thank you!'

His eyes dropped to their joined hands, then lifted to meet hers, a stunned expression on his face. Belatedly, Juliana regretted her impulse and removed her hand. The warmth of his stayed with her, though, and she was conscious her nerve endings were tingling from touching him.

Charlotte laughed shakily. 'Oh, Juliana, I am so glad you did not lose your temper! I, too, was sorely tested, but I am glad we did not lower ourselves to their level.' She frowned. 'I must tell Adam of this.'

'It is a worry, Charlotte.' Harry looked unusually sober. 'If they behave this way towards their staff in public, who is to say what may be going on in private?'

'Can they not leave?' asked Juliana. 'They are not slaves, after all.'

'It is not so simple,' said Harry. 'Many of them have been there their whole lives. Mrs Campbell, for example, has worked at Glenbrook Hall since she joined the staff as a housemaid when she was a girl. It is the only home she knows.'

'What of the grooms? Did you speak to them?'

'I did, for Wakely disappeared briefly to speak to his steward.' He stopped to reflect, running his thumb pensively along his lower lip. Juliana watched, temporarily mesmerised. 'The grooms seemed well enough, but then, they may have little contact with the Wakelys. The only horses were the farm animals and the carriage horses. The Wakelys do not pretend to be connoisseurs of horseflesh.'

'You know we cannot interfere in matters between servants and their master or mistress,' said Charlotte. 'But it does not sit well with me to ignore this. If only we knew whether today's incident was their normal way of behaving towards their servants.'

'They were desperate to impress you, Charlotte,' Juliana pointed out. 'Perhaps under normal circumstances they are more benign.'

'I certainly hope so,' agreed Charlotte.

They travelled on in silence, and Juliana's thoughts roamed from the disgraceful behaviour of the Wakelys towards Mrs Campbell to Harry's intervention, and to the fact that she suddenly felt in such charity with him. She had seen Harry in a different light today, had admired his sympathy for Mrs Campbell, his anger at the injustice they had witnessed and the adroit way in which he had handled the situation. As they travelled home to Chadcombe, each lost in their own thoughts, Juliana reflected that the silence between them held none of the tension of only a few hours ago. It was, in fact—she struggled to find the right word, then discovered it—companionable.

Harry lunged, then retreated. He repeated the move six times, each time working on his accuracy and control. The rapier shone menacingly before him, steel glinting in the sunlit stable. Fencing was popular with young men of fashion as a sport, but Harry knew the discipline of practice could be vital to all his skills as a soldier—including the realities of wielding a crude bayonet in battle.

He had been in the stable for nearly two hours, working with *epée*, rapier and foil, practising moves again and again, and yet again. He had stripped down to his shirt and loosened it at the neck. His body was slick with sweat. Rather than dry his sword hand, he continued, knowing he needed to master control of a weapon even when it was dangerously slippery.

A small sound behind him alerted him to the fact

that he was no longer alone. He spun in an instant, raising the rapier and drawing his arm back in a threatening pose.

It was Juliana. Her eyes widened briefly and she caught her breath, but she stood stock still.

'What on earth are you doing?' he demanded, lowering his weapon. His heart pounded with the fear of what might have happened. 'I might have run you through! Don't you know not to creep up on a swordsman when he is engrossed in practice?'

She tilted her head to one side and regarded him evenly. 'I didn't know that, actually. How could I?' She walked to his sword case and picked out a short sword. She examined it carefully, before grasping it in an approximation of a sword hold.

He tutted. 'Not like that. It would be knocked from your hand on the first strike if you were to try to wield it with that weak grasp. Here.' Acting on impulse, he moved behind her and closed his hand over hers. Adjusting her grip, he moved the thumb to the correct position and moved her fingers down slightly. As he did so, he was conscious of a vague floral scent emanating from her and mixing with the foul odour of his own sweat. He stepped back quickly and picked up his own sword.

He adopted the posture and she copied, devilment glinting in her eyes.

'Now, carefully, bring your sword up like this.'

She watched him carefully, mirroring his every movement. Once her sword was up, he tested her with a gentle lunge.

'Block!' he ordered, and she did. It was inexpert, but she managed to instinctively move her weapon to block the progress of his.

'Now, other side!' he said. She blocked again. He kept testing her, teaching her the basics of the four block directions. The intense concentration on her beautiful face was a dangerous distraction.

'Now,' he said, stepping back. 'Your turn.'

She smiled gleefully and launched an attack. He, of course, held her off with ease, but he could not help but be impressed both by her fervour and evident enjoyment. His heart felt light as he fenced with her and her whoops of excitement lifted his spirits. *Oh, but she was a woman in a million!*

She kept thrusting, stepping forward as she did so. The clang of their blades rang out through the stable, punctuated only by Juliana's spontaneous expressions of delight.

Eventually they stopped, both a little winded. 'That was wonderful!' breathed Juliana. 'Oh, I sometimes wish I had been born a man! It is unfair you get to fence, while we must embroider!'

'Really?' Harry had never thought of it that way

before. He supposed some of the male pursuits were probably more exciting than female ones. He was certainly looking forward to their move to London tomorrow, where he would practise fencing with his friends and visit Jackson's Boxing Saloon, and indulge in all his favourite sports. He imagined having to embroider, and shuddered. 'Would you truly wish to be a man?'

'No, of course not,' said Juliana, setting the sword back in its case. 'I am glad to be a woman, though I do wish women were allowed to practise sports.'

'Good,' he said gallantly. 'I am very glad you are not a man, for then I would be deprived of your female beauty!'

Her relaxed expression vanished, replaced with clear exasperation. 'Oh, why did you have to go and spoil it?' she exclaimed, before turning on her heel and stomping out of the stable. Harry watched her go in some bewilderment. What had he done wrong?

Chapter Seven

The Fanton town house was a three-bay, elegant edifice located near St James's Square. Charlotte delighted in showing Juliana around—from the attics to the basement—and was clearly proud of it. She had made small changes since her marriage, including opening up for her own use a little-used parlour at the rear of the house which was warmed by the afternoon sun. It was a cosy room, with a pretty Aubusson rug, comfortable armchairs and a lady's writing desk. Here she had placed a portrait of her mother—deceased when Charlotte was still a child—and she had just taken receipt of a recent one of her father, Sir Edward.

'It is a good likeness, Charlotte,' said Juliana, tilting her head to one side to consider the matter. 'The artist has caught something of his spirit, I think. Sir Edward has such energy, such vitality. It reminds me of that other portrait—the one of Lord Cowlam and his family. The Baron had a decided air of mischief.'

'He did,' said Charlotte. 'They say the Baron was impetuous in his youth and his ill-fated son inherited his headstrong nature.'

'Such a sad tale,' mused Juliana. 'I still think of that poor housekeeper and of how the Wakelys have cut up her peace.'

They had been in London for a sennight and had settled into an easy routine. In the mornings, Juliana and Charlotte retired to the parlour after breakfast to talk, and plan, and enjoy each other's company. Afterwards they often accompanied Olivia and Mrs Milford to the shops, or on house calls, and later in the day they frequently went riding in one of the many parks nearby. Harry and Adam usually accompanied them, if Harry was not needed in Horse Guards and Adam was free from his responsibilities. Juliana was beginning to feel she really *knew* them and was becoming more comfortable in their company.

She liked Adam more and more, helped by his obvious adoration of Charlotte. He was naturally solemn and a little reserved, until in his wife's company, when he seemed more relaxed, open and warm. They made a good couple and were clearly very much in love. Some days they missed breakfast entirely, often retired early, and spent a lot of their time together kissing and holding hands. Juliana was delighted to see her friend so happy and loved.

Juliana's thoughts turned to her relationship with Harry. This was much less comfortable. He was as sociable as his brother was taciturn, and his ready smile and open nature was in stark contrast to Adam's reserved character. Harry still insisted on flirting with her and she continually rebuffed him. The incident during the fencing was typical. Just when she started to feel in charity with him, he would get that *look* on his face—the false, flirtatious one—and turn into the jester that so angered her.

It had become quite a contest between them, as Juliana still felt irritated by his extravagant praise and easy compliments, feeling sure these were not sincerely meant. However, since the incident at Glenbrook Hall, she had also understood he had good qualities—a matter of regret, since it made her opinion of him far too complicated.

Mama, thankfully, was at ease, having formed a firm friendship with Miss Langley—whom they both now addressed as Great-Aunt Clara, as she had requested. Clara's gentle conversation and warm nature made them perfect companions. Juliana had rarely seen her mother so contented, and she was glad of it. Perhaps the decision to bring her to England had not been so bad, after all. It was, she admitted, sometimes hard to be constantly catering to Mama's needs.

Adam and Harry's sister, Olivia, was experiencing her first Season and was thrilled to be visiting dressmakers and milliners in preparation for the parties, picnics, routs and balls she would attend. Town was becoming increasingly busy, as more families returned from the country, and invitations were piling up on Charlotte's desk. She opened each one diligently, then put them into different piles, some to be accepted, others rejected.

'Oh, Juliana,' she said suddenly, 'look—it is the Almack's vouchers!'

'Finally!' breathed Juliana, 'Now we shall see what all of the to-do is about.'

Charlotte handed her one of the vouchers. It was a small, thick card and had the dates inscribed on it, along with the initials of Lady Jersey, one of the Patronesses.

'Olivia will be thrilled,' said Juliana.

'Never mind Olivia—*I* am thrilled!' said Charlotte excitedly. 'We have heard so much of Almack's—even in Vienna it was talked about! I was so disappointed that my aunt did not allow me to attend any balls or assemblies when I was living with her in London, and I have not had the chance to go since my wedding. I am glad now, for it means we can go together.'

'Do you remember how we used to dream of going to an Almack's ball?' asked Juliana. 'We imagined dancing with dozens of handsome men.'

'Of course I do! We said we would be courted and fêted, and our dance cards would be filled!' She took Charlotte's hand and the two of them danced a quadrille step, giggling and laughing as they had when they'd learned the steps together at school. Neither noticed the door opening.

'Bravissima!' It was Harry, smiling, and looking devilishly handsome in morning dress. Juliana's heart skipped a beat—possibly because of the unaccustomed exercise of dancing in a parlour. For once, his smile actually looked genuine. 'Ladies! Might I request the honour of a dance with each of you, whenever we finally have the opportunity to go to a ball?'

'That would be on Wednesday.' Charlotte grinned, showing him the voucher.

'Almack's? Olivia, too?' Charlotte confirmed it. 'Then I must be off—to procure men's vouchers for myself and Adam. He hates Almack's—always has—but he will need to show his face for Olivia's sake. Shall we ride later?'

Juliana nodded. 'We shall.'

He leaned towards her, his breath fanning her cheek. 'I am counting the hours.'

'You may think your charms are working, but I am unmoved,' she said evenly, though her heart was still beating quickly. *Oh, no! Was she finally starting to accept his silly emptiness?* She steeled herself to stand rigid, her face frozen in a mask of disapproval.

A raised eyebrow and wide smile signalled his scepticism and he bowed out of the room.

'Oh, what a flirt that man is!' said Juliana crossly.

'He has been that way as long as I have known him,' agreed Charlotte. 'He has a good heart, though... But you shake your head at me, Juliana. You disagree?'

'I will admit to his *sister* having a good heart. His great-aunt has a most generous heart. His brother, a warm heart, for he married you, my dear friend. But Harry? Harry has the smile of a wolf, for sure...but I am not entirely certain he *has* a heart.'

'Juliana!' Charlotte looked shocked. 'I know you and he began badly, when you first met in Dover, but surely, now you have spent time with him, you can see his good qualities?'

Juliana looked at Charlotte, who seemed genuinely stunned. 'I am not sure of him,' she admitted slowly, though the memory of his intervention at Glenbrook Hall nagged at her.

'Then let me urge you,' said Charlotte, 'to get to know him better. I do not ask that you *favour* him, but I should hate for you to dislike each other.'

'Well…'

'Please? I do not wish my best friend and my brother-in-law to be at odds.'

Juliana sighed. 'Very well. I will try. But only because you have asked it of me.'

'Oh, come now, Juliana, it will not be so difficult, surely?'

'Not difficult for you. But he delights in teasing me and I find I always take the bait, then regret it afterwards.'

'So I have observed. It is amusing to watch—though not, of course, to experience. Now, let us go and tell Olivia we are finally to go to Almack's.'

'Well, I was never more disappointed!' declared Olivia. 'After all the talk of Almack's, I expected a *palace*, not this!' She gestured around, indicating the plain ballroom, its arch-top windows draped with simple curtains, the spaces in between decorated with mirrors and paintings. 'Why, our ballroom at Chadcombe is a thousand times more beautiful!'

'But the attraction of Almack's, you must understand,' asserted Harry, 'is not in its appearance, but in its *exclusivity*. For every maiden here tonight, there are dozens—perhaps hundreds more—who will never be admitted.'

Olivia, who looked stunning in a white evening gown, with small rosebuds threaded through her dark curls, studied her dance card. 'It is all country dances and quadrilles, too. Are we not to dance the waltz?'

Adam took the card to check. 'You are correct, Olivia—no waltzes. That is probably because Countess Lieven is not here. Of all the Patronesses, she is the one who promotes the waltz.' He turned to his wife. 'Charlotte, I have been brought here on false pretences. The only reason I came was so I could waltz with you again, my love. I have been deceived!'

Charlotte blushed prettily, but retorted, 'Tosh! The reason you are here—why we are all here—is so we ladies can see what all the fuss was about. And I must say, Olivia, so far, I am in agreement with you.' She glanced around. 'Adam, some seats are free there. Can we procure them?'

Adam made an ironic bow, smilingly saying, 'Yes, my Sergeant!' but moved to reserve the seats. They followed him swiftly, the ladies seating themselves while the men stood nearby.

As the room slowly filled, Juliana was content to sit and gape at all the ladies and gentlemen. With Charlotte and Olivia, she discussed the fashions, demeanour and identities of the other guests. Juliana's own gown of cream-coloured silk, worn over an amber underdress and trimmed with Vandyke lace, was quietly elegant. Charlotte, too, looked pretty in a deep yellow evening gown and fetching cap. As a trio, they attracted more than a few admiring glances and knew themselves to be properly turned out for the occasion.

The only beverages on offer were tea and lemonade, so many of the young men had taken their fill of wine before arriving, which left them in varying states of abandon. It did, however, give them often misplaced confidence in their dancing abilities, and they gleefully circled around the ladies like birds, securing partners for the dances. All three ladies soon found their dance cards filling up. Olivia seemed particularly impressed by one young man who likened her eyes to sapphires and begged for the honour of bringing her a drink. She dimpled prettily and accepted with demure politeness, but her eyes followed him as he crossed the room.

'What a handsome young man!' observed Juliana.

'Oh, Juliana,' said Olivia with enthusiasm. 'I do not think I have ever seen anybody as handsome as he is. His name is Mr Nightingale—is that not a romantic name?'

'Do you think so?' asked Juliana doubtfully.

'Oh, yes,' said Olivia happily, 'I have long believed the nightingale to be the most romantic of birds.'

Juliana returned a non-committal answer, reflecting, although Mr Nightingale was probably close to her own age, she was not sorry his eye had fallen on Olivia rather than herself. Not that she needed another admirer—she had her own circle of beaux tonight and was quite enjoying the sensation.

One young man in particular seemed very interested in Juliana. His name was Mr Attwood and he was not inebriated—which impressed her from the start. He was a good-looking, fair-haired gentleman in his early thirties, with a solemn eye and a sober taste in clothes. His knee breeches, black evening coat and dancing slippers were *de rigueur*, but his neckcloth was tied plainly and he wore no jewellery, save a single ring on his little finger. They danced together and he made polite, sensible conversation. He was a real contrast to the half-silly youths making extravagant compliments, and Juliana found herself intrigued by him.

Between dances, Juliana could not ignore Harry. Standing slightly to one side, he eavesdropped on her light conversations with the young men. His expression was one of tolerant amusement, which was decidedly irksome. Why did he insist on being interested in her personal business? She wished he would leave her be.

He had solicited her hand for the supper dance, which she could hardly refuse—indeed, it could perhaps be deemed an insult if he had *not* danced with her, as she was a guest of his family and part of his party. She was surprised to find he danced well, without flamboyance, and that she quite enjoyed dancing with him. He also refrained from saying anything to vex her during their dance, which was a relief. Guiltily, she admitted dancing with Harry was much more entertaining than dancing with any of her other partners—including the worthy Mr Attwood. Afterwards, Harry escorted her into the supper room.

'Oh, dear,' exclaimed Juliana, looking at the paltry array of food. 'Olivia will be sorely unimpressed!'

Harry grimaced. 'Almack's prides itself on offering a meagre supper. The Patronesses want us to remember we are here on their sufferance, rather than by desire.'

'Captain Fanton?' A female voice intruded on their conversation. 'Oh, it is you! I am so happy to see you again!'

Juliana turned. A young lady stood there—a beautiful young lady with deep-auburn hair, warm brown eyes and creamy skin. She looked similar in age to

Juliana and wore a stunning evening gown of rose silk, trimmed with dark-pink rosettes.

'Miss Etherington!' Harry, all smiles, lifted the lady's hand to kiss it. Juliana slipped her hand out of the crook of Harry's arm, where it had been resting. 'How wonderful to see you. You look delightful, my dear! What a charming gown—the exact colour of your beautiful lips.'

Miss Etherington blushed and stammered, and was flattered. 'Please tell me,' Harry continued, his full attention on the newcomer, 'you still have a place on your dance card for me? Do not break my heart!'

'Well... I do have a country dance free, later,' said Miss Etherington coquettishly, her eyes dancing.

'I cannot conceive how that has occurred, with so many men here tonight and you looking like an angel! Yet, their error is welcome and I will take my opportunity with delight.'

'Oh, Captain Fanton! You flatter me!'

'Not at all—every word is true!'

Juliana opened her fan and wafted it smartly. Harry, sensing it, turned towards her. 'Miss Milford, may I present Miss Etherington.' The two ladies smiled insincerely at each other and curtsied politely.

'Delighted!' said Miss Etherington civilly, casting

an assessing eye over Juliana's gown, before turning her attention back to Harry. 'Captain Fanton, I have often remembered our drive together, during my stay at Chadcombe. You did promise to take me driving in London…'

'But of course! And I mean to keep my promise. May I call on you tomorrow?'

'Please do—we shall be at home between two and four. And I must call on dear Lady Shalford—it has been too long since I have seen my dear friend Charlotte!'

That was enough for Juliana. Catching a glimpse of Olivia at the far side of the supper room, she said quickly, 'Excuse me—I see my friend calls me.'

Harry made a brief acknowledgement, but seemed to barely notice when Juliana slipped away, embarrassment and anger reddening her face. Making her way through the crowds, she eventually reached Charlotte and Olivia.

'Oh, Juliana—there you are! Look—for supper, there is only dry cake, and bread and butter!' Olivia indicated her plate. 'Why, any hostess should be ashamed to offer such scanty fare to her guests! I declare it is all a take-in!'

Charlotte was studying Juliana's face. 'Are you well, Juliana?'

'I am quite well,' lied Juliana, 'though I confess it is warm in here.'

'You are right—this supper room is such a crush!' Charlotte indicated the nearest door. 'If you don't mind doing without the bread and butter, we can go back to the ballroom where it is quieter.'

'Yes, let us do that,' agreed Juliana. As they left, her gaze found Harry, who was still with Miss Etherington. As she watched, Harry bent closer to speak into the young lady's ear, causing her to blush charmingly and slap him playfully with her fan. Juliana gritted her teeth, lifted her chin and walked on.

Harry was feeling deeply uncomfortable. Having spent so much time with Juliana recently, he was in danger of becoming too focused on her. Yet no matter how he tried, he could not seem to divert his attention elsewhere. When that dull dog Attwood seemed to be making headway in attracting Juliana's interest earlier, he could have cheerfully throttled him!

It would not do. He must behave as he always had—enjoying the company of many ladies, without becoming attached to any one in particular. Yet there were moments when he felt a real sense of peril—as if he was not in control of his own emotions. Fencing with her in the barn, walking with her at Chadcombe, enjoying a gallop through a London park—she exhilarated him and *it would not do*! In the carriage, after the trip to Glenbrook Hall, Juliana had gripped his hand briefly and it had shaken him to his core. He barely understood what was happening to him, but he felt bewitched—as if he was not in control of his own mind. He must master this!

Only he knew how flawed he was, how unworthy of love. The thought that someone might wish to know him better was terrifying. Why, she might discover his true nature! He needed to keep everyone at a safe distance.

The appearance of Miss Etherington tonight was a relief. He knew her to be on the catch for a husband, yet willing to flirt outrageously with him—and others—in the meantime. He enjoyed the game, yet always forgot her instantly when she was out of sight. She had appeared at exactly the right moment tonight, because he had been aware of a strange feeling of lightness—euphoria, almost—while dancing with Juliana. Having Juliana's hand on his arm as they moved to the supper room had filled him with unexpected feelings of pride, possessiveness and longing. There was nothing he had needed more in that moment than to escape from himself, and from the unwelcome feelings coursing through him.

Juliana's departure had been abrupt. Had he hurt

her feelings? He reviewed his actions. He had been perfectly polite, had even introduced the two young ladies. He knew Juliana did not take his flirting seriously, so there was no reason to think she had been upset by his compliments to Miss Etherington.

Steeling himself to get through the rest of the evening, he quickly developed a plan. He would focus on Miss Etherington and put Juliana out of his head completely. Juliana wasn't upset—of course she wasn't. What strange notions he took, sometimes! He reflected again on the conversation in the supper room. On reflection, he thought, Juliana might be simply annoyed with him again—seeing the whole situation as evidence that he was nothing but a shallow flirt, made of 'all mirth and no matter'. *Good*, he thought grimly. Better that than the chance she might genuinely feel something for him. He must at all costs remain remote. Love and marriage were for other men, never for him. He had faced many enemies in battle, but the one adversary he had never slain lived within him.

Chapter Eight

Juliana sighed. After the incident at supper, the whole evening now seemed flat. Faced with this new evidence of Harry's empty insincerity, she should have been feeling triumphant and vindicated. Instead, she was struggling to identify anything in herself other than anger. She went through the conventions of the ball, dancing with different partners and engaging in light, witty conversations with people she could not afterwards remember. How dared he be so rude! He had completely ignored her when Miss Etherington appeared. And as for the compliments he had been paying the other young lady—why, he had said almost identical things to her!

During the second-last dance of the evening, Juliana was doubly unfortunate. Firstly, she had the felicity of dancing with the portly Mr Ryan, who trod on her foot three times, and, secondly, she was in the same set as Harry and Miss Etherington. As they wove through the figures, Juliana tried to maintain an air of elegant disinterestedness, which survived only as long as her unbruised toes.

'Ouch!' She could not prevent the expletive.

'Oh, my dear Miss Milford! I apologise!' Mr Ryan blushed and stammered.

Juliana tried her best to reassure him, while desperately trying to ignore Harry's devilish grin.

A moment later, during an intricate step, her unfortunate partner did it again. This time, Juliana was forearmed and did not cry out. However, she could not prevent a small stumble. As the dance continued, Harry swept around her as part of the figure. 'I do hope nothing is bruised, Miss Milford?' he said silkily.

Juliana awaited the return figure. 'Only my pride, sir.'

He circled back. 'Such a pity you could not have only accomplished dancers to partner with.'

'I prefer a clumsy, honest man to a fork-tongued snake!'

He laughed mechanically, then looked slightly startled as a new thought occurred to him. 'You cannot possibly be referring to me!'

She arched her eyebrows. 'It is interesting you should immediately think so!'

The dance took them apart again, he returning

to his beautiful partner and she to Mr Ryan, who was becoming, it was clear, increasingly anxious. His conversation had petered out and he was now focused fully on his steps, to such an extent that his tongue was protruding and his face frowning in concentration.

At the far end of their set, Harry sent her a wicked glance. Juliana sighed.

The next figure brought them together again. 'Now,' said Harry, his eyes dancing, 'you must tell me what I have done to offend you.'

'I have not said that you have offended me,' she replied haughtily.

'I am no green boy, Miss Milford. My reading of women is usually accurate. Now, tell me. Or shall I guess?'

His 'reading of women'! Such arrogance! 'I have nothing to say to you. Please do not bother me with your conversation.'

'Ah, is that why you and your…er…light-footed partner are not on speaking terms? Are you taking a silent vow?'

In her head, she uttered a silent vow which would have shocked him, but managed to say evenly, 'Please save your dialogue for Miss Etherington. I am sure she will appreciate it.'

'Miss Etherington?' His eyes narrowed. 'Jealous, Juliana?'

Before she could respond, he swept away from her, to the next lady in the set.

Juliana felt ready to explode—like the famous fire mountain in the East Indies. She felt the anger build within her. How dared he? *Jealous?* Of him fawning over the insipid Miss Etherington? She did not care who he practised his lies on! She only wished he would leave her alone.

How she got through the remainder of the dance, she did not know. But thankfully, the music finally came to an end. She was then forced to endure a full two minutes of heartfelt apology from Mr Ryan, who was mortified at his clumsiness. Making up for his reticence during the dance, he held her with a litany of apologies, followed by advice on how to best treat her bruised feet. She was just beginning to wonder if she would ever escape, when a male voice intruded.

'Ah, Mr Ryan!' It was *him*. 'I fear I must claim your delightful partner, as she I believe she is promised to me for the last dance.' Juliana glared at Harry, paralysed by indecision. If she denied him, exposing his lie, she would be stuck with the frankly tiresome Mr Ryan for goodness knew how long, yet

Captain Fanton was the last person she wanted to spend time with.

He forced her to choose, offering his arm and waiting. To refuse him now would be the height of rudeness and he knew it.

Murmuring a goodbye to Mr Ryan, she rested her fingers lightly on Harry's arm—making sure there was minimal touch involved. After just a few steps, she removed her hand and stepped slightly in front of him, relieved that the crowd of people in this part of the room meant there was no space for them both to pass at once. Neither of them spoke, but she could *feel* his amusement.

The dancing area was still thronged with people taking the opportunity to talk in the break between dances. As they picked their way through to its edges, a tall man in front of Juliana was suddenly jostled by a rather drunk youth. The man took a step back, almost treading on Juliana's foot. What was it with Almack's and clumsy men! Taking evasive action, she stepped slightly to the side, where she and the tall man half-collided.

He turned and apologised. He was older than she'd realised—probably nearly seventy, judging by his lined face and silvering hair. He was lean and sprightly, and moved with an ease belying his advanced years. His eyes were a pale, faded blue and were filled with polite apology. Glad she hadn't knocked him over—or suffered the embarrassment of falling over herself—she murmured something appropriate and was about to walk on when the tall man spotted Harry.

'Fanton! Captain Fanton!'

'General!' Harry smiled. The two shook hands warmly. 'It is good to see you again, sir.'

'Badajoz, wasn't it?'

Harry looked grave. 'It was. I am surprised you remember me.'

'I remember you well, Fanton.' They looked at each other solemnly, piquing Juliana's curiosity. What was happening here?

Harry swallowed, then squared his shoulders. 'Sir, may I present Miss Milford, who is a house guest with us at present? Miss Milford, this is General Hunter.' Juliana curtsied, noticing as she did so that the General was looking at her intently.

'Milford, eh?' said the General sharply. He frowned. 'It is a common enough name...' He stood, lost in thought for a moment, before turning back to Harry 'What is your direction in London, Captain?'

Harry gave it. The General nodded curtly, bowed and walked on.

'Well!' said Juliana. 'What a strange man!'

'The General is eccentric, to be sure,' said Harry,

'But a first-rate leader, with excellent qualities. I fought under him in Spain.'

Juliana looked at him curiously. There was a strange expression on his face—sadness, strength and something else, a shadow that she could not quite name. Something to do with the General and Badajoz.

She of course had heard about the battle there, during the Peninsular Campaign, and the rumours that it had been particularly harrowing. And now she knew Harry had been there. She felt a pang of compassion.

He saw her intent regard and his demeanour immediately changed. 'Now, Miss Milford, am I to enjoy the next dance with you, or are you promised to another?' He smiled charmingly. 'I do hope your card is free, especially after such an invigorating country dance. I'm sure your enjoyment of Mr Ryan's company has made you hungry for more.'

Juliana felt disorientated. Harry's moods could change so quickly, from sunshine to storm and back again. This time, she did not react angrily to his flirtatious tone, instead tilting her head to one side and enquiring seriously, 'Captain Fanton, are you quite well?'

He stilled and her eyes caught his. Briefly, something flashed there before he laughed lightly, saying,

'I was never better! For here I am, in the company of the Incomparable Miss Milford, and all Almack's is envious of me! Now, let me see your card.'

Juliana showed it and half-listened as he bemoaned cruel fate, which had placed Mr Attwood's name there for the final dance of the evening. As Mr Attwood appeared and Harry relinquished her into the young man's company, Harry continued with his usual light banter, but Juliana only half-heard it. She had much to think about.

Juliana picked up her embroidery tambour with a sigh. Much as she tried, she could not pretend she was good at needlework. She turned the frame over. As usual, all of the threads were completely tangled. Why was it that other women were so good at these traditional tasks, while she just saw them as pointless?

'Can I help you with that, Juliana?' Great-Aunt Clara, bless her, was looking at the tangle with barely concealed horror.

'Please do! For I do not know where to begin with it!' Taking the tambour, Juliana moved to sit with Clara.

The ladies were all seated in the main parlour, awaiting guests who might call. They had just said goodbye to Mr Nightingale—Mr Alfred Nightingale—whose first name had proved to be just as romantic as his surname, according to Olivia.

He had brought a Poem for Miss Fanton. She had listened and blushed, and stammered her thanks after he had recited his poem, which celebrated her beauty and innocence in a wordy, flowery manner. He had delivered his verse with confidence because, he said, he knew himself to have a Talent for his Art—a lucky chance denied to other, more limited souls. Juliana and Charlotte had exchanged amused glances, but Olivia and the older ladies seemed impressed by Alfred's recital.

Mr Attwood had also called, which Juliana was pleased about. She liked his quiet solemnity and plain-spokenness—no flirtatious games with him, though she believed he admired her. He had been a regular caller since their first night at Almack's and Juliana quite looked forward to his visits. She was always comfortable with him; here was a man who was straightforward, consistent and respectful—in short, everything she admired. Sensible. Yes, that is what she liked about him. He was sensible.

Losing interest in her embroidery as Clara separated the threads, Juliana looked around the parlour. Charlotte was writing a letter, Olivia was flicking through the fashion plates in *Ackermann's*, a dreamy half-smile on her lips, and Mama was reading a book. The ticking of the clock on the mantel was the loudest sound in the room, as they all focused in companionable silence on their tasks.

The door opened. 'Mrs Etherington, Miss Etherington!' intoned the footman, stepping to the side to allow the ladies to enter.

They all rose and curtsied, and the introductions were made. Miss Etherington—she of the auburn hair and creamy skin—looked stunning in a day dress of green crape. Juliana, whose pretty sprig muslin had seemed perfectly adequate until just now, noted the other girl's stylish coiffure, modest jewellery and soft kid gloves with antipathy. She had a certain fashionable air which Juliana found decidedly off-putting. Her mother was similarly elegant, and they were clearly well known to Charlotte, Olivia and Clara.

The guests were invited to sit, tea was ordered and silence once more settled on them all.

'Lady Shalford, I am so happy to see you again!' Mrs Etherington, a delicate widow whose sloped shoulders and harassed visage indicated unspoken Trials in her life, spoke softly. 'We so enjoyed our trip to Chadcombe last summer. Miss Langley, you were a most excellent hostess!'

'We were happy to have you there,' said Clara graciously. 'Such a busy time at Chadcombe, with you and Charlotte, and Charlotte's cousins!' She turned to address Juliana and Mrs Milford. 'Charlotte's cousin Henrietta is married to Mrs Etherington's son. The match was made at Chadcombe—as was dear Adam's marriage to darling Charlotte!' She reached out and took Charlotte's hand as she spoke. Miss Etherington did not look pleased, which Juliana wondered at.

'Yes, indeed,' said Mrs Etherington, 'my dear Hubert and his wife will return to town next week.' She leaned forward and added confidentially, 'Henrietta is increasing, you know—my first grandchild!'

'I did know,' confirmed Charlotte. 'She wrote to me last week. I am looking forward to seeing her again.'

'Oh, but she may not be well enough for house calls,' proclaimed Mrs Etherington. 'I remember how ill I was when I was in the family way. Why, when I was confined with Millicent—' she indicated her daughter '—I kept to my room for an age! My poor husband was distracted with worry!' She sighed sadly, pulled a lace handkerchief from her reticule and dabbed gently at the corner of her eye. Juliana watched, fascinated.

The door opened again, this time admitting Harry and Adam. Immediately, Charlotte looked more relaxed, while Miss Etherington sat up straighter and smiled warmly in Harry's direction. Harry and Adam greeted their guests with the ease of long acquaintance. Adam sat with his wife on the red sofa, while Harry chose a chair next to Miss Millicent Etherington. She flashed a brief, triumphant glance in Juliana's direction—as if Juliana cared where he sat! The anger Juliana had felt at Almack's returned immediately and with full force. Harry and Miss Millicent were a good pair, it seemed—equally preoccupied with games of flirtation. They deserved each other.

The refreshments arrived and the next few minutes passed with Charlotte pouring tea and ensuring everyone had been served with their preferred pastries and sweetmeats. Mama helped, as she usually did. Harry and Millicent talked convivially of mutual acquaintances, while Clara and Mrs Etherington chatted about the weather and the impact of damp on old bones and joints. Juliana, not wishing to appear discomfited by Harry and Millicent, asked Olivia to show her some of the fashion plates. Olivia moved to sit with her and they put their heads together to peruse bonnets, gloves and the latest fashions in sleeves.

Mrs Etherington turned her attention to Juliana's mother. 'Mrs Milford,' she said, 'I understand you are guests here. How long do you stay in London?'

Mrs Milford's eyes opened wide. 'Our plans are not yet fixed,' she mumbled.

Mrs Etherington was not satisfied. 'Where is your home?'

A slight frown appeared on Mama's brow. 'We normally reside in Brussels.'

'Brussels? That is in France, is it not? Where that monster Napoleon hides? I declare I shudder at the very *thought* of Brussels!'

'Oh, but, it is not so bad,' said Mama, fidgeting with the book on her lap. 'That is, we have always lived there peacefully.'

'I have heard,' asserted Mrs Etherington, 'that these places are full of Disease.'

'Oh, no!' said Mrs Milford helplessly. 'No more than any other place.'

Harry spoke up. 'I have been to Brussels many times, Mrs Etherington, and I can assure you I have never had so much as a stomach ache!' He smiled winningly at the older lady. It seemed to work.

'Fie, Captain Fanton! That means only that you have been blessed with a strong constitution—unlike my poor son Hubert! He was a most delicate child, you know.'

No one knew how to respond to this.

Millicent spoke, breaking the awkward silence. 'Captain Fanton, at Almack's I saw you conversing with General Hunter. He lives near us in Kent. Are you well acquainted with the General?'

'I fought with him in Spain,' Harry affirmed. Then, as if to temper his tone, he added, 'But I would much prefer to speak about *you*, Miss Etherington. When shall we drive out together?'

As they made arrangements to meet, Juliana became aware something was ailing Mama. She was pale, and her hands trembled where they held her book. Meeting Juliana's eyes, she immediately glanced away, as if to hide from her daughter. Was she unwell? Juliana kept observing until her mother looked up again. She was clearly distressed, but she shook her head slightly, clearly signalling she did not want Juliana to say anything.

Thankfully, the Etheringtons rose to leave a few moments later, having stayed the required twenty minutes. Juliana said everything that was proper, aware that she must seem very dull to their guests— certainly Miss Etherington seemed to have dismissed her as being of no consequence.

Juliana watched with annoyance as Harry kissed Millicent's hand and reminded her of their driving arrangements. The irritation she felt towards Millicent and her tedious mother was nothing in comparison to her exasperation with Harry. Now the Season had started, she knew she would frequently see him in the company of young ladies, flirting and playing games. It would provide constant reminders of why she should be on her guard with him.

Her prime concern just now, however, was Mama. As soon as the Etheringtons had left, she moved to sit beside her.

'Mama! What ails you?' She took her mother's hand.

'Oh, Juliana! It is just as I feared! I knew how it would be if we came to England.' Her hand trembled in Juliana's and her voice wavered. 'We must return to Brussels immediately!'

'My dear Mrs Milford!' Harry was first to react. The others were all looking at her, their faces a mix of shock and anxiety. 'Why should you return to Brussels? Have we done something to upset you?' He looked genuinely concerned, Juliana noticed.

'Oh, no, dear Harry, of course not!' said Mrs Milford tremulously. 'I cannot speak of it! Juliana, please take me to my room!'

Juliana stood immediately and supported Mama as she walked slowly to the door. She seemed truly indisposed. As they walked, Juliana's eyes met Harry's. As well as worry and concern, there was a clear question in his gaze. Juliana shrugged slightly, indicating she had no idea what troubled her parent.

Reaching the safety of her mother's room—a

pretty chamber overlooking the street—Juliana saw Mama settled in the comfortable armchair beside the small fireplace, before enquiring gently, 'Mama, please tell me what troubles you.'

Mama looked at her sorrowfully for a moment, before covering her face with her hands, muttering distractedly, 'I can't! Oh, I can't! I thought maybe, after all these years, I would be safe, but I will never be safe! My wickedness will haunt me for ever!' She burst into noisy tears, still mumbling incoherently.

Juliana, distressed, crouched beside her, offering what comfort she could. 'Hush, Mama, please, tell me the whole.' She was met with an anguished refusal. Juliana could not recall ever seeing her mother so unhappy. 'Would you like a tisane? Some laudanum?'

'No, no, I do not want anything! Please do not ask me!'

Eventually, her mother quietened, her tears eased and she agreed to lie down upon the bed and rest. Juliana closed the curtains, then sat in the armchair until the sound of Mama's breathing indicated that she slept.

Moving silently, she slipped out of the room, closing the door quietly behind her.

Chapter Nine

Harry paced up and down the hallway. What on earth was wrong with Mrs Milford? She had seemed so happy, so contented recently. Knowing how much she and Juliana relied on each other, he had been pleased to see Juliana gradually relax into life in London, as her concerns about her mother eased. Having watched his own mama decline and slowly die of a wasting illness a few years earlier, he understood a little of Juliana's anxiety. No one could replace one's mother.

Mrs Milford was not ill, but she was vulnerable. She was clearly a woman who had always relied on others—albeit in a gentle, loving way. Juliana and her mama had come to depend on each other and there was a closeness between them that was heart-warming to see. However, Harry did wonder at times, although Juliana never complained, if she felt the burden of carrying the sole responsibility for her mother. At times it seemed as though Mrs Milford was the helpless child, while Juliana stood in the role of mother, father and guardian. Right now, while Harry was fretting about Mrs Milford, more importantly, he was worrying about how her incapacitation was impacting on Juliana. Despite his vow to keep Juliana at an emotional distance, seeing her carry her burdens alone was proving too much for him.

It never occurred to him to question why he should care. If someone had asked him, he would have said it was a combination of factors—they were guests in his home and, as such, deserved his care and attention, and, as a responsible army officer, he was used to taking charge and sorting out problems. The fact that it was his *brother's* home, not his, and that neither Juliana nor her mother were under his care as an officer, was, evidently, of no possible relevance.

Juliana glided down the staircase, surprised to see Harry waiting for her. 'Juliana!' He took both her hands, concern etched on his face. 'How is she?'

'Sleeping.' He led her to a *chaise longue* in the hallway and sat with her.

'What has happened to upset her so?'

'She would not tell me.' Juliana's shoulders slumped. 'I know not what to do. I have never seen her like this.'

His eyes searched her face. 'How can I help you?'

Moved, she squeezed his hands, which remained locked in hers. 'Thank you for your concern. You are already helping.' This was true, if surprising. It was remarkably comforting to see his compassion, which looked genuine. His demeanour had changed from his usual, light emptiness. He seemed serious, thoughtful, as if he actually *cared*. She did not know what to make of it but, in her current state, could only be grateful.

'You look so pale, Juliana.' Letting go, he reached up to smooth a stray tendril of hair that had escaped from her Grecian knot. His eyes met hers and her heart began to race. The intensity of his regard was creating strange flutterings in her stomach. His gaze dropped to her mouth and instantly Juliana felt it— as if he had actually kissed her! She held her breath. What was he going to do? Their eyes met again. Neither spoke.

Juliana heard the clock tick in the hallway, the beating of her heart, the sound of her own breathing. Time stood still.

Harry exhaled, shook himself slightly, then spoke lightly. 'You are much too quiet. Where is the lively Miss Milford, who would never normally allow me to be this close to her?'

His words recalled Juliana to the moment. He was

right—she could not afford to be weak, least of all with him! She must be strong and look after her mother. She sat up straighter and schooled her features to impassivity.

'I thank you, Captain Fanton, for your kindness. But this is none of your concern.'

He looked uncertain. 'Please do not disappear on me again, when finally we were almost friends.'

She regarded him mildly, safe in her self-containment. 'I am sure I do not know what you mean,' she said primly. 'I have not disappeared. I am still here.'

'No, you are gone again,' he muttered. 'And it *is* my concern,' he insisted. 'You both are.' He stared into space. 'You are too much my concern.'

Abruptly, he stood, bowed and walked away, leaving Juliana feeling confused, disappointed and more than a little deflated. He was so mercurial! One moment, all concern, the next, distant and grim. Yet another indication that he could not be relied upon. She straightened her shoulders. She must not be distracted. Mama was her priority. Nothing else mattered.

Harry spurred his horse to a gallop. He was a fool! Despite all his self-discipline, the control he thought he had established over his emotions, he had gravely erred. Juliana had managed to get through his defences. He galloped at full speed through the park, glad there were not many other riders around at this hour. He was not in the right temper to be polite.

He was forced to admit it: he was beginning to care for Juliana. He wanted to ensure her happiness, to take away her worries, to ease her pain. The thought of her distress over her mother filled him with compassion, worry and the need to *act*. He pictured her beautiful face, creased with concern, as she had accompanied Mrs Milford out of the drawing room. He then recalled that moment later, in the hall, when he had spoken softly to her and time had stood still…

How had this happened? How could he have been so foolish? He had been drawn to her from the first, and, as he had come to know her better, he discovered every day new things to admire about her.

The fact that she was a guest in their home had not helped matters, of course. They had naturally spent time together and he could not help but get to know her. Mrs Milford, too. His heart sank as he thought of Juliana's mama. What on earth ailed her? She was so emotionally *frail* that nothing should be allowed to vex her. He genuinely cared about her, as if she were a long-lost aunt or a lifelong family friend.

Perhaps that explained it. Perhaps he saw Juliana as a member of his family, or a close friend.

He developed the thought, seeing a possible escape from his turbulent emotions. *Yes!* He would naturally worry about Olivia, or Charlotte, if something ailed them. He thought about others in his life. Great-Aunt Clara. His aunt, Lady Annesley. Adam, of course. Without a doubt, he would help any one of them, if they were in a fix.

He turned his thoughts to his Army colleagues. If Evans needed support, Harry would do all he could—within the constraints of his own vile, cowardly nature. And, since that terrible incident at Badajoz three years ago, he had ensured he always considered the needs of ordinary citizens he had encountered while on duty.

Badajoz. Seeing General Hunter again had stirred up the old memories—of what Harry had seen and done, and how he had failed.

He brought his thoughts back to the dilemma at hand. Perhaps that was his solution. It was perfectly acceptable to care about people. Everyone else treated Juliana and her mother as part of the family, so why should he not? Pulling up his horse, he turned and began trotting back the way he had come. The difficulty, he decided, was that he was so attracted to her. She was in his home. He saw her every day. It was only natural that two unattached young people would notice each other. It did not mean he had to act on it, or attach a deeper meaning to it than was necessary. He ignored the small voice that reminded him of Miss Etherington's visit to Chadcombe last year and how he had found it an easy matter to resist her charms.

Reassured by his own logic, he continued on, past the lake, through the copse. All he had to do, then, was to stand Juliana's friend, without taking advantage of her. He was the experienced one, having played games of flirtation—as well as having had encounters with courtesans—for years. Juliana, an innocent, if tempestuous, young lady, needed him to behave with propriety at all times.

He must forgive himself this one lapse. It would not happen again.

The Etheringtons were regular visitors after that, and were sometimes joined by Millicent's brother, Mr Hubert Etherington, who fancied himself a leader of fashion. Today, his coat was a glaring yellow and he had paired it with an appalling puce-and-green waistcoat and salmon-pink breeches. He described it as being 'all the crack' and delighted in reporting that he had been followed all the way down St James's Street by a group of street urchins.

Mr Etherington's wife, Henrietta, was now in town and came to visit with the others. She appeared not to notice her husband's startling attire and, indeed, matched his eye for discordant colour. Today she wore a reddish-purple satin gown trimmed with rows of cream lace. She looked a little like the sugary confections Juliana remembered from the Brussels bakeries. Henrietta, who was Charlotte's cousin, was engaging in what her mother-in-law stated was a shocking level of social intercourse for a woman in her 'condition'.

'Oh, fiddle!' said Henrietta, as they all sat in civil conversation in the drawing room. 'I never felt better! After the dreary tiredness left me, I felt cooped up at home, so I persuaded my dear husband to take me to London. I missed the company and the excitement, you see.'

Juliana thought she did see. Henrietta was a stunning blonde, with deep-blue eyes and a sullen pout, and—interestingly—was not, it seemed, well liked by Millicent. This was hardly surprising, since, in the half-hour since they had all been conversing, Henrietta had twice referred to Millicent's unmarried state and in a manner guaranteed to rouse her sister-in-law's ire.

'But, my dear Henrietta, you must think of your child,' insisted Mrs Etherington.

'I do think of my child,' countered Henrietta, 'for

my child needs a mother who is happy and content. Is that not true, Hubert?'

Sensing the trap, her husband refused to intervene in the debate between his wife and his mother, muttering about his having no opinion on female matters and inviting them instead to admire his new waistcoat.

Harry, who had been watching the by-play with amusement, immediately caught Juliana's gaze. She could not resist letting him know, with a wry smile, her opinion of Hubert's waistcoat. His eyes danced in response.

They had developed something of a truce, she and Harry. He flirted less often—though seemed incapable of quitting completely. In response, Juliana was less antagonistic. Neither had spoken of that strange moment in the hall. Now they were wary, a little guarded, but much friendlier in their everyday relations.

As Henrietta, Charlotte and Millicent began to discuss mutual acquaintances, fuelled by an enquiry from Henrietta as to who was in town, Juliana stole a glance at her mother. She sat on an upright chair near the door, her hands resting in her lap and with an air of serenity about her. Juliana was not fooled by this. Her mother had not revealed the reason for her distress the day the Etheringtons had first called and refused even to discuss the incident. There was no more talk of returning to Brussels—though Juliana had offered this, should Mama truly want it. With Napoleon gathering his armies again, Mrs Milford said, she could not consider putting Juliana in danger.

'As if I should care about that, when you are unhappy, Mama!' Juliana had said.

'I am not unhappy,' Mama countered quietly.

'But you are not happy, Mama.'

'And what of it? I am content. I long ago accepted my fate.'

'What do you mean?' Juliana was perplexed. 'What fate?'

'I do not wish to discuss it. Now, where is my Indian shawl?'

And that was it. She would not be moved. Juliana had noticed, though, that she went out less frequently, preferring to keep to the house or the garden, often pleading 'tiredness' or 'a headache' when the others went shopping, walking or visiting. In the evenings she stayed with Clara, saying she had no taste for soirées and balls. She seemed outwardly content, but Juliana was not convinced.

'It is so unfair that I am not permitted to dance, just because I am increasing,' said Henrietta petulantly.

'Oh, Henrietta, please tell me you will not even consider it!' said her mother-in-law, shocked.

'Well, I suppose I must concede, though I do think it is stupid. After the baby is born I will go dancing *immediately.*'

As Mrs Etherington gasped in horror, her son intervened in the growing argument. 'I have it!'

They all looked expectantly at Hubert. 'The theatre! We shall all go to the theatre.'

'Hubert, what a wonderful idea!' cried Henrietta, clapping her hands. 'You are the cleverest person in the world!'

Hubert accepted the accolade with equanimity, clearly in agreement with his wife's assessment of his intellectual capacity. Juliana couldn't resist glancing at Harry. Sure enough, he was awaiting her gaze and once again they shared their appreciation of Hubert and Henrietta's absurdity. Juliana broke eye contact first, suddenly perturbed by how attuned she was to him. It would not do! She had responsibilities and could not afford to be diverted by a friendship where she was unsure if she could truly trust the other person.

As the conversation washed over her—they were all discussing which performance to attend, and when—she considered the matter. Harry was, in many ways, no different to many other men of her acquaintance. He charmed and flirted, praised and complimented, playing the game of courtship without, she had noted, getting too close to any particular young lady. So why was it he irritated her so much? Why did she object so much to his easy charm? When she met other men at Almack's or at private balls, she was happy to play the game of flirtation and thought no less of herself or the men who tried to charm her. So how was it that Harry could rouse her to anger so quickly, by flirting with her or another young lady?

The answer, she felt, was connected to the strange affinity she felt for him. Charlotte said he had a good heart. Juliana had been forced to acknowledge it—she had seen his genuine concern for Mama and remembered his compassion for the housekeeper at Glenbrook Hall. It was as though there were two of him, she mused. There was his public face—the charming, shallow flirt. But there was also, she felt, a kinder, more serious person who was hidden from view. She looked at him. Like her, he was taking no part in the conversation just now, but was listening contentedly. His handsome face was relaxed and open, and she was sure that a witty remark or warm compliment was only a moment from his lips. She knew him so well!

Suddenly, looking at him, she was assailed by a

strange burning sensation in her chest. It reminded her of the warmth she felt for those she was close to—Mama and Charlotte—but the scale of it was much more intense. If the warmth she felt for them was a banked fire, what she was feeling just now was a furnace.

Discomfited, she raised a hand to her breastbone, as if by pressing it she could quell the feeling flowing through her. What did it mean?

Lord! She hoped no one would notice what was happening to her. Dropping her hand, she schooled her features into polite indifference. She sneaked a look around the room. No one was paying her any attention, thank goodness.

The door opened. More visitors! At this rate they would soon run out of chairs. The footman held the door, announcing the latest arrival. 'General Hunter!'

Chapter Ten

General Hunter strode into the room, his tall, imposing figure seeming to shrink the space. In daylight, his gaunt, lined face and morose expression seemed even more marked. He wore plain pantaloons, gleaming Hessians and a well-cut black coat, in the style favoured by older gentlemen. His demeanour bore the hallmarks of a military life and the authority of command.

Harry stood immediately, offering his hand. 'General Hunter! I am happy to see you, sir!'

The General shook his hand unsmilingly. 'Fanton.'

Harry made the introductions. 'My brother, Lord Shalford. His wife, Lady Shalford.'

The General shook Adam's hand and bowed to Charlotte. His expression was inscrutable, and Juliana wondered about the reason for his visit. There had been something unspoken between him and Harry, that night at Almack's—a reference to shared memories that had seemed important to both of them. Was that why the General was making a house call to a family that he was clearly not well acquainted with?

Adam took over the introductions. 'General, I am delighted to make your acquaintance. May I introduce our guests?'

General Hunter cast an eye over the room. His gaze paused briefly when he reached Juliana, then moved on. 'Please do,' he said evenly, 'though I already know the Etheringtons—' he bowed '—and Elizabeth.'

What? He knows Mama?

Juliana was shocked. She looked at her mother. She was pale as a ghost and her hands were shaking. Once again, her mother was reacting with fear. Juliana did not understand why; she simply knew she must protect her from all harm.

Adam smoothed over the moment, saying only, 'Excellent—I will not introduce Mrs Milford to you then. Are you acquainted with Miss Milford?'

The General's eyes blazed into hers. 'We have met,' he said curtly, bowing his head towards Juliana.

Juliana dipped in the smallest of curtsies, aware that all eyes were on her and her mother. Though she did not understand exactly what was happening, she would be equal to it. She lifted her chin and eyed the General levelly. She would not be intimidated!

'This is my great-aunt, Miss Langley, and my sister, Olivia.' Adam's voice diverted the General's attention to the others in the room. The General bowed to the ladies. Charlotte then bade him sit and offered him tea, which he declined.

There was a tense silence in the drawing room. The expressions on everyone's face showed various forms of confusion. Harry had described General Hunter as eccentric. Well, he was certainly that!

Surprisingly, it was Mrs Etherington who eased the situation. 'General Hunter, I declare we have not seen you for an age! What do you think about this new turnpike road they are building in Kent?'

'The state of the roads is abominable,' said the General curtly. 'I do not mind paying a toll if it means my wheels do not get stuck every winter!'

'I must say I agree with you, General. I know not why they must riot about it!'

'Oh, those awful people!' said Millicent crossly. 'Do you know they threw mud at my coach last week?'

Henrietta agreed. 'And they tried to break the toll gate near our village.'

Despite being distracted, Juliana was intrigued by this. 'Why are people rioting?'

Charlotte explained diplomatically. 'Each time a new turnpike trust is set up, a free road becomes a toll road and often the local people don't like it.'

'Well, that is understandable, surely. Why should they pay a toll for something that has always been free and open?'

General Hunter's eyes narrowed. 'Because, Miss Milford, the road will be improved with the toll money. Holes will be filled, milestones posted and the rules of the road will be enforced. If people would all keep their carriages to the left, I dare say we would not have so many accidents.'

Juliana was undaunted. 'What about the poorest people? How do they pay?'

General Hunter looked taken aback for an instant, then shrugged. 'It is not a large amount. I had not thought much about it.'

That does not surprise me, thought Juliana. She had the bit between her teeth now and was enjoying standing up to the overbearing General. He had aroused her ire by making Mama feel uncomfortable. Well, she would not be so easily cowed!

'Well, someone *should* think about it! The poorest villagers may not be able to afford even a small toll. There ought to be some sort of free passage for those living in the area.'

The General looked at her with interest. 'And how,

Miss Milford, do you propose enforcing this?' His tone was deceptively mild. 'For any token would be abused and sold on.'

Across the room, Juliana caught Harry's gaze. He looked like he was quite enjoying her exchange with the irascible General. His look contained admiration, more than a little confusion, and something else...something she could not quite fathom.

She turned her attention back to her adversary. 'For shame, General Hunter. As a great leader, you can surely see the obvious solution!'

Perhaps I should not have referred to him as a great leader, she thought. *He is clever enough to detect my meaning.*

'Enlighten me.' His face was impressively grim.

Juliana shrugged. 'Leave it to the gatekeeper. Locals will always be known at the toll gate.'

The General laughed briefly, a sharp bark. 'You speak your opinions without fear, Miss Milford.'

'And why should I fear speaking my opinion?' she threw back at him, undaunted. Out of the corner of her eye, she could see a shocked expression on Millicent's face. It encouraged her to be even more reckless. 'I have a heart, and a brain, and a stomach, and I have a taste for debate. Why should I remain silent?'

'Others may disagree with you,' he said, but there

was a gleam in his eye. 'Or they might think such strong opinions not suitable for so young a person. Particularly for a young lady.'

She tossed her head. 'I like it when others disagree with me. I enjoy the battle and sometimes I learn new things that way.'

'Your way of learning is most unusual,' he muttered thoughtfully. 'A spirited character through and through—I admit to being surprised, Elizabeth.'

Everyone looked at Mrs Milford. She still seemed unable to speak, but nodded mutely, clearly desperate for him to take everyone's attention away from her.

'It has been some time since we were last in company together. Might I have a word with you in private?' The General was addressing Mrs Milford.

Her jaw dropped and a look of sheer panic came over her face. Juliana had to intervene.

'Mama, you are unwell! I shall take you to your room.' She moved quickly to her mother's side. Her mother rose immediately and squeezed Juliana's hand gratefully.

'General, I am sure you will excuse Mrs Milford,' said Harry calmly. 'She is clearly unwell.'

General Hunter frowned. 'Very well, Elizabeth. But you cannot avoid me for ever, now I have found you.'

Juliana's mother did not respond. And the last

thing Juliana saw as she left the parlour was the General's piercing gaze.

'And your mother will not tell you anything?'

'Nothing. She is clearly troubled, but she will not let me help her.'

Juliana and Harry were walking arm in arm through Green Park. Ahead of them, Charlotte and Adam meandered happily along the path, oblivious to everything except each other.

This was becoming quite a habit. The four of them would walk out together, but would then immediately break into couples, which left Juliana spending much of her time with Harry. With Charlotte and Adam still acting as newlyweds and Mama so distant, Juliana was conscious she was becoming accustomed to sharing her worries with Harry. Relying on him was becoming rather a habit with her, since the drama with the General. He seemed genuinely interested and concerned. Indeed, she believed he truly cared about Mama. When he acted like this he was dangerous to her peace of mind, precisely *because* he ceased his irritating flirtation. This Harry was hard to resist. If pressed, she would be forced to admit she counted him her friend.

Mama was resolutely refusing to explain how she knew General Hunter, and became so distressed when probed that Juliana had—for now—admitted defeat. Mama now kept to her room during many visits and refused to leave it. She was becoming a recluse and dwindling before Juliana's eyes.

'What do you know of your mother's life before her marriage?'

'Very little.'

'Your father?'

'I know almost nothing about my father, how they met, or where. He died soon after I was born.'

'Pardon me for all these questions, but—what of your mother's family?'

'Again, I know almost nothing. They were wealthy, I think. Mama once referred to a plan they had to marry her off to a rich, old gentleman, which outraged her because, she said, her family had no need of more wealth.'

'Hmm. I did wonder…something in the General's approach to her…'

'What do you mean?' Juliana could barely think straight. She was consumed by concern for her mother. 'Do you think they wanted to marry her to General Hunter? No wonder she ran away!'

He looked at her, then shook his head. 'No, that wasn't it. Just a passing notion.'

Ahead of them, Adam and Charlotte stopped to

kiss. Juliana glanced sidelong at Harry. He, too, had seen them.

'Ah.' Harry raised his voice. 'Dear brother, can you please confine your…er…marital activities to the…er…marital chamber?'

Despite herself, Juliana giggled. Adam and Charlotte broke off their kiss, Charlotte blushing profusely.

Adam seemed undaunted. 'I shall thank you, Harry, to keep your opinions to yourself!' He smiled tenderly at Charlotte. 'I shall kiss my wife whenever I choose.'

Charlotte returned his smile with a shy one of her own. Juliana felt a sudden ache in her chest, a tightness in her throat. Charlotte was so happy! That was what was different about her now. Happiness surrounded her, like an invisible glow.

As they walked on through the park, Juliana mused on Charlotte and Adam's evident contentment. Charlotte had found her home—not the elegant London town house, nor the grand country estate. It was Adam. Adam was her home.

Why the thought should make her sad, she simply did not know.

The new Theatre Royal in Drury Lane had risen from the ashes of the dreadful fire which had put

paid to Sheridan's ambitions, and it had now confirmed its place as London's leading theatre. The
presence of Kean—held to be the greatest actor of
his time—meant the theatre had enjoyed continuous success since reopening three years previously.
Juliana was fascinated by the huge interior, ornately
gilded boxes and elaborate Safety Curtain which had
been included to protect the audience from harm.

Their party was large, as it included the Etheringtons—apart from Mrs Etherington, who was at
home, enjoying a bout of indigestion. Olivia, Charlotte and Juliana, along with Millicent and Henrietta, were escorted to delicate gilded chairs in the
front row of their box. Henrietta asked for a stool
for her feet and two cushions, which the footman
arranged behind her as directed. Behind the ladies,
a row of chairs was arranged for the gentlemen. Hubert and Adam took up the places directly behind
their wives, while Harry sat behind Millicent, who
was next to Juliana. Alfred Nightingale, Olivia's
poet, had been invited to make up the numbers, as
well as Mr Attwood. Juliana was pleased to see Mr
Attwood again, despite some gentle teasing earlier
from Olivia.

Juliana was pleased with her gown for tonight—a
blue silk with pale-blue gauze and a pretty flounce
along the hemline. She had added a simple string of

pearls, long evening gloves and a delicate painted fan. Mr Attwood had told her she looked beautiful, in a straight, unadorned way, which she appreciated. His words seemed so much more sincere than Harry's fulsome compliments, which she had received back in the town house before the carriages had been brought round. In addition, Mr Attwood did not make her feel uncomfortable. He was easy company without making her feel anger, or warmth, or anything much at all.

That, she told herself, was *exactly* what she wanted. She had seen with Mama what happened when someone became lost to their own emotions. Mama had been overwhelmed by her own fear, and fear had become the defining feature of her personality and her character. Juliana adored Mama, but she knew her mother's life was limited by her many and varied fears and anxieties.

Juliana had been determined to stand up to her own fears. When she felt anxious about something, her immediate reaction was to meet it directly, to face it down and to defeat it. She knew it led her on occasion to do something others would see as foolhardy or unnecessary. It mattered not. To let fear win, even once, would set her on the wrong path.

Harry challenged her in different ways. With him, she felt irritated, sometimes angry, and occasionally she felt that intense fire for him which had threat-ened to overwhelm her that day in the parlour. It was an entirely new sensation and she was still not entirely sure what to make of it.

Yes, spending time with Mr Attwood was much less challenging.

Alfred was currently sending glowing looks in Olivia's direction and had brought a pink flower for her. 'A rosebud,' he said, 'the only flower you should ever wear.'

Olivia blushed and thanked him, while Juliana mused silently that, if someone had told her she should only wear rosebuds, then she would make a point of wearing everything *except* rosebuds af-terwards.

Not to be outdone by the poet, Hubert announced dramatically, 'Ladies, permit me to tell you that you outshine all the angels in the skies tonight!'

Millicent grimaced at her brother's extravagance, while Juliana and Charlotte suppressed small smiles. Henrietta responded with exasperation, curtly ask-ing her husband to secure some lemonade for her.

He duly did so and what might have been a dif-ficult display of disharmony was averted. Juliana, determined to enjoy herself, kept her eyes on the actors as the play began. There was no hush in the brightly lit theatre and the assembled guests conversed and commented and laughed throughout the performance.

Juliana's enjoyment was a little dimmed by Harry, who pulled his chair forward to easier converse with her, and with Millicent, who was to her right. Mr Attwood had taken the seat behind Juliana, next to Harry, and so Juliana pointedly concentrated on him, leaving Harry to focus on Miss Etherington.

The more Millicent simpered and tittered, and told Harry how much she admired his wit, the quieter Juliana became. Mr Attwood diverted her with a string of rational questions and comments, and they maintained a polite discourse during the first interval, while Adam and Alfred sourced refreshments for the ladies.

Lord! thought Juliana. How am I to get through two more hours of this? She pursed her lips and steeled herself for what would surely be the most tedious evening of her life.

Chapter Eleven

Their box was in a prominent position and Juliana took the opportunity during the break to scan around the theatre, enjoying the spectacle of the revellers in the pit—some of whom were using quizzing glasses and opera glasses to better ogle the ladies. Juliana lifted her gaze to the patrons in the boxes opposite. Suddenly she stiffened. 'Charlotte!'

Charlotte turned towards her. 'What is it?'

'Look there! Someone is waving at you!' Juliana indicated the largest box to the left of the stage. In it was a couple, the lady portly and dripping with jewels. Behind her stood a man, rake-thin and slightly hunched, giving instructions to one of the theatre staff. 'I think it might be your friends from Glenbrook Hall!'

Charlotte gasped. 'It is, though they are no friends of mine! Lord, I hope they do not intend to renew the acquaintance!' She lifted her hand slightly, the smallest of movements, to acknowledge Mrs Wakely's frantic waving, which was already attracting curious stares from other patrons. It had the desired effect. Mrs Wakely beamed broadly and stopped waving.

A moment later, she signalled to her husband. He looked across to where they sat, before performing an obsequious bow in Charlotte's general direction. Juliana shuddered, while Charlotte moaned slightly in mortification.

Thankfully, the footmen signalled that the interval was now at an end and Juliana averted her eyes from the Wakelys.

The second show—a farce which was shockingly ribald at times—eventually came to a close and soon the curtains were closed for the second interval. This was the longest break and, throughout the well-lit theatre, people were up and moving, visiting acquaintances in other parts of the building. Mr Attwood excused himself, having discovered an old schoolfriend signalling to him from the upper circle, while Millicent and Hubert, with Henrietta, went to visit one of Mrs Etherington's friends, to report on their mother's health. Olivia agreed to walk with Alfred, who looked pleased when she took his arm. Adam and Charlotte sat talking quietly, which left only Juliana and Harry.

He invited her to walk with him to order refreshments and she, reluctantly, complied. She did not expect to enjoy the experience. She had noted before that social settings such as this brought out the worst of his behaviour. He played to his audience, and was particularly frivolous with young ladies. Listening to his flirting with Millicent had set her teeth on edge and she was in no mood to be charitable towards him.

'Are you enjoying the plays?' he ventured, as they walked along the flagged corridor behind the boxes.

She eyed him balefully. 'I would enjoy them more if you were not constantly chattering about nothing!'

'Oh, come now—not "nothing", surely! I have been entertaining Miss Etherington with my thoughts on the play and the actors.'

'I dare say your *wit* has been most entertaining to Miss Etherington,' she retorted scathingly, 'but some people wish to see and hear the plays without such commentary!'

'I must confess,' he ventured, 'I was trying to ensure you could also hear my remarks. I feared you would die of boredom otherwise.'

'There was no danger of that—I was being most ably entertained by Mr Attwood.'

'Exactly.' She glanced at him. Gone was the light-hearted look. Now he was most definitely glowering. She wondered about his sudden change in mood.

'And what do you mean by that?'

He raised a quizzical eyebrow, all lightness gone from his tone. 'You are surely not serious about Mr Attwood?'

'I am sure I do not know what you mean.'

'A beef-witted clodpole like him would bore you within a week. You would rule him easily and hate him for allowing it.' His eyes pinned hers. He was not jesting. He was actually daring to comment on her character, her choices and Mr Attwood's disposition.

'And what gives you the right to comment on my wishes, or my choice of friends? Mr Attwood seems to me to behave just as he ought.'

'Precisely—he is much too staid for someone with your passion.' There was a charged air between them. His expression remained stormy.

Juliana was outraged. How dared he speak so frankly to her! She stopped walking and removed her hand from Harry's arm. 'I shall thank you to keep your opinions to yourself!' she snapped.

'Then thank me, if that ever should happen,' he replied, turning to face her. 'For now, though, you can thank me for this!'

Without any further warning, he bent his head and kissed her.

Shocked, Juliana could only feel the warmth of his lips, the taste of him, the brief scent of his breath, before he was gone again. Not a moment too soon, as some guests appeared round the arc in the corridor. He had timed the kiss to perfection, in the brief instant when they were alone. In that split second, Juliana's senses swam, her stomach flipped and her nerve endings tingled.

Her heart was pounding with what must be outrage. 'Thank you? I should *thank* you for kissing me without my permission?' Her voice squeaked a little. She cleared her throat. 'Why on earth would I wish to do such a thing?'

'Because, my darling Juliana, I wished you to know yourself. The passion within you. A passion that would be smothered by the wrong man. You would end up half-alive.'

'You have no right to make such remarks—or to kiss me!' Surprisingly, Juliana felt close to tears. What was happening to her?

He looked closely at her and his gaze softened. With a rueful half-smile, he murmured, 'You must believe me when I tell you I have only your interests at heart.'

They had reached the refreshments area and a

footman approached to offer them lemonade, wine or ratafia. With an urbane smile, Harry ordered drinks and asked for them to be delivered to their box.

Juliana was seething and more than a little shaken. Harry had no right to pass comment on her friendships, or her temperament. He had certainly no right to kiss her, uninvited, or to speak to her with such familiarity. *My darling Juliana*, indeed! Mr Attwood would never do such things, she was certain. Mr Attwood was worth ten of him! He had all the sincerity, the constancy and the integrity that Harry lacked.

No. That was too much. She did not truly question Harry's integrity. Indeed, she knew he could be as generous and as upright a person as his brother. It was his *behaviour* that frustrated her. He pretended to be shallow, trivial and vacuous, and lessened himself by doing so. Kissing her fitted with the shallow flirt that he pretended to be—though he should reconsider his seduction technique, she thought wryly, suddenly seeing humour in the situation. Insulting young ladies was not, she concluded, a technique likely to lead to his getting many kisses. She stole a glance at him. He was still glowering, and she fought back a sudden urge to giggle.

She remained resolutely silent as they returned to

the box, her heart rate slowly returning to a more normal rhythm. Perhaps, she mused, she was the one who was mistaken about him. Everyone else— including Harry's family—accepted his behaviour with tolerant amusement. Harry the wit. Harry the flirt. Harry the lively artiste. Was she wrong to believe it was all a trick? Like the actors on the stage, he was playing a part. The role of the happy entertainer. But she had seen another side to him. Knew there was more below the surface, that he cared deeply about certain things. Certain people.

She had seen evidence of his compassionate and caring nature, more than once. At Glenbrook. When Mama was upset. When he put himself out to support others. The shallow charmer that he pretended to be would not do that. She had seen *more* in him. There was depth there, and integrity. The thought was strangely unsettling and sent strange ripples whirling through her mind and her heart. Resolutely, she stopped her train of thought. She had no more right to assess his character than he had to assess hers. Though at least she had never spoken about her suspicions to anyone. It was not her place.

That kiss, though! Her heart skipped a beat at the memory. As a young lady of quality, she had had only a few opportunities for kissing. Never had a kiss affected her as this one had.

Perhaps it was because it was so unexpected. The other kisses had been shared with her permission, with young men who were respectfully adoring, not argumentative and passionate! She was surprised to find it made a decided difference. If she wasn't so angry with Harry, she would admit that she would quite like to experience it again.

Harry was berating himself in his head. He had kissed her, after all his promises to himself. And what a kiss! Never had he needed to kiss a woman so much, and never before had the simple, brief touch of a woman's lips left him feeling so elated, uncertain and confused at once.

He had been doing so well, allowing their friendship to develop at its own pace, while resisting becoming emotionally involved. In truth, he genuinely enjoyed and valued her company. Yet it was more, so much more than friendship. His mind, heart and body were consumed by her. She terrified him. He had known it would be a mistake to kiss her and had resolved to resist. Until just now, he had been successful in avoiding all temptations to get near her—and there had been many.

Tonight, though, there had been extreme provocation. Her attentions towards Attwood had finally broken his self-control. It had been, he thought grimly, a choice between kissing Juliana, or challenging her dull beau to a duel. On reflection, he thought perhaps, after all, his choice had been the right one.

As they reached the box, Juliana's heart sank. There, just in front of them, were the Wakelys, approaching the door to their box and entering. She glanced at Harry, who seemed lost in his own thoughts. They reached the door. Harry opened it and motioned for Juliana to enter before him. As she passed, he muttered in her ear, 'I do hope Mr Attwood has thought of some new witticisms with which to entertain you.' She glared at him, but said nothing.

They were only a few steps behind the Wakelys, stepping into the box in time to see them go straight to Charlotte, who was seated by herself. Adam had disappeared—he must have left the box while they were out.

Keen to assist her friend, Juliana hurried forward—and heard Mrs Wakely's opening words.

'Oh, my dear Lady Shalford! I am so glad to find you without Miss Milford, for I have something to tell you—terrible news about your friend that will shock you!'

Juliana stopped walking. *What?* Had the Wakelys, somehow, seen Harry kiss her? But, no, that was not possible, as they had come from the opposite direction. She was aware that Harry had followed and was also listening. He laid a hand lightly on her arm. Juliana stood stock still, transfixed by her view of Mr Wakely's back and Mrs Wakely's half-profile. Neither were aware of her presence. Charlotte, too, was focused completely on Mrs Wakely and had not yet noticed Juliana and Harry.

Juliana knew she should alert them to the fact she was there, knew she should not be eavesdropping, but somehow, her mind could not function.

'I regret to be the one to bring you such bad news, but, my dear Lady Shalford, I know you would not wish to support a cuckoo in your nest.'

'Mrs Wakely, please do not say anything further!' Charlotte sounded distressed. 'Juliana is my dear friend and there is nothing you can say that would ever change that!'

'Ah, you are loyal, my lady, and that is to be admired. But—forgive me—you only know the young woman from school, is that not correct?'

Young woman? thought Juliana. *Why does she not say young lady?*

Juliana did not hear Charlotte's response. Mrs Wakely went on. 'You must brace yourself for bad news, my lady. We have reason to believe that Miss Milford—and I knew the name could not be correct—that Miss Milford is the illegitimate by-blow of some general or other! There! Now what do you think of that?'

Chapter Twelve

Charlotte drew herself up and haughtily replied, 'I should think it a great deal of nonsense and I am surprised you should repeat it to me.'

Mr Wakely coughed. 'Permit me,' he said politely, 'but I'm afraid there is proof.'

'What do you mean? What proof?' Charlotte's voice trembled a little.

Juliana became aware of Harry's strong hand clasping her elbow. She glanced towards him. His gaze seared into hers. In that moment, she wanted no one else beside her.

'As you know, we are not without financial resources. While one does not wish to boast about one's wealth, at times it can be an asset. An asset indeed.'

Charlotte's tone became even sharper. 'I do not understand you, sir. And I do not wish to continue this conversation.'

'You *must* hear this, my lady. My investigations have confirmed the General in question has been sending money to Brussels for many years. He has also been sending money to a certain school for young ladies.' He named the school—the one which Juliana had attended, and where she had met Charlotte.

'*No!*' Juliana was unaware she had spoken out loud until Mr and Mrs Wakely, and Charlotte, turned towards her.

'Juliana! Oh, my dear!' Charlotte stood. 'Mr and Mrs Wakely, please leave us.'

'Of course, of course!' Mrs Wakely was all agitation. 'Only trying to help—thought you should know—wouldn't want you to be embarrassed...'

'Mrs Wakely!' Harry's tone was forceful. Both Wakelys looked at him, more than a hint of anxiety in Mrs Wakely's face. 'There has clearly been some mistake. Miss Milford's character and family are unassailable. You will speak to no one of this.'

'Of course not!' said Mrs Wakely. 'We should not dream of adding to poor Lady Shalford's pain.'

Mr Wakely agreed, 'We shall be as silent as the grave, Captain Fanton. After all, rumours are evil things, are they not?'

Harry fixed him with a steely glare. 'Indeed! And I shall ensure that *anyone* spreading false rumours

about my family—and those close to my family—
will be suitably dealt with!'

Mrs Wakely looked severely daunted. 'Yes, Captain Fanton. Why, we wouldn't *dream* of—'

'Just go!' he told them.

If it could be accurately said that a thin gentleman and a plump lady could scurry, then Mr and Mrs Wakely scurried out of the box, avoiding Juliana's eyes.

Juliana was in a daze. Her world—everything she had thought, known and believed about herself—was crashing down around her.

It all made sense! General Hunter's cryptic comments, Mama's distress, the way she had avoided coming to England—everything was clear now. Her mother—poor, dear, innocent Mama—had somehow been impregnated by that man. Had he attacked her? Or seduced her? Either way, she was sure General Hunter was to blame for all the ills in Mama's life.

It had to be true.

Everything she believed, or thought she knew, had changed in an instant. This news was significant—and confirmed Juliana's worst fears. It meant Juliana herself was a fraud. As a bastard, she should not be socialising in polite society. Should not be on easy terms with a family such as the Fantons. Should not be friends with a lady such as Charlotte. Her mother's reticence had given Juliana a false sense of who she was, the wrong idea about her place in society.

She became aware that Charlotte, her face pale as paper, was speaking to her. Juliana could not hear the words, could not understand anything. Someone—Harry—brought a chair and gently pressed her to sit. Charlotte placed a cup of ratafia into Juliana's hands and made her drink.

The potent liquid swirled sweetly round Juliana's mouth and down her throat. She spluttered.

'…is too much! That awful woman! It is lies, Juliana, do not fret over this!' Charlotte's words began to seep into Juliana's ear. 'Harry, call the carriage—we are going home!'

Harry hesitated. 'That will add credence to their story, Charlotte. Best to brazen it out.'

Juliana could not think. While her instincts were to run, away from the gaze of the Wakelys, the Etheringtons and everyone in the theatre—for surely they would all be looking at her—she did not know if she could sit through the final play. She lifted her eyes to Harry's in mute appeal.

'Juliana!' His handsome face was creased with anxiety. 'I know this is difficult, but we must not give authority to their lies. Can you stay? Can you bear it?'

No! she thought. *I cannot stay here for one minute more!* But his earnest, concerned expression gave her pause. Charlotte's reputation, not just hers, was at stake here.

'I will stay.' Her voice was little more than a croak.

He took her hand and squeezed it. 'I knew you would. You are the strongest woman I know.'

His tender gaze sent warmth through her, but still her mind remained sluggish with shock.

'If you are sure, Juliana?' Charlotte still looked dubious.

'I am sure.' Juliana's voice sounded a little firmer. *I must do this.*

Behind them, the door to the box opened. It was Millicent, along with Hubert and Henrietta, who were bickering over something. Immediately, Harry's mask returned. Stepping away from Juliana and Charlotte, he made an effusive bow.

'Ah!' he said dramatically, drawing all eyes to him. 'We begin to gather together again! I was sadly lost without you! Our little party was diminished by your absence, for friends—true friends—will always add to society!'

Juliana had never before felt gratitude for Harry's ability to dissemble. Skilfully, he kept everyone's attention, ushering them to their seats and ensuring Juliana was placed among them with little ceremony.

Olivia and Alfred arrived next, soon followed by Adam, and Harry engaged them all in meaningless prattle, asking Millicent and Henrietta what they thought of the rosebud as a flower. Had the poet the right of it? Could a flower become the symbol of a person?

Mr Attwood was last to rejoin them. Slipping quietly into his chair, he seemed slightly irritated by Harry's performance. Juliana, on the other hand, had never been more appreciative of it.

As the final play progressed, she sat in mute shock, unable to think clearly. General Hunter—her *father*! Her mind recoiled from the idea. He had treated Mama dreadfully. He must be a monster! He had banished Mama abroad and assuaged his conscience by sending an allowance and paying for Juliana's education. Such behaviour was not uncommon, Juliana knew. It was considered honourable among gentlemen to provide for their by-blows, those unwanted consequences of their lechery.

Honour! Honour would be resisting their lecherous, bestial urges in the first place! Juliana's hands hurt. Looking down, she saw she had clenched her fists so tightly that the fingernails had dug into her skin. *Oh, how I wish the General was before me right now! I would rake his face with those same fingernails! I would punch his stomach! If I had a sword, or a pistol, I would surely murder him!*

How could he? Mama was so naïve—she would have stood no chance against an older man like the General. Had he violated her with force, or with seductive words? Oh, Mama! Poor, vulnerable Mama! Now Juliana knew why they had never been to England before. Why Mama was so anxious. Why she had reacted to General Hunter with such terror.

And how dared the evil General comment on Juliana's spirited behaviour? He had been almost *admiring*, Juliana recalled. As if she was livestock that he was distantly responsible for. A filly, bred from his stallion.

Juliana's thoughts swirled around and around, fuelled by hot anger. Outwardly, she remained calm, aware of the need to protect Charlotte and her family. Mr Attwood's comments on the play were met with short answers and he eventually subsided into silence.

As the final play mercifully came to an end, she apologised briefly to him, claiming a slight headache.

'It is the stultifying air in the theatre, Miss Milford,' he said soberly. 'I feel a little the same.'

Grateful for his lack of perception, Juliana murmured a suitable response. As the ladies busied themselves with cloaks and the men took possession of their hats and canes, Juliana yawned theatrically, to cover her silence. It was late and the other ladies were also claiming tiredness—particularly Henrietta, who was demanding that Hubert forge a path for her through the departing crowds.

Despite everything, Juliana still noticed Millicent's flirtatious glances towards Harry as she asked him when they would drive out again. His reply was curt and non-committal, citing commitments at Horse Guards, and she gave him an arch look, clearly put out. Seeing it, he immediately set out to charm her again. Juliana, watching, could tell his attention was not fully engaged. Millicent, who responded with enthusiasm, seemed not to notice.

It was all too much. The headache she had invented to satisfy Mr Attwood now began to pound at her temples. Hiding towards the rear of the group, she moved with the others along the crowded corridor. In the crush, someone took her hand and squeezed it comfortingly. She turned her head and met Harry's eyes. His expression spoke of concern, and reassurance, and something more intense.

The crowd moved on, and he let go of her hand

before they were discovered. She could still feel his warmth though. She felt it in her mind, and it lasted all the way home.

Juliana could not settle. She had woken frequently during the night, her thoughts disordered and her heart pounding. She had imagined conversations with the General—what she would say, how she could best express her outrage and disdain for him. She had imagined his response—everything from anger to arrogant disregard—and planned how she would react. Her ideas went nowhere, crowding on top of each other as every scenario was imagined and re-imagined. As the first light of dawn filtered through the curtains, she finally fell into an exhausted, but unsatisfying sleep.

She breakfasted in her chamber, leaving the food mostly untouched. Though her thoughts were less feverish than they had been in the depths of night, nevertheless she was unsure what to do. Her first thoughts were for Mama and how best to protect her. She would be distressed if she knew Juliana had discovered the truth about her parentage and would be slain by the thought that people in society were gossiping about them both. No, Juliana could not speak to Mama of this.

In addition, she was no longer sure of her own place in the world. Despite the show of loyalty from Charlotte and Harry last night, Juliana knew it would not be appropriate for Lady Shalford to be intimate with a bastard—someone with no legitimate family and lineage. England—London in particular—was the strictest, most rigid society in Europe. Juliana knew enough of the *ton*—the aristocratic part of society—to understand this.

Pacing the floor, filled with pent-up energy and frustration, Juliana tried to think. Nothing worked. Her brain was weakened by the anger which threatened to overwhelm her. The room was too small to contain her. She felt like a lit firework just before it spewed out its starry explosion.

There was a timid scratching on the door. 'Enter!'

'Miss.' It was Lily, the first housemaid. 'Milady says please to accompany her walking in the park.'

Good! thought Juliana. 'Tell Lady Shalford I shall accompany her. Then return and assist me to dress, please.'

'Yes, miss.'

As the maid buttoned her into an elegant day dress of mauve cotton and silk, Juliana reflected on Charlotte. Her friend was so kind-hearted it was likely she would try to persuade Juliana to make little of the news. She must do the right thing—once she had worked out what that was—and not be swayed by Charlotte's tender heart.

And so it proved. They were barely away from the house before Charlotte, with an anxious tone, asked Juliana how she did.

'Well, I can hardly say I am well, Charlotte. This was evil news. But it explains so much, so I must be grateful to know who I am at last.'

'Oh, my dear Juliana. You are exactly the same wonderful girl you were yesterday. Nothing has changed!'

'Everything has changed, Charlotte,' Juliana said flatly. 'We cannot pretend otherwise.'

'But Mr and Mrs Wakely are merely repeating vicious gossip. You know how people are—always ready to consider the worst, always looking for a new drama. They are surely mistaken.'

'You heard Mr Wakely. He has proof that General Hunter—' she almost choked on the hated name '—has been paying for my schooling, as well as providing an allowance for Mama. It must be so.'

'But you always said your mama's income came from her own family and from the Army. After all, your true father died a soldier.'

'I know not who John Milford is, or whether in fact he even exists,' said Juliana, with some bitterness. 'He may be a phantom created by Mama to cover her shame. A dead husband is a useful creature.'

'Juliana! You know full well, as I do, your mama would not be capable of sustaining such a ruse. Nor indeed—and I mean this kindly—would she be able to make up such a thing!'

Juliana's shoulders slumped. 'It is true that Mama is guileless and not good at dissembling. I grant you that.' She considered for a moment. 'In that case, I contend that it was General Hunter himself who came up with the conveniently dead husband. And Mama has struggled with the falsehood for over twenty years. I told you how she wept and spoke of her shame and her wickedness.'

'She may have meant something else entirely.'

'Charlotte, you are so good that you wish to see only good in others. Mama is a good person, but she has been grievously wronged by that man. Oh, I wish I were a man—I would call him out!'

'And as I told you before, I am glad you are not a man,' said a familiar voice behind them. They turned. Harry caught up with them. 'Did you not hear me call you?' he asked. 'I have been trying to catch you since you turned yon corner. Adam is still in Westminster, but I am returned earlier than I expected from Horse Guards.'

'We did not hear you,' said Charlotte, 'for we have been deep in conversation.'

'I can see that,' he said soberly. 'Juliana, how do you do? You look troubled.'

She looked directly at him. About to deny it, she saw the sincerity in his blue eyes and relented. 'I am distressed, naturally.'

'I do not doubt it. Those Wakelys, spouting nonsense—dangerous nonsense! How dare they attack the reputation of two ladies they barely know, as well as that of a long-serving general?'

Juliana gave an unladylike snort. 'The General,' she said scathingly, 'has wronged my mama! Although I must acknowledge the evidence that he is my father, I cannot think well of him.'

Harry shook his head. 'Something is not right here. General Hunter is autocratic, and at times overbearing and arrogant, but I swear he has always been honourable in all my dealings with him.'

'Male notions of honour seem restricted to their behaviour in male company. Are you certain you know about his dealings with women?'

Harry frowned. 'I know he had no dealings with the—with the women who followed the army. He was not one who sought opportunities for female company, though I believe he was married and widowed many years ago. I do know some men who have had children with…er…with women they were not married to, but such men would have had a reputation for enjoying the companionship of women. Occasionally such relationships were almost like marriages, but without the benefit of church.'

'I am one-and-twenty,' said Juliana bluntly. 'Can you really know what General Hunter was, and whom he seduced, twenty-two years ago?'

Harry shook his head. 'Of course not.'

'Well then! Besides, I am here. I exist. That is proof enough of his predilections.'

Charlotte intervened, her expression anguished. 'Oh, Juliana! Do not say so! It may yet all turn out to be a mistake.'

Juliana eyed her cynically. 'And that butcher's boy may suddenly sprout wings and fly over the rooftops. I am sorry, Charlotte, I see no miracle here.'

'At least let us check the veracity of the Wakelys' so-called evidence.'

'How should we do that?' Juliana pondered for a second. 'I could seek out the General and ask him face to face if he is my father.'

Charlotte paled. 'Oh, no! Please do not! Only imagine if it should turn out to be untrue! To make a false accusation of that nature…!'

'I have a better suggestion.' Harry's brow was creased in thought. 'I could do what Wakely did and pay someone at the bank for details of General Hunter's account.' He looked at Juliana. 'Or your mother's.'

'Very well,' said Juliana. 'But I know it is true. Why would the Wakelys make up such a malicious falsehood? They barely know me and have nothing to gain. And it fits with the mystery of my past and my mother's behaviour towards the General. It *must* be true.'

She saw the uncertainty on Charlotte's face, the doubt in Harry's expression. They did not wish it to be true. Nor did she, but she must be realistic. She explained to Harry that her mother's bank was in Brussels, so he could seek information only through General Hunter's transactions. He undertook to make discreet enquiries.

For the rest of their walk, Harry made light conversation, endeavouring to ease the heavy mood that had settled over them all.

He did not succeed.

Chapter Thirteen

Harry was, in fact, desperately trying to find a way in which he could relieve Juliana's pain. Were it not for the assertion about the money sent to Brussels, he would have dismissed the Wakelys' accusation as vindictive tittle-tattle. They were *exactly* the sort of people to do such a thing, he thought, though how they believed bringing bad news would help ingratiate themselves with Lady Shalford was unclear.

He had barely slept last night, haunted by the stricken shock on Juliana's beautiful face. It had not lasted long, for she had been in fighting spirit by the end of the night. He expected no less from his tempestuous beauty! How was he to stop her acting in haste, in ways which might prove damaging to her or her mother? He knew, from the incident in Dover, how impulsive and stubborn she could be, especially when fuelled by righteous anger. But he could not yet say what was to be done about it. He would investigate the financial question and pray the answer that came back was the right one.

On returning to the town house, the maids came scurrying out to assist the ladies with their boots, while Harry gave his hat and cane to the footman. That young man, who had worked in the household for many years, gave Harry a speaking look. Seeing it, Juliana's heart sank. What was amiss?

Mounting the stairs with the others, Juliana heard raised voices coming from the drawing room. A man's voice. Exchanging worried glances with Harry and Charlotte, Juliana hurried faster up the stairs.

As they got closer, they made out some of the man's words.

'...this stupid! To foist an illegitimate girl on polite society! How *could* you? Answer me, Elizabeth!'

Harry opened the door with a crash, Juliana following on his heels. There was General Hunter, wagging an irate finger at Mrs Milford. She was weeping softly, her hands wringing a small handkerchief.

'But, no!' she was saying. 'Please listen to me!'

Hearing the door open, they both turned to see Harry and Juliana in the doorway, Charlotte just behind. Harry reacted immediately.

'General Hunter, how kind of you to visit us again!' He swept forward, bowing to the General.

'However, you may not be aware Mrs Milford is unwell, so I am afraid I must ask you to leave us.'

'Must you, eh?' snapped the General. 'Young hothead! You have no idea what you are about.'

'I know Mrs Milford is upset, sir.'

'Bah! When was she ever sensible? Greatest watering pot I ever knew!'

Juliana had heard enough. 'General Hunter,' she said, 'go out of this house and do not return!'

Charlotte gasped. 'Juliana!'

The General gave a short bark of amusement. 'Spirited, like before. She did not get that from you, Elizabeth.'

'Please,' begged Mama. 'Juliana, please do not—'

'Do not? *Do not?*' cried Juliana. 'I cannot bear to see him abuse you, Mama.'

'But you are not aware—you do not know who he is!'

'I know what I see. I know what I hear. I can judge a man as well as any.' Juliana looked scathingly at the General.

'You would judge me, eh?' Approaching, he touched her chin with his knuckle. Her eyes flashed fire at him. He chuckled. 'Very well, child, I will go. But you would do better to return to Brussels.'

'Mama and I are perfectly capable of making our own decisions. We need no advice from you!'

'Nevertheless, you have it. It is kindly meant—I have your best interests at heart, no matter what you think you know.'

Turning back to her mother, he said, in a tone that was almost kindly, 'Goodbye, Elizabeth. I hope you will see sense.'

He strode towards the door, where Juliana stood aside to let him pass, her face set with suppressed rage. He nodded to her, bowed to Harry and to Charlotte, and was gone.

'Mama!'

Juliana dashed forward, too late to catch her mother, who had slumped to the floor in a dead faint. Harry swept her up and laid her on the nearest couch. Charlotte, who was still beside the open door, directed the servants to bring hartshorn and laudanum. The two housemaids and the footman who had found reason to be within earshot of the Interesting Event dispersed quickly.

Mrs Milford was not unconscious for long. Within a short time, she moaned softly. Her face was deathly white.

'Mama!' repeated Juliana, with urgency. 'All is well. He is gone!'

Mama's eyelids fluttered open. 'Juliana!' she said weakly. 'I am so sorry!'

'Hush, Mama! You are not to blame. It is that man! That overbearing, autocratic monster!' Mama made a high-pitched keening noise. 'No, Mama, please be well. You are safe. Listen to me. You are *safe*!'

The housemaid soon returned with the hartshorn, quickly followed by the footman who had brought a vial of laudanum. Harry opened the hartshorn and wafted the pungent scent under Mama's nose. It revived her a little. She coughed forcefully, and struggled to sit up. Juliana assisted her, feeling the trembling in her slight body.

Charlotte passed Juliana the laudanum.

'Mama, here is laudanum. Will you take it?'

Mama reached out a trembling hand and took the glass. She drank a small amount and spluttered as it hit her throat. Her hand shook even more. Juliana took the glass from her.

'Would you like to stay here, or go to your chamber, Mama?' Juliana asked gently. There was no response. Her mother's eyes were closed again.

'If she wishes to retire, I will carry her, if she permits.' Harry was all concern. Juliana did not know how she had come to rely on him so much, but in that moment she was again grateful fate had brought him into her life.

'Thank you, Harry.' He looked at her and his eyes softened.

Turning back to Mrs Milford, he asked if she would like to be carried to her room and this time she nodded. He lifted her, carefully and gently, his strong arms carrying her as if she was no burden at all. Juliana and Charlotte followed, Charlotte quietly directing the housemaid to fetch a hot brick for Mrs Milford.

Mrs Milford. A name that was likely fabricated, like Juliana's own. Her mama was not Mrs Milford. Juliana was not Miss Milford. Yet she was certainly not Miss Hunter! The idea disgusted her. Whatever else the General had done—and it galled her to think of the conscience money he had been paying all these years—he had not married Mama, not offered her respectability. So Juliana had no name. She was simply Juliana.

Harry left them as soon as he had deposited Mama on her bed. He squeezed Juliana's shoulder as he left. Juliana and Charlotte, working quietly and gently, divested Juliana's mother of her outer garments and made her comfortable under the covers. She barely stirred.

'Come, Juliana,' whispered Charlotte. 'Let her sleep.'

'She will need me when she wakes.'

'I will ask one of the maids to sit with her. Susie, perhaps. Your mama likes Susie.'

'Very well—but I will stay until Susie arrives. And I will tell her she must send for me immediately when Mama wakes.'

'Of course.'

True to her word, Juliana waited until Susie, the young, shy housemaid, arrived. Charlotte was on her heels. 'Come now, Juliana. You can do no more here.'

Reluctantly, Juliana left. Mama was sleeping soundly, as the laudanum had taken full effect.

She did not wake at all during the evening. Juliana, already exhausted from her own lack of sleep and distress, spent the evening in a haze. She responded when spoken to, but her mind was again not functioning. Worry about her mother's distress, coupled with the knowledge of her status—her lack of status—haunted her. It was all just too much. After checking on her mother, she sought her own bed and fell into grateful oblivion.

Harry was experiencing similar disorder in his thoughts. He had arranged to meet two friends at his club and kept the engagement. But all through the evening he found himself wishing he was back at home. How was Juliana faring? Was Mrs Milford sleeping peacefully still? What was to be done about their situation, about General Hunter? The conversation they had overheard left little room for misinterpretation. The 'illegitimate girl' could be none other than Juliana herself. Yet he could not help hoping for some miracle.

Earlier, he had met with a man he had used before, one who had contacts throughout London. Money had changed hands and the promise of more. The man undertook to find out if General Hunter had, indeed, been sending money to Brussels and to Juliana's school. He promised his enquiries would be discreet.

Harry frowned. What would he do with the information, when he had it? If it simply confirmed what they all expected, how would that change things? Harry thought no less of Juliana for being illegitimate—after all, she was not to blame for her parents' sins. He knew Mrs Milford was good, kind and honourable, but her behaviour clearly signified guilt. And Juliana was right about General Hunter—who knew what his character had been twenty-two years ago? Perhaps the birth of Juliana had made the General forswear intimacies with women. The General's wife might have still been alive when Juliana was born—indeed, it would explain why the General had been unable to marry Juliana's mother. He shuddered. The entire debacle was a mess.

And my Juliana is in the centre of the storm.

He frowned. *My Juliana?* When had he begun thinking of her as *his* Juliana? He shook his head slowly. That way led to disaster. He could not marry, he had nothing to offer a woman—least of all someone as proud, headstrong and passionate as Juliana. She deserved someone who was whole, someone dependable and reliable. Someone who was clean from the taint of evil and cowardice. Not like him. He had never before wished so much that he was like other men—able to love, and to marry, and to claim love for himself.

Yet when he pictured her, his heart swelled. Juliana, defiant and angry with General Hunter, defending her mama like a stubborn ewe protecting its lamb. Juliana, white and anguished as she listened to the Wakelys in the theatre. Juliana, quiet and unnaturally subdued as she tended to her mother today.

Damn it! Someone should look after her! Strong as she was, he knew that Juliana deserved to cry, or rail against her fate, or share her worries about the future. Instead she would try to carry all of it on her own slight shoulders. Charlotte was a good friend to her, he knew, but Charlotte, like Juliana, had grown up in Europe, not England, and could not fully advise her friend on Juliana's next steps.

As he travelled home, his mind circled around

and around the problem. If the worst was true and it became widely known, Juliana and her mother would no longer be welcome by many in society. Almack's vouchers would be out of the question, and even appearing in a public place would expose them to potential insults. The *ton* guarded itself fiercely and even those who had fathered or borne illegitimate children themselves would criticise anyone who failed to keep their 'mistakes' away from public view. Unfair as it was, everyone knew the rules.

Should Juliana marry, her husband would join her in being exiled from the higher reaches of society. In the Army, making a bad marriage would affect the progress of one's career, as it would be held up as evidence of a man's bad judgement.

Juliana, married. His heart stilled briefly. He could not imagine any man being worthy of her—least of all himself. Just for a moment, Harry imagined being the one who would become her husband. What a joy and a privilege that would be!

He pictured himself telling his Major that he was marrying a girl of dubious parentage. Major Cooke would rail at him for stupidity and suggest he bed her instead.

In his head, Harry gave a defiant speech back to the Major, asserting his right to marry whomever he chose, for, of course, a woman like Juliana would be worth any sacrifice.

If he were a different person, if he were free to marry, then he would count it an honour to win the hand of such a woman.

But she needed a better husband than him.

Averting his thoughts from his own inadequacies, his mind turned instead to the meetings he had attended earlier, at the War Department. The news had been troubling. Napoleon was on the move and his armies were gathering. It looked like war would be upon them again before long. Dark clouds were gathering in Europe and the sense of foreboding he felt had its echo in the troubles of those closest to him.

As he sipped a last brandy before finding his own bed, he was suddenly, unexpectedly, assailed by old memories. Dust, heat, the smell of blood, death and fear. His stomach felt sick, his hands shook and his heart raced uncontrollably.

No! He thought. *Not now!* He had not had one of his turns for months. Not now, when he needed to be strong. Breathing slowly and carefully, he sat the glass down, seated himself in the comfortable chair by his bedroom fireplace and tried to avoid thinking about the war. About that day.

Concentrating on his own breath, he slowly drew

air into his lungs, noticing how his chest expanded, how the air cooled his throat. Holding his breath for a count of five, he then exhaled as deliberately as he could, gradually emptying his lungs. He closed his eyes and did it all again. And again. Bit by bit, moment by moment, his heart rate returned to normal, his tremors settled and his stomach gradually became stable.

Opening his eyes, he returned to reality. Exhaustion made it difficult to even stand up. Moving slowly and carefully, like an old, old man, he prepared for bed.

Why had this happened now? In the three years since Badajoz, he had worked hard at controlling his weakness, his cowardice. He had managed to conceal it from his senior officers, thank goodness.

Evans knew, of course, and had roused him from nightmares many times in the early weeks and months after the incident. By the time he had come home after the Spanish campaign, Harry had built a careful mask of gaiety to conceal his rotten brokenness. He had built it on memories of his youthful persona—the wit and humour that had carried him from school to Oxford to the purchase of his Army colours. With practice, it had become a way of life.

He climbed wearily into bed, watching the flame

on his nightstand candle guttering in the slight draught.

Why now? Why had his demons returned tonight?

General Hunter, who had been there. That was part of it. The other part was Juliana. This he knew, without fully understanding why. She had pierced his armour, that circle of distance he held around himself. Concern for her, combined with the escape and return of Napoleon, threatened his path ahead. Why it had triggered memories of what had gone before, he could not be exactly sure. Was it fear? Perhaps. Or was it his conscience reminding him he should not become close to any woman? He would not want Juliana infected by his poison. She deserved better.

He blew out the candle.

Juliana woke with a start. Confused for a few seconds, she suddenly heard a faint cry and was instantly wide awake. *Mama!*

Fumbling for her flint, she eventually succeeded in lighting the candle beside her bed. Without even stopping to grab a robe, she padded quickly in bare feet to her mother's room.

'Mama?'

Silence. She approached the bed. Her mother was sleeping soundly, her features relaxed and peaceful.

Pausing for a moment, listening to her mother's even breathing, Juliana shook her head in confusion. Had she imagined it?

There it was again! A faint cry, coming from somewhere else!

Moving quickly, she exited her mother's room, closing the door carefully behind her. She moved to the centre of the landing and waited. There it was again—an anguished, strangled sound, coming from the room to her right.

In her confusion, she could not quite remember whose chamber it was. She had been told in a long list when Charlotte had showed her around the town house—but that had been an age ago.

Juliana did not hesitate. Someone was in trouble, so she must act. She opened the door, stepped inside and lifted her candle.

It was Harry! And he was clearly in the throes of a nightmare. His hands gripped the sheet, which had been pushed down below chest level. His lean, muscular torso glistened with sweat and his body was shaking. There were tears trickling down the sides of his face.

What should she do? Before the thought was completed she had already taken the three steps needed to reach him. Placing her right hand on his shoulder, she spoke softly.

'Harry. Harry! Wake up!'

He responded instantly, sitting up dramatically and staring straight ahead. He was clearly confused and not yet quite awake.

Juliana spoke soothingly. 'Harry, all is well. You are having a nightmare.'

He looked at her unseeing, his eyes wide and unfocused.

'I am sorry,' he muttered. 'So sorry!'

Why was he apologising?

'Harry, wake up. You are at home and all is well.'

This time, he did awaken. 'Juliana!' He looked at her directly, his eyes sweeping from her face down to her thin nightgown and back again. 'What the devil are you doing in my room?' His voice croaked a little. He ran a hand through his already tousled hair.

'You were having a nightmare. I thought it was Mama.' She studied his expression. Why was he so angry?

'You should not be here. Have you no care for your reputation?'

'Pfft!' Juliana indicated with a toss of her head how little she cared about her reputation in such a moment. He looked at her again, deliberately making a leisurely examination of her form, half-revealed through the thin cotton of her white nightgown. His eyes met hers again, a challenge in his expression. *Oh, he was clever!* 'Very well, I shall go! But do try not to wake the whole household again!'

As she left his chamber, knowing his eyes were on her, Juliana could not help smiling. Indeed, it was shocking that she, an unmarried woman, had gone into his room. She really ought not to have done it. Even if she was illegitimate and likely to be outcast from society in the near future.

Regret was not, however, an option in this case. She enjoyed the feeling of *daring* it had given her and the fact that she had made him flustered. She had also enjoyed the flutterings in her body caused by his perusal of her and by the sight of his bare torso. In the midst of all her trials, it was good to have a moment of rebellion and excitement.

As she climbed back into bed, she wondered about his nightmare. What had caused him to be so distressed? Everyone had nightmares from time to time, she knew. Despite his disapproval, she was glad she had woken him. He had done so much to support her, it was satisfying to be able to offer him some help in return.

She blew out the candle and closed her eyes. Her thoughts this time were not of Mama, or of General Hunter. Instead she saw only Harry. His body—a thing of beauty, such as she had seen recreated by artists with paintbrush and chisel. His gaze as he made that leisurely tour of her form with knowingness and need. Harry, she thought. *Harry.*

Harry's mood was rather different. She had seen him! Seen him in the midst of his nightmares. Seen his ugly, twisted soul. How long had she stood there? Did she pity him, perhaps? She knew now that he was weak. Dashing away the unmanly tears that she had surely noticed, he sat now in the darkness, dejection in every line of his body.

At least he had spoken like a man of sense, chiding her for being in his room. What had she been thinking? A young lady, in a man's bedchamber! Much as he had ached to see her in his chamber—under what unlikely circumstance, he could not imagine—the reality was bittersweet. She had looked stunning in the candlelight, wearing nothing but a flimsy nightgown and with her long dark hair unbound and flowing over her shoulders.

He tried not to think of her expression, but knew he would be awake for hours, searching his memory for signs of disgust in her beautiful face. Self-loathing and physical frustration were not a combination that led to peaceful sleep. Clasping his arms around his knees, he sat in the darkness and cried like a child.

Chapter Fourteen

Juliana awoke feeling strangely hopeful. It seemed that, despite everything, her heart believed all would be well in the end. She was unsure about the source of her confidence. She was still the bastard daughter of a dishonourable general. She had no clue about her own future and the lack of knowledge about her past still bothered her. Her mama was still ill and likely to remain so for a while. Despite all of this, Juliana could not ignore the fact that there was a warm glow sited somewhere in her chest.

She took a moment to recall again last night's incident. In her mind's eye, she replayed the scene. Harry, half-naked, vulnerable and gorgeous. How he had looked, sitting in that bed, the candlelight adding a glow to his smooth skin. The way he had looked at her.

The whole thing had a dreamlike quality, yet was also immediate and visceral. Her heart was pounding. In an attempt to calm it, she tried to find another aspect to last night's incident to focus on. She soon found it—his nightmare.

Nightmares were horrible, distressing experiences. Juliana wouldn't wish them on anyone. Yet, assuming that he—like herself—only experienced a bad nightmare on a few rare occasions, it was almost fortuitous he had experienced one on the very night when she was sleeping lightly, worrying about Mama. The walls in the town house were thick. Under normal circumstances she would never have woken from sleep on the basis of the faint sounds coming from his chamber.

Knowing all was well as soon as she had woken him, Juliana acknowledged that seeing him as she had—tousled, handsome and sleepy—was extremely endearing. There was a beautiful vulnerability about him that touched something within her heart. Any helplessness had soon vanished though—once he was properly awake he had reverted to typical opinionated Harry. Remembering his ire, she chuckled slightly as she rang the bell for the maid. It had most definitely been worth it.

Dressed and ready, she went directly to Mama's chamber before breakfast. Scratching at the door, she heard her mother's voice, weakly calling her to enter. Good, she was awake then.

'Good morning, Mama!' Juliana drew back the curtains, allowing sunlight to flood the room. She turned to face her mother—and stifled a gasp. It was like looking at a statue. Her mother's expression was devoid of feeling, of reaction. Her eyes were dull and lifeless.

Knowing her mother was too fragile for questioning, Juliana instead behaved as though all was well, chatting to Mama about the weather, the prettiness of her room and which dress she should wear that day.

Her mother gave monosyllabic answers, but she at least responded. Yes, she believed she had slept quite well. Yes, she had woken naturally, had already used the chamber pot and, yes, she had washed. Was she ready to dress? Yes.

Juliana took all of this as encouragement.

'You do not need a maid this morning, Mama, for I shall button you up myself. It will be quite like old times! Why, in Brussels, every time Sandrine was ill or visiting her family, we had to tend to each other. It was one of the best things about having only one maid.' Mama stood and allowed Juliana to dress her.

'I wonder how Sandrine is faring.' Excellent—her mama had spoken a full sentence!

'We shall see her soon, Mama. We never intended to stay here long.'

Mama clutched Juliana's hand. 'Can we go home, Julie? I do not wish to stay here. Though Charlotte—everyone has been most kind—I cannot—I…' Her voice tailed off.

Juliana placed her other hand over her mama's. 'Yes, Mama. We shall go soon—though perhaps we should wait until Napoleon is defeated. It might be difficult to pass through France right now.'

Mama seemed content with this and sat to allow Juliana to brush her hair. She sighed and closed her eyes.

Juliana bit her lip. Mama was reassured and that was a comfort, but Juliana was troubled. She had spoken confidently just now, but in reality she knew not what to do. How long would the campaign against Napoleon last this time? Would the Allies finally defeat him? If the self-styled Emperor marched again, even Brussels might become a battlefield.

And what would they subsist on? Pin money from General Hunter? That awful man's money had paid for everything Juliana and her mother owned—including this hairbrush. Juliana's jaw hardened with anger. Setting down the hairbrush before her strokes became too harsh, she twisted her mother's fair hair into a pretty Grecian knot and fixed it with hairpins.

'Mama, you look beautiful! See?' She showed her mother her face in the glass, but Mama's expression remained blank. 'Now, let us go and join the others for breakfast.'

Harry did not appear at the breakfast table. Juliana tried hard not to watch the door, which was constantly opening, with servants bringing food, hot chocolate and strong coffee. Charlotte had stood to embrace both her and her mother when they had appeared, but no one mentioned yesterday's drama.

'We are at home today,' Charlotte reminded Olivia. 'Perhaps Mr Nightingale will call.'

Olivia blushed, and tossed her head. 'What care I if he calls? There are many young men in London.'

'But none who writes such romantic poetry, surely?'

Olivia muttered something unintelligible and stared down at her food. Then, as if having found courage, she lifted her head.

'Alf—Mr Nightingale would like to show me Vauxhall Gardens. He says there are pretty walks and there is to be a show with acrobats. Please may we go?'

Charlotte looked dubious. 'As you know, Olivia,

I have only lived in England for a relatively short time, but I have the strong impression that Vauxhall is not a suitable place for debutantes.'

'Oh, please, Charlotte. I should so love to go!'

Juliana saw Charlotte's discomfort. She was unwilling to agree to something unless she was certain it was appropriate. Steering her young sister-in-law through the Season had its complications.

'I shall discuss it with Adam and I will let you know.'

Olivia had to be content with this. Juliana reflected that Charlotte was doing well as Olivia's sponsor. After all, at twenty-two, she was only a few years older than her young charge. Juliana now felt older than all of them. It was strange to sit through a normal conversation and to wonder if she would ever appear in public with Charlotte and Olivia again.

Mr Nightingale did call, and soon after he left, they received Millicent, Henrietta and Hubert. Juliana's heart sank when she saw them. She was, of course, perfectly polite in her greeting and did her best to make sensible conversation—or, as much sense as the artless trio were capable of.

It was almost an hour later when Harry finally appeared. He did so just as the Etheringtons were finally rising to leave. Juliana looked at him admiringly, recognising that everything about his appearance was perfection. His regimental coat and pale breeches hugged his fine form, and his black boots gleamed. In the midst of the confusion, worry and uncertainty surrounding her, seeing him was like the sunshine breaking through clouds.

Naturally, their guests decided to prolong their visit for a few extra minutes, Millicent in particular dominating the ensuing conversation. Harry was all smiles, flirting expertly with the redhead, yet today, Juliana was not irritated by it. She saw, for the first time, that Harry was not serious in his attentions to Miss Etherington. Knowing every expression on his face, every gesture made by his strong hands, she understood his mind was elsewhere, even as he paid outrageous compliments to Millicent's new gown.

Juliana had finally, it seemed, decided to trust him.

Not to be outdone, Henrietta fished for a compliment on her own attire and her husband, recognising his cue, duly obliged. In that moment, Harry's gaze sought out Juliana's and the corners of his eyes marginally softened as their eyes met.

Juliana's world shifted. Her gut, stomach, womb and heart reacted with joyful glee. *This* was real. This was a true connection. Not the extravagant words Harry gave to Millicent, but the quiet glance he gave to her. It was so subtle that no one else could be aware of it, but Juliana knew his heart was singing in the same key as hers.

Harry was terrified. He felt lost, adrift on a sea of uncertainty, fear and hope. He looked at Juliana. Her eyes met his and his heart turned over. She was his nemesis, his judge—but she was also, he realised, his anchor.

The realisation filled him with joy, but also with dread. It would not do! He had nothing to offer her—he was too flawed, too broken. Yet he saw the light inside him reflected in her eyes. *Juliana!* He wanted to touch her—to take her into his arms and kiss her forever. To take away all her worries and make everything right for her and her mother. To protect her from all harm.

Yet, he reminded himself, he must not speak, must not act. Self-restraint was his only option. War was coming and he would again be tested—and found wanting. His soldier's uniform made him look competent, dashing—heroic, even. He felt sick at the false impression he was projecting. He was not whole, not worthy of being loved. To pretend to be otherwise would result in more pain, for when Juliana discovered the truth about him—his insides froze at the possibility—she would surely recoil in disgust. No, better to resist now, and avert disaster.

During their visit, Henrietta and Millicent had focused their conversation on Charlotte and Olivia, and later Harry, ignoring Juliana and her mother almost completely. Juliana had not remarked much on this, as she had already made a fair assessment of the young ladies' characters. Henrietta was vain and self-centred, while Millicent saw Juliana as a rival in her flirtation with Harry. *Oh, if only you knew*, thought Juliana, not without a little smugness, *how he looks half-naked in candlelight. How he gazes at me, as if hungry. How he looked at me just now.*

Instinctively, she knew. There was a profound connection between her and Harry, something patently missing from his superficial interactions with Millicent. Watching the young ladies titter and giggle at his witticisms, Juliana felt as though she and Harry were benevolent parents, indulging their children with silly games while saving their true energies for each other.

As the Etheringtons rose to leave, Juliana realised Millicent's antipathy towards her was more marked than ever. Both Henrietta and Millicent afforded her mother and herself only the slightest of courtesies, their manner bordering on insolence. Mr Etherington, seemingly unaware of his wife's and his sister's disdain, performed equally courteous bows to all of the company, which made the ladies' rudeness even more apparent.

Having been aware of Millicent's ill feeling towards her from their first meeting, Juliana was only a little surprised. It was now apparent that Millicent had extended her hostility to her own poor mama, who, thankfully, seemed unaware, still lost in the fog of yesterday's trauma. And Henrietta was taking Millicent's part, throwing Juliana an equally disdainful look as she moved towards the door.

'Dear Charlotte!' she said gushingly. 'I do so enjoy spending time with you! And with *dear* Lady Olivia, of course! One can tell a person's quality when spending time with them and you and Olivia are two of the most gently bred ladies in all of London!'

Millicent's expression was one of unholy glee. 'I must agree with you, Henrietta! The Fantons of Chadcombe are one of the noblest families in England and must of necessity be particular about the company they keep!'

With this obscure statement, the whole party finally departed, leaving Juliana, Olivia and Charlotte heaving sighs of relief as they retook their seats.

'I honestly thought they would never leave!' said Charlotte, with some feeling.

'It is all your doing, Harry,' added Juliana teasingly, 'for we had just about succeeded in encouraging them to go when you appeared.'

Harry, it seemed, was in no mood to be amused. 'I never saw them behave so rudely before. They were downright vulgar just now.' His brow was furrowed in thought. 'I cannot account for it.'

'Oh, come now, Harry,' chided Charlotte. 'You know Henrietta of old! And Millicent, too.'

He shook his head. 'I know them to be two of the silliest girls in England—though I never before saw Millicent behave as badly as Henrietta. Something about today's insolence seems different. I cannot exactly identify what it is.'

'I wondered the same thing,' said Charlotte. 'But perhaps we are imagining it.'

'Hmm...' he said, clearly unconvinced. 'Are we walking today? Adam is home and said we should rescue him from his secretary as soon as we may.'

Charlotte rose immediately, her eyes lighting up. 'Adam is home? Why did you not tell me?'

'But I have just done so!'

Charlotte was already opening the door, charging them to be ready to walk out in ten minutes.

Olivia declined immediately, reminding them the dressmaker was to call on her shortly. Juliana's mother, with clear relief, indicated her intention to go and lie down. Olivia took her arm and accompanied her out of the room.

Which left only Juliana and Harry. They were alone for the first time since their encounter in his chamber. Juliana felt uncharacteristically hesitant.

'How is Mrs Milford today?' His voice was a little husky. He coughed, as if to clear his throat. 'She still looks poorly.'

'She is, though thankfully she slept well.' Juliana blushed, wishing she hadn't mentioned sleep. Sleep meant beds and bedchambers and led inevitably to memories of her uninvited visit to his room. 'Er… she is too frail to speak about difficult matters, but she has eaten a little today. I am hopeful she will recover in time.'

An awkward silence grew between them. Abruptly, he walked to the window and looked out, his back to her. She saw tension in the line of his shoulders. She was at a loss for something to say. Why was it she could feel so connected to him in public, not half an hour ago, yet in private she was overcome with awkwardness? She pushed through it. 'I shall walk with you and Charlotte and Adam. Indeed, if I stay indoors for much longer I believe I should burst!'

He turned to face her, then threw his head back and laughed. '*Burst?* Burst, indeed! Oh, Juliana—you are truly unique!'

Juliana threw him a mischievous smile, glad to see she had punctured the tension. 'I am sincere! Being at home to visitors is so tiresome. I feel as though I am held in a cage today, imprisoned by doors and walls and *la politesse*!'

'Then let me release you, my beautiful captive! We shall walk out together and escape the cage of London society for a time.' They shared a smile and all was right again.

St James's Park was the oldest of the Royal Parks, and Juliana had already come to know it very well. She and Charlotte linked arms as they crossed the tree-lined Mall to reach the greenness beyond. They were discussing Juliana's mother, of course, and General Hunter, but were no nearer to finding any solutions. Charlotte kept repeating the hope some other explanation could be found, though even she admitted it was unlikely.

Juliana held no such hope. She was not denying the reality of her parentage, but strangely, she felt distant from it. Bad things were coming—any position she had in society was gone, along with the opportunity to maintain a close friendship with Charlotte, Adam or any of the Fantons.

Today, with visceral memories of Harry's sleep-tousled form and the feeling of connection with him, she could not imagine *not* being part of him. It was acting like a warm blanket, protecting her from thoughts of the troubles ahead. Her greatest worry, though, was her mother. Mama cared about such things as reputation and what others thought of her much more than Juliana did.

They wandered towards the lake, where Adam broke off his conversation with Harry to reclaim his wife. Juliana fell in beside Harry as they followed the lakeside path. Taking her hand, he tucked it in the crook of his arm and they walked in silence for a few moments, following Charlotte and Adam, as they usually did.

'Mrs Milford is lying down again?' His voice was a little husky.

'Yes.' Juliana bit her lip. 'She still does not speak about anything important. It has always been her way. She prefers to pretend the problem doesn't exist, refuses to speak to me about it, yet she is clearly suffering. I feel so helpless, so useless! I do not know what I can do for her.

'She told me earlier she wishes to leave London. She wants to return home as soon as possible.'

'Is that what you wish?'

Home? Away from Charlotte, from London, from *Harry*? Coldness gripped Juliana's stomach. Somehow she could not think clearly. She stared blankly up at him.

Searching her face for a moment, he suddenly stopped walking. 'Oh, Juliana, if only I could take this burden from you!'

Grateful for his words, Juliana felt the fear inside her subside a little. She squeezed his arm. 'You are already diminishing it, Harry. Indeed, I am sure I do not know how I would manage without our conversations!'

'Nonsense!' he said gruffly. 'You are like an Amazon! I admire your strength of character—I do not know how you can bear it!'

Tears sprang to her eyes. 'Thank you.' Her voice shook slightly.

'Damn it, Juliana!' His face twisted. 'Do not show me weakness!'

Then, suddenly, somehow, she was in his arms.

Afterwards, she could not remember whether he had embraced her, or whether it was she who moved towards him. She only knew his lips were on hers, his strong arms were around her and she was lost in him. They kissed, and kissed, and kissed again. Juliana reached her arms around him, feeling through his well-fitting coat the strength in his back, the warmth of his body. Another kiss and now their tongues danced with each other. Juliana's heart was racing, her breathing was laboured and heat was coursing through her. Never had she felt a fire like this!

They broke off to look into each other's eyes. What she saw in his was both terrifying and wonderful at once. He felt what she felt! She knew it! He looked at her mouth, then swooped again, kissing her with a fierce intensity that she returned, measure for measure.

'Juliana!' he murmured against her mouth. 'My love!'

Joy coursed through her. He was right—this was love. *Love!*

Suddenly, it all made sense. Her connection to him. Her irritation with his flirtatious mask. The way she knew, always, where he was in the room. The way they both, subtly, contrived to spend time together, talk together, walk together, whenever possible. The way he looked at her—as if she was a puzzle he was compelled to solve. As if she was wonderful.

'Harry,' she murmured. Inside, her heart sang. *Harry.*

Chapter Fifteen

They broke apart, as consciousness slowly returned. They were in a public park, with Adam and Charlotte walking up ahead, and anyone might see them! Juliana took a small step away, noting as she did so that Harry seemed as shaken as she felt. He stood staring at her, then lifted his left hand and slowly ran his fingers down her cheek. The look in his eyes was so tender that it melted something inside her. She felt like she could cry. Or fly.

Time slowed as she took in every detail. His face, framed by windswept dark hair. The look in his deep-blue eyes. His physical presence, that sense of his strength, warmth and solidity.

Harry lifted her hand and tenderly kissed it. He then tucked it into his arm and indicated with a gesture that they should walk on. It echoed the events of just a few minutes before, when he had left Adam to take up his place by her side. In those intervening moments, the world had changed.

Neither spoke as they walked along. Juliana was content to simply enjoy the feelings flooding through her—elation in her heart, warmth in her belly and a sense of wonder at what was happening. Her eyes followed the flight of a lark, as it ascended, dipped and climbed higher into the clear blue sky.

They had nearly caught up with Adam and Charlotte when they suddenly spied a horseman coming towards them from the left. Harry squeezed Juliana's hand in warning as they realised who it was.

The rider reined in and touched his hat to them.

'Afternoon, Captain. Miss Milford.'

'General Hunter.' Harry's tone was polite, but held no warmth. Juliana remained silent, but inclined her head in the shallowest of acknowledgements.

'It occurred to me,' said the General, addressing Juliana, 'that you may be anxious about my difference of opinion with your mother. I did not wish to cause her further distress by calling on her again, so I determined to seek you out directly—your footman indicated I would find you here.'

Juliana found her tongue. 'You did right not to call upon my mother.' Her tone was curt. 'Indeed, I advise you not to approach her again. She has been seriously affected by your last visit.'

'Taken to her bed, eh?' The General shook his head. 'She was always weak-willed.'

Juliana forced herself to maintain control. 'She is *not* weak-willed. And she has *not* taken to her bed. Why, we shared nuncheon not two hours ago.' Juliana decided not to mention that Mama was, at this very moment, in bed. 'She is a strong woman, who has raised me by herself in a foreign country, with no assistance from anyone.'

'I give her credit for that. She has done well in raising you, despite your bitter tongue and opinionated conduct.' There was a glint of humour in his eye. Seeing it, Juliana's rage boiled further. About to unleash it, she paused when Harry placed his other hand over hers.

'Was there something in particular you wished to say to Miss Milford?' he enquired.

The General gave a bark of laughter. 'Young puppy! Think you stand as her guard dog, eh?' He turned back to Juliana. 'I wish you to know I will continue to send money to your mother. I am displeased she has come to England and brought you with her, and I have told her so. However, it will not deter me from what I know to be my duty. Should you need additional funds to cover your journey back to Brussels, you should let me know. Here is my card.'

Immobilised by rage, Juliana did not immediately respond, so Harry took the card and pressed it into her hand. After a brief glance at Juliana, he addressed the General again. 'Did you pay for Miss Milford's education?'

'Permit me to tell you, Captain Fanton, it is none of your business—though I confess you are providing me with some rare entertainment this day! You are not related to Juliana and should not ask impertinent questions.'

'Then I shall ask.' Juliana glared up at him. 'Did you, General Hunter, pay for my education?'

'Every penny of it. I have provided a generous allowance for Elizabeth and for you for over twenty years.'

'Generous? You dare to describe yourself as *generous*? When my poor mama has been exiled for those twenty years, ashamed to return home, because of *you*! And you have the conceit to call it *duty*!' Anger boiled through Juliana.

'You go too far, miss!' All humour left him. His eyes flashed. 'Elizabeth's shame was her own doing and she did right to stay in Brussels all those years. It is a pity you cannot have what should have been rightfully yours, but Elizabeth's foolishness has condemned you both. I have already indulged you enough. You will keep a civil tongue in your head when you address me. I shall wish you good day.'

Then he was gone, in a thunder of hooves and arrogance.

'Ooooh! He—that he can say such things!' Juliana dropped her hand from Harry's arm and watched the General fade into the distance. She began to pace up and down in barely articulate rage. 'I hate him! I actually hate him. To speak to me so—to say such things of Mama! And I must stand helplessly and allow it!' She paced for a moment, before forcing herself to stop. She looked at Harry. His handsome face was creased with concern. 'Thank you for standing my friend.'

He shook his head. 'I am sorry I could not do more. He is correct, though, I have no right to speak for you. Only a close relative can do so—because the matter is so personal. *Damn!*' He glanced at her. 'My apologies for the profanity.'

Juliana was only half-listening. She stood, pale and unyielding, her hands clenched into small fists. 'Is this how it feels, when you want to kill an enemy?'

Charlotte and Adam, who had belatedly realised what was unfolding, hurried over to them.

'Juliana!' cried Charlotte. 'Are you well? What did he say?'

Juliana could not even speak to Charlotte. Focusing intently on Harry, she asked again, 'Do you hate your enemies?'

Harry, looking rather pale, let out a breath. 'No. I do not.'

'Then how can you kill them?'

'Because I must. I am a soldier. Those who hate do not survive long.' His eyes held hers—his expression calm, testing and concerned all at once.

'Oh, Juliana!' Charlotte made as if to embrace her, but Juliana stood rigid. There was no softness in her. She was only anger, and hatred, and rage. Something in what Harry had said was important, though. There had been a challenge in it.

'I am well, Charlotte,' she said shortly. Charlotte bit her lip, but subsided. She had seen Juliana like this before. Throughout her school years, Juliana had worked to master her emotions, to control them rather than allowing them to control her. She had made progress in working out which battles were the important ones and how to apply rationality to fury. Since arriving in England, she had been sorely tested, and the challenges were becoming tougher by the day.

Juliana looked at Harry again. Though she had not asked another question, he said, as if answering her, 'To survive, one must be calm enough to see things clearly and to make the right choices. There is—' He frowned. 'There is a killing rage which comes over some men. They go berserk and lose all sense of danger. They forget about the safety of their comrades. To kill is more important than to live. Sometimes, they lose their honour. Such men die quickly.' A pulse beat rapidly in his neck. 'Others spill their rage on the innocent, knowing them to be helpless.' His voice was measured, his gaze intent. It gave her pause.

They were all looking at her expectantly. She needed to say something. Her head was spinning. 'May we turn back? I wish to return to the house.' Her voice sounded even. Good.

They all turned and walked in silence through the park. Harry's words reverberated through her, like the striking of a gong. Despite the darkness that had briefly threatened to overpower her, she was an innocent child in comparison to those who had been through the horrors of war.

Gradually, Juliana became aware of her surroundings—the chirp and chatter of birds, the susurration of the breeze in the branches. Harry's solid presence by her side. Yellow primroses and nodding bluebells punctuating the green landscape all around. Adam and Charlotte, walking together behind her and Harry. Beauty, warmth, friendship, love. These were stronger than anger and hate.

Her rage slowly, steadily subsided. Recognising, finally, the concerns of her friends, she stopped to make them a frank apology.

'I am the vilest creature!' she said. 'I do not lose my temper often, but when I do it is not safe to be near me.'

Charlotte, with a muffled exclamation, enfolded her in a tight hug. This time, Juliana leaned into it.

'Nonsense!' said Harry gruffly. 'You were severely provoked. You managed the situation well in the circumstances. I believe you really did want to run him through—if you'd had a sword.' He grinned. 'I did wonder if you would try to seize mine.'

'I did—but only for a moment. It was a thought, but acting on it did not occur to me.' She frowned, recognising that for all her intemperate words, she had no notion of actually *killing* anyone. Even General Hunter, her enemy.

She gave Harry a rueful grimace. 'I cannot imagine actually doing it. For all my bravado, I could not, I think, be a soldier. I wonder at those who can kill, yet keep their humanity.'

The smile faded from his face. 'It is not so easily achieved. The killing is hard.' He added softly, his gaze focused on a distant point, 'Keeping hold of one's soul is much, much harder.'

Adam and Charlotte exchanged glances, but said

nothing. Juliana recognised this was not the best moment to ask more questions, but her hunger to know more of Harry would take her back to this. She laid her hand on his arm and squeezed gently. Coming back to the present, he placed his other hand on hers. They walked on.

Juliana still had much to think about. General Hunter's words gave the worst confirmation about her identity, and the anger she felt towards him remained sharp. How dared he blame Mama for the scandal? Why was it always the woman who was condemned by society? Never the man.

Much more importantly, though, she needed to think about Harry. As they walked along the well-trodden path, Harry's steps in rhythm with hers, everything suddenly seemed as though it was not real, as though the events of the past half-hour were a play she had watched or a book she had read. She searched for the elation she had felt after Harry had kissed her, and she could not find it. General Hunter had stolen it away with his untimely arrival. Love and hate had come to her, and she was all perplexity.

Harry, too, walked through the park with a sense of confusion. Momentous things had happened—were happening—and, despite his calm exterior, his mind and heart were awhirl. *He loved her!* Of course he did, for who could fail to love her? She was magnificent, beautiful, fiery, quick-witted… What seemed entirely wonderful to him, though, was that she seemed to return his regard. His heart quickened. He had felt it in her passionate response to his kiss.

Or had he? He frowned. He had kissed many women, yet he had never before had the notion that any of them loved him. Indeed, he always tried to ensure they did not. He had shared passionate kisses—and more—with his *chères-amies*, and never wondered if they held warm feelings for him. This time had felt different, but he must not be too hasty to make assumptions. The only distinction he could be sure of was that *he* loved Juliana. It did not follow that *she* also loved him.

He stole a glance at her. She remained lost in thought, frowning slightly—she was probably still reflecting on her angry encounter with General Hunter. Oh, why had the damned General come along at that precise moment, before Harry had had the chance to properly read Juliana's reaction to his kiss, his mutterings of love? Juliana might assume he said such things to all the women he kissed! Indeed, it would not be unreasonable of her to make such a judgement, he admitted, for had he not worked hard to display himself to her as a flirtatious fribble?

He berated himself. *Undone by your own frivolity, Fanton!*

Perhaps, to Juliana, this was nothing more than a little light romance, like many others being kindled in Almack's and elsewhere this Season. She certainly did not seem to be disturbed by what had occurred between them. He knew Juliana's feelings about General Hunter—she had engaged heartily in the skirmish with the General, her emotions plain to read in the line of her body, the tone in her voice and the range of expressions flitting across her face.

Should he not, then, have seen signs of loving feelings for him, if they existed? There had been no coyness, maidenly shyness or any of the usual signs that maidens were expected to display to signal their interest in or feelings for a man. She had simply kissed him with passionate abandon, then continued their walk as though unmoved. He knew she valued his friendship. Charlotte loved him as a friend, too—and neither he nor Charlotte had ever had a thought of a different sort of relationship. Harry had never thought of Charlotte in that way and, from very early on, Charlotte had had eyes only for Adam. Yes, Juliana's friendship was assured—and he valued it tremendously. But it was not enough. It would never be enough.

General Hunter's words had wounded him, though not as much as they must have hurt Juliana. Confirmation that the General had indeed been funding Mrs Milford, and that she had stayed away from England because of past scandal, provided yet more evidence that Juliana's origins were dishonourable in some way and that the General was likely her father. Not that Harry cared. It made no difference whatsoever to his feelings for Juliana—though, as he had previously concluded, to marry her would affect his career and his social standing. A small price to pay, if she actually wanted him.

General Hunter's words had hurt simply because of the blunt reminder that Harry had no status in Juliana's life, no right to stand with her and fight with her. She did not *need* him—she had handled the encounter with credit—but, as he well knew, having strong friends and family to take your part made difficult situations easier to bear. She was fiercely independent—one of the many things he loved about her—but some of his most precious memories since he'd known her were the brief moments when she had allowed him to see her vulnerability.

He looked at her again. Her beautiful face was creased with concentration, as she worked through the thoughts in her lively mind. Should he say something?

He could not.

The truth was he had no clue what to say or, indeed, whether to speak at all. His usual instincts were letting him down. He shook himself internally. This was a new experience, this uncertainty. He was Captain Harry Fanton, dazzler of women, leader of men! He *always* knew what to say...until today.

Chapter Sixteen

Juliana's recovery continued as they walked together without speaking. Her pulse had calmed, her
breathing eased and she knew it was safe for her to
be in company again. It was important to protect
Mama from the General and from his harsh words
and opinions of her. Juliana's mother knew her better than anyone and might figure out that something
had upset her.

Juliana also wanted to hide her newly discovered
feelings for Harry from everyone. She barely understood what was happening to her, never having
been in love before, and the sensations he aroused
in her were as confusing as they were pleasant. She
wanted to hug it all to herself, until she understood
it better.

They left the park and ambled through the noisy
streets towards St James's Square. Coaches and carts
rumbled past, horses toiling in the spring warmth.

A young street-sweeper jumped out in front of them to brush away the dung. Harry threw him a coin.

As they strolled up the street towards the Fanton town house, the front door opened and two figures emerged. First, a man—a small, slight man, who moved with the care of age. His clothes were black, neat and sober and signalled his membership of the professional classes. He carried a leather folder of the type that usually held papers.

He paused on the top step to await his companion—a woman, dressed in charcoal-grey. Her hair was a lighter grey and secured in a neat bun. Juliana was too far away to see either of their faces and when they descended the steps they turned away, walking east along the Square. Some people of business, perhaps, visiting Adam's steward. Strange to think everyday life continued and that, for everyone else, things were more or less the same as they had been this morning. When she left the house around an hour ago, Juliana had not known that Harry loved her, or that she loved him. Now that the ill effects of General Hunter's interruption were fading, the glow of happiness which had surrounded her earlier was beginning to return. She resolved to simply enjoy the feeling for a little while.

They entered the house and Juliana readily allowed the housemaid to help replace her walking boots with soft slippers. Harry and Adam were still being assisted out of their coats and boots by the footmen, so Charlotte and Juliana went ahead to the drawing room. Juliana could not resist one last look towards Harry. He was ready for it and, as their eyes met, a tingle ran down her spine.

'Mama!' Juliana could not keep the surprise from her voice. Her mother was in the drawing room, seated at the writing desk, and *not* sleeping still. *Taken to her bed*, indeed! It just showed that General Hunter knew nothing of Mama now. 'Did you have a good rest earlier?'

'Oh, Juliana! Charlotte! No. Yes. I—what?'

Juliana seated herself in one of the upholstered chairs by the fireplace. She shook out her skirts, checking that the only stains she had picked up in the park were along the hemline of her petticoat, where it had brushed the longer grasses and picked up pollen and a small trace of dried mud. The delicate fabric of her printed muslin was perfectly clean. Thank goodness the style was for slightly shorter dresses over long petticoats!

Charlotte picked up her darning from a side table and brought it to the sofa.

'Earlier?' Mama seemed finally to take in what Juliana had said. 'Oh, yes, it was—quite...quite... yes.' She sat down her pen, but her mind was evidently elsewhere. Juliana's heart melted. This was such a trial for dear Mama and she was coping so well—much better than Juliana had hoped.

'Are you writing letters, Mama?' Juliana looked carefully at her mother. She seemed a little more agitated than she had been, but there was also something different about her. Juliana could not quite work out what it was.

'No, not yet—though I will need to write some later. There will be work in it, but it must be done, for the possibilities...' Mama's voice tailed off and she gazed into space. Juliana and Charlotte exchanged glances.

'Juliana!' Mama's voice was suddenly strong, decided. Juliana looked back at her in surprise. That was a tone she had not heard in a very long time. 'I must speak with you!'

'Of course.' Juliana glanced at Charlotte, who shrugged slightly.

'I need to speak to Cook anyway, so I shall leave you alone,' said Charlotte, rising and setting her darning back on the table.

Her mother waited until Charlotte had closed the door behind her, then rose and paced the room in some agitation. Juliana waited, a little bewildered by her mama's unusual behaviour. Finally she turned, stood straighter and spoke.

'Juliana, there are things I cannot tell you. Things that you want to know. Information you *ought* to know. But I—I simply can't. Not yet.'

Should she tell Mama that she already knew? That General Hunter had, not an hour ago, confirmed it all himself?

'I promise I will tell you all of it—even the parts I am ashamed of. But not yet and not here.'

Juliana's eyes misted. Mama was being so strong, so brave. 'I do not need you to tell me anything right now,' she murmured. 'We can talk when it seems right to you.'

'I have made a decision, Juliana. We are going home, to Brussels.'

Juliana frowned in confusion. 'Do you mean when the war is over?'

'No. We must go as soon as we may—within a few weeks.'

'So soon?' Juliana was aghast. 'But why?'

'It is necessary.' Mama began pacing again. 'We must reach Brussels safely before Napoleon moves his armies too far north. We will travel via Ostend. We either go soon, or we may be stranded in England for months.'

'And would that be so terrible? We have good friends here, a comfortable situation. You do like it here, Mama? Don't you?'

'Of course! Dear Charlotte has been so kind and her Adam is a true gentleman.'

Juliana had to ask. 'And you like all of them, don't you? Olivia and Great-Aunt Clara, and Harry?'

She slipped his name in at the end of her list, *needing* to talk about him, desperate to hear that Mama liked him.

'Yes, I do. Olivia is a delightful young lady and Clara is a dear friend.'

'And Harry?' Juliana held her breath.

Mama gave her a stern look. 'If you remember, I appreciated Harry's good qualities from the first time we met—unlike you, who wanted only to fuss and argue with him.'

'That is true.' Juliana blushed a little at the memory of how rude she and Harry had been to each other, that first day.

'I will tell you something now, Juliana. Harry is the most amiable, the most charming and the most *reliable* young man I have met in many a year. He is like a son to me. I have come to depend on him and to appreciate how he cares for us both. I know you have not always seen eye to eye, but I truly believe he has your interests at heart.'

Juliana felt her blush mount. Seeing it, her mother looked a little surprised, then her eyes narrowed. Shying from her mother's perceptive gaze, Juliana attempted to divert her. 'I still do not understand why we must leave soon. It would be much less dangerous to wait until the armies have battled and we will then know if it is safe to cross France.'

'It must be soon. There are reasons—but I do not wish to dwell on it. It will take a few weeks to arrange everything. I will ask Adam if his steward can organise our passage. We will also need to hire a coach to take us to the coast. Then there will be inns to be written to, a coach to take us through France… I have begun to make a list. I do not wish for you to be involved in the arrangements, as you did when we travelled here. Coming to England was your project, your mission, so you had the organising of it. Returning home is mine and I will do it myself.'

'But, Mama,' Juliana protested, 'We cannot simply—'

'You will heed me in this, Juliana. My mind is made up.'

Juliana looked at her, recognising a new firmness in her mother's expression. For some reason, Mama believed it was important to return home now, war or no war. And she was absolutely determined, that was clear. What did it all mean?

She nodded. 'Very well, Mama.'

* * *

Dinner that evening was a strange affair. The conversation was led by Mrs Milford, who normally was the quietest person at the table. It was as though she had found a new energy—a zest and vigour that had not been there before. Juliana had never seen her so animated. She sparkled and questioned, and was interested in everyone and everything.

Juliana did not know what to make of it. Her own mother had transformed before her eyes. While it seemed to be a good thing, part of her wondered if it was in fact some sort of feverish manifestation of a continuing underlying malaise. She watched, bewildered, as Mama drew Olivia out with some gentle teasing on the topic of Mr Nightingale.

'Does he still encourage you to arrange a picnic in Vauxhall, Olivia?'

A slight crease appeared on Olivia's brow. 'He does. I believe a picnic would be an excellent adventure, but I should not like Mr Nightingale to think—that is to say, he might inadvertently have had the wrong impression—'

Adam looked at her keenly. 'What is it, little one? Has he said something that he ought not?'

Olivia smiled briefly at her brother's endearment. 'Oh, no! He is ever the gentleman! But...'

Harry, who was seated in his usual place on Juliana's left side, chortled softly. 'I see it! He has fallen out of favour.'

Olivia blushed and applied herself to her asparagus. 'He seems to think he is the only man I should talk to. He is most agreeable, but I do not like it when he thinks he has some sort of special position.'

'You must be bold, Olivia!' It was Mrs Milford. 'If you are not careful, you will become a passenger in your own life. You must steer your ship, make your choices and follow what your heart tells you.'

Juliana knew her mouth was hanging open. She shut it and exchanged a look with Harry. His was filled with admiration—and a good deal of amusement. Juliana, while understanding how the others were enjoying this new, assertive Mrs Milford, was mostly confused. What on earth had happened to create this change?

'But what if I choose wrong?' asked Olivia, in a small voice. 'I was so looking forward to my first Season, but it is much more difficult than I anticipated.'

Mrs Milford gave her a kind look. 'What does your heart tell you?'

A series of expressions flitted over Olivia's face—surprise, doubt, then certainty. She squared her shoulders. 'I must let Mr Nightingale know that, while I admire him and I like him, I cannot—I mean, I do not think I could like him above all others.'

'You see? You know what is right. Now, do not doubt yourself.' Mama's gaze dropped and she added softly, 'I wish someone had advised me so, when I was young.'

'We can still have a picnic, you know,' offered Charlotte, 'but we will go with Adam and Harry, instead of Mr Nightingale. Perhaps in a couple of weeks.'

'Really?' Olivia's eyes were alight with excitement. 'And can we stay into the evening, to see the fireworks?'

Adam nodded. 'If it will make you happy. But you must stay with us at all times.'

'Oh, I will!' Olivia smiled happily. 'But what about Mr Nightingale?'

Harry leaned forward and, in a conspiratorial whisper, told her, 'I will advise you. I know all the ways by which you can rid yourself of Mr Nightingale, without ever enacting a drama. You will need to be tactical, and disciplined, but together we will make a plan.'

Olivia clapped her hands in delight. A moment later, she frowned. 'You will not ask me to be unkind? I sincerely admire Mr Nightingale and I would not do anything to upset him or hurt his feelings.'

'Never fear, chit. You are in the hands of an expert. You will do it gradually, but firmly. He will come to understand that he holds no special place in your affections. All will be well.' Harry winked at her and Olivia replied with a tremulous smile.

Juliana, watching, felt a shadow of doubt. This reminded her of the old Harry. She shook off the feeling—after all, she knew him much better now. And he was right. It would be good if he could advise Olivia how to extricate herself from Mr Nightingale's expectations without hurting his feelings.

After dinner, when the gentlemen joined them in the drawing room, Harry drew Juliana to one side. 'I must speak with you, for I have news that may interest you.' He took her hand and led her to a satin-covered sofa near the window, out of earshot of her mother and the others, who were eagerly discussing the possible picnic.

The touch of his hand sent a thrill through Juliana and she gladly sat with him, keen for a private moment's conversation. Checking with a glance that the others were not watching, he gazed at her hungrily. Juliana's heart began to pound. It really was amazing how, now she knew her own feelings, everything about him was interesting to her. She searched his face, thrilling in committing to memory his beloved features.

'I have news for you, too—and you may not like it.'

He frowned. 'Tell me.'

'No, you first.' The thought of leaving him—leaving all of them—to return to Brussels sat like a lead weight in the bottom of her stomach. While she knew he would soon travel to France himself, to risk his life in the war against Napoleon, she preferred not to think of it. Somehow, she needed to pretend everything would stay the same. That they could talk and walk in the park, and kiss each other, without threat of war or scandal to pull them apart. It was coming. She knew it. He might be killed in the war and, even if he wasn't, there was no way for them to marry—an Earl's brother simply could not marry beneath him, and an illegitimate girl could not expect anything from him.

There was no point in thinking of marriage, anyway, with the threat of war on the horizon. Thousands of young men had died in the last engagements with Napoleon. Now the Emperor had escaped his prison and was once more amassing an army, further conflict was inevitable. She knew it. And Captain Harry Fanton knew it, too.

All they might ever have would be these last

weeks, before she and Mama left for Brussels. Her mother had talked of organising their return for next month. A cold hand gripped her heart as she imagined trying to say goodbye to Harry. How had he suddenly become so dear to her? The answer came immediately. It had not been sudden at all. Her love for him had been growing since the day they met. That intense attraction could not be ignored, which was why she had gone through the agonies of questioning him, challenging him and, finally, concluding she could trust him.

It was too late. He was as essential to her as breathing. She knew he felt it, too, for how could he not? While it seemed amazing to her that he should love her, she knew in her heart, in her bones, that he did. Never had she felt so attuned to another person. His large, strong hand enveloped hers, his eyes held hers and she felt the strangest combination of excitement and peace.

'Today I met with my informant—the man who has contacts in the bank.'

Juliana was puzzled. 'But we already know General Hunter has been sending Mama's allowance to Brussels.'

'Yes—though we did not know that for sure when I engaged him. But he had more to tell me—and not all of it was clear.'

'Go on.' Juliana had no idea what to expect.

'He says information on General Hunter's financial affairs has never been more in demand. His source claims to have been paid by at least two other parties for the same information—details of the General's funding for you and your mother.'

Juliana thought quickly. 'Presumably the Wakelys were one source of his lucrative bribes! Mr Wakely already told Charlotte he had used some of his unexpected fortune to seek out information which would be harmful to me and Mama.'

'Yes—and I presume the Wakelys were motivated by a misplaced desire to gain Charlotte's gratitude. He says Mr Wakely mentioned that General Hunter had called on your mama here—which means that the rumours, I am sorry to say, must have their source in this house. Some of the staff, or possibly a guest, has been indiscreet.'

Juliana gave an unladylike snort, thinking of Henrietta and Millicent's recent disdain. 'Or vindictive.'

He pondered this. 'Possibly. I will ask Charlotte to discreetly question the butler and housekeeper about their staff.'

Juliana kept her opinions to herself. 'So who was the other person asking questions about us?'

'My contact would not say—save to mention that

they were a perfectly respectable party, seeking information in respect of a legal matter.'

'A legal matter? What legal matter?'

'He could not say. I do not believe he knew anything else. Now, tell me, have you or your mama ever had any dealings with lawyers, or come under threat from anyone with respect to the law?'

'No! We have been boringly and consistently honest in all our dealings. It is possible, I suppose, that Mama has been holding some other secret from me…' Juliana glanced across at her mother, who was laughing gently at some witticism from Adam '…but you understand Mama by now. Why, she is the sweetest, most transparent person I know! Her life is limited only by the fears and anxieties in her head—and breaking the law would not, I think, be something she would ever do.'

He considered this. 'That is my impression, too. Do not forget, though, she does talk of being ashamed and seeks to hide from people. We know she carries some secrets in her heart. If there is something dangerous, like a legal matter where she is at risk of some action against her, then we can only help her if she reveals it.'

'Yes, but we know her secrets relate to my birth and parentage. She was attacked, or seduced, and ran away—or was sent away—to hide that shame.

Coming back to England, meeting General Hunter again, must have been so trying for her, yet she has done it.'

'Is that why she has changed, do you think? I have never seen her so well as she is today. Are her burdens lighter?'

'She is certainly transformed. Perhaps meeting the General again has been cathartic for her. Though he wounded her when he came here, she has recovered well and she can now perhaps look forward to the future with a new perspective.'

His thumb was gently caressing her palm. The sensation was wonderfully distracting and was causing disturbing responses throughout her body. She swallowed and dropped her eyes to their joined hands. Without quite understanding why, she felt her breathing had quickened. There was not enough air in her lungs. His thumb continued its work, slowly, gently. She took a deep ragged breath, and exhaled heavily. Raising her eyes to his, she was silenced by the passion blazing there. 'Juliana!' he groaned quietly.

Chapter Seventeen

She could not speak. She could only look at him, lost in the same ecstatic agony. They remained like that, for a terrible, wonderful moment, then a change came over him. His jaw hardened. He set her hand into her own lap, and disengaged his. She saw his chest heaving—his breathing was as disturbed as hers! Casting a sidelong glance at the others to ensure they weren't being scrutinised, he muttered, through clenched teeth, 'I do not understand this power you have over me, Juliana. I have never felt this way.'

Her eyes widened. 'Never?'

He nodded grimly. 'Never. I am not sure I like it.'

She understood exactly what he meant. There was a vulnerability in it. They each had the power to inflict tremendous hurt on the other. And while she could not imagine them doing so deliberately, the shadows that would separate them were already gathering.

'I am leaving England.' The words were out before she had time to even consider them.

'What? When?' He looked shocked.

'Soon. Mama has decided she wishes to return to Brussels as soon as it may be arranged.'

'But—it is not safe! War is coming. Napoleon's power increases by the day, along with his armies. He aims to conquer all of Europe.'

'She believes we will be safe and wants us to get through France before the battles begin. She wants to go home to Brussels.'

'Keeping to northern France is certainly a little less dangerous, but the situation is changing by the day. Can she not be persuaded?'

'I was unable to manage it. The thought of being home is, I think, part of the reason why she is so happy today.'

Distractedly, he ran his hand through his hair, leaving a lock falling forward on to his brow. Juliana resisted the temptation to smooth it back.

'May I speak with her? Try to dissuade her?'

'Of course! I wish you would. But—' Juliana spoke earnestly, needing him to understand this '—if she truly wants to go, then I will not deny her.'

'I know.' His expression was grim. Juliana could

hardly blame him. She, too, was concerned at the notion of travelling back to France on the eve of war. While she knew many society families living in mainland Europe had vowed to stay in their homes, very few would choose to return from safety to danger. Memories of the Terror that had happened a generation before, when so many people had lost their lives, still haunted those Juliana had grown up with.

'I know I must go there myself—it is my duty. But I expected to go knowing that everyone important to me would be safe here.' His gaze became unfocused. 'At once, I have someone to fight for and someone to worry about. Make no mistake—' he brought his focus back to her '—I *will* fight for you and for my family. I will do whatever it takes to keep you from harm.'

She rested her hand on his arm. 'But you must fight *safely*, if there is such a thing. You told me about those men who fight in a passion of hatred. Please, do not be blinded by emotion when you are in battle. I need you to be safe.' Her voice dropped. 'I need you to live!'

His eyes blazed into hers. 'Juliana, can you promise me you will take no unnecessary risks as you journey into danger?'

'Of course!' She had no intention of risking herself, or her mother. She needed to get them safely to Brussels, then hope that Napoleon's imperial ambitions would pass them by. Perhaps she could persuade her mother to delay a few weeks more and the situation with Napoleon might become a little clearer.

'Mama will not allow me to help her plan our journey. However, she might listen to you. If she insists on travelling, can you advise her on the safest route and help her engage guards as outriders?'

'Naturally I will. Though it fills me with dread just to consider you making such a journey.'

'Juliana!' Mrs Milford was calling. 'We need you to help us decide between these two fashion plates for Olivia's new ballgown!'

With one last look at Harry, Juliana stood and rejoined the others.

Two weeks had passed with heavy rain and blustery showers, and Mama would be put off no longer. The arrangements were made, a sea crossing booked and Juliana accepted she now had only a few days left in England. Napoleon was continuing to make his plans, but he had not yet made his move. Mama insisted they must go and that they would be safe in their little house in Brussels. Juliana, determined to enjoy these last few days of happiness, tried not to think of the future.

Finally, a day dawned fair and dry, and, after checking with the head groom, Joseph, that it was likely to remain dry all day, Adam and Charlotte confirmed they would go ahead with the much-delayed picnic. Juliana, in a bout of silliness she hadn't enjoyed since she was seventeen, took an inordinate length of time over choosing her dress.

'I am so sorry, Priddy,' she said, apologising to Charlotte's personal maid, whom she had known for years. 'I do not know why I am so demanding today!'

'It is not like you to be unsure of yourself, Miss Juliana,' Priddy said, with a knowing glint in her eye. 'So are you decided on the green crape?'

'Yes!' affirmed Juliana, turning from side to side as she once again checked her reflection. 'I have a matching spencer for this one, in a deeper green. And, somewhere, a parasol.'

'I know exactly where they are,' snorted Priddy, opening the oak armoire in the corner of Juliana's room, 'for I take pride in my work. I have always believed if I do something to the best of my ability, I am immune from criticism.'

'But surely disapproval can still occur, even when we do things correctly?'

'If I have truly done all I can, then any such censure is none of my business, but rather reflects poorly on those who criticise. Words that try to wound have therefore no power over me. Here you are, miss.'

'I see what you mean.' Juliana shrugged her way into the spencer and buttoned it up. Priddy's philosophy might serve her well should she experience insult or disdain from anyone at Vauxhall today.

'If you know your own true worth, then no one can truly hurt you.' Priddy eyed her levelly through the glass. 'Yes, that spencer matches perfectly. Here are your gloves and parasol.'

Taking them, Juliana smiled and thanked Priddy. In truth, she felt immune from any hurt today. The sun was shining, she was in love and she was to spend the entire day with Harry!

And with Mama, Charlotte, Adam, Olivia and Great-Aunt Clara. While she loved them all and looked forward to the entertainments the day would bring, in truth Juliana knew it was Harry who was at the heart of this happiness. She moved along the landing and started down the stairs, aware she was blessed to have found a love like this. While neither of them had actually made an open declaration of love, they understood each other. She was under no illusions about her beloved. Harry was stubborn— as stubborn as she. He was also capable of irritating superficiality. But she knew him. Knew his true heart—his integrity, sense of duty, his deep love for his family. She recognised his great capacity for compassion and marvelled at his big heart. These past two weeks had been blissful. It was extraordinary that this wonderful man loved her!

He was waiting at the bottom of the stairs. His eyes kindled as he saw her. Her eyes fixed on his, Juliana moved unthinkingly toward him.

'My love!' he murmured huskily, lifting her hand to kiss. *I am glad I have not yet put on my gloves*, thought Juliana, thrilling at the touch of his warm lips on her skin. 'You look stunning!' he continued, his other hand coming up to touch her face. She tilted her head to lean into his caress, and he caught his breath.

'—which is why I have ordered the phaeton, as well as the coach.' Adam's voice came to them from further down the hallway, and they both moved apart, a little guiltily.

'So will Harry drive the phaeton?' asked Charlotte, approaching. 'Oh, there you are, Harry! Would you mind driving Juliana in the phaeton, for we would be better taking the other ladies in the coach? Adam can ride alongside us.' If Charlotte had noticed the culpable behaviour of her friend and her brother-in-law, she gave no sign. As usual.

'An excellent notion! I should treasure the opportunity to drive Miss Milford in the phaeton,' confirmed Harry, beaming.

'I thought you would,' said Adam, his expression inscrutable.

The other ladies soon joined them and they all bustled outside, an air of excitement fuelling the ladies to chatter, and exclaim, and compliment each other's outfits. Mrs Milford meanwhile was continuing to behave with more energy, confidence and happiness than Juliana could ever remember. It gave her hope this truly was a new era in her mother's troubled life.

Harry handed Juliana up into the high-perch phaeton—a dashing model more suited to racing than to sedate jaunts through the city streets. He jumped up beside her and grinned as he took the reins from the groom. 'I have a plan!' he said conspiratorially.

Caught up in his infectious humour, Juliana grinned back. 'Oh, yes?' she murmured. 'Impress me, then!'

'Oh, I shall,' he returned, every word a promise. 'Adam, we shall meet you at Vauxhall!'

Adam, who was busy supervising the loading of two large picnic baskets on to the back of the ladies' carriage, waved abstractedly.

'Hyaa!' cried Harry, setting the matched bays in

motion. In a neat move, he manoeuvred the phaeton out from behind the coach and into the stream of traffic. Juliana waved at Charlotte as they sped past, then the others were behind them and they were driving through London.

Juliana had heard Adam and Olivia tease Harry on his driving skills—apparently he was a notable whip. She frowned slightly as she remembered he had taken Millicent out driving, then reassured herself. It was she who was with him now, and she truly believed he had never felt anything for Millicent.

She cast an eye sideways, enjoying the sight of Harry's muscular legs, encased in tight-fitting breeches and top boots. He braced himself against the footboard as the phaeton sped and turned, and she could see the play of muscles there and in his strong forearm as he expertly handled the reins in his left hand.

Her gaze moved on, upwards… His clothing today was particularly striking, and, as always, of the finest quality. The cravat was expertly tied and spotlessly white, while his waistcoat was an attractive pale gold, embroidered with a tracery of gold leaves. Over this he wore a snug-fitting coat of deep blue, which now drew her eyes to the breadth of his shoulders, the near one so close to her. He turned his head towards her and she immediately looked ahead, not wanting to be caught studying his form.

He chuckled softly. 'Patience, my love.'

She found her voice. 'Where are we going?'

He grinned. 'Since the coachman will take at least half an hour to drive them all the way to Vauxhall, you and I have time for a diversion.' He turned and murmured in her ear, '*They* will travel directly down Whitehall, while *we* will divert through St James's Park.'

His mouth briefly brushed her ear as he spoke, sending a delicious shiver through her.

'Whoa!' Harry's attention was back on his driving—he had narrowly missed careering straight into a large coach which had decided to pull out in front of them. Juliana gripped the side of the phaeton and vowed to remain silent, as Harry expertly manoeuvred the vehicle through the narrowest of gaps, leaving the lumbering coach in their wake.

'Nicely done!' she ventured, exhaling in relief. He just grinned.

Thankfully, they had now reached the gates of the park. Their path ahead was clear, so Harry gave the horses their heads. They sped through the park, travelling at a faster pace than Juliana had ever experienced. She held on to her bonnet as the air rushed by and could not resist letting out a hoot of glee. She had never known such exhilaration!

Harry whooped, too, then glanced at her. Raising his voice against the thunder of hooves and the whistle of the air whooshing by, he yelled, 'Take my arm!' He lifted his elbow to allow her to slip her hand inside the crook of his arm, then warmly clamped her arm close to him.

All too soon he slowed, the trees ahead necessitating a more measured pace. Pulling the horses to a gradual halt under the trees, he spoke softly to them, then turned towards Juliana.

'I think I know the answer to this, but tell me—were you frightened?'

'Frightened? Of course not! I have never felt so...' She paused, looking for the right word.

'Exhilarated?'

'No—though it was certainly exhilarating.' He waited, his eyes intent on her. 'I have it! *Alive.* I felt truly alive. As though everything had come together in a perfect moment.'

His eyes widened, then he swallowed hard. When he spoke, his voice was low and intense. 'Juliana, I am not a man much given to prayers, although like all soldiers I speak to the Almighty in times of need. But I am moved to say that He has sent me a remarkable woman to care for and for that I am grateful.'

Her heart swelled as he bent his head to touch his lips to hers. This kiss was unlike any they had shared so far. While her body responded as it did each time their mouths joined, this time Juliana felt a purity, a reverence that moved them both. They pulled back to look at each other.

'May I ask something of you?' His voice was husky and his expression uncertain. She tilted her head quizzically. 'I have taken the liberty of bringing these with me today.' He fished in the small compartment beside his seat, emerging with a small pair of scissors. 'I would consider it an honour if you would gift me a lock of your hair.'

'Oh, how romantic!' Juliana had heard of such customs, but only in the pages of novels. To have Harry demonstrate his passion for her in such a way was extraordinary. In the novel, the lady involved usually responded with coy archness, making a game of extracting every last ounce of drama from the request. Juliana, incapable of dissembling, simply smiled and assented.

She removed her bonnet and sat still, as Harry took time to touch her hair, before eventually selecting a dark curl from the left side. 'May I?' he asked again.

Juliana felt for it, in the location where his hand lingered. Their fingers touched as he passed the small curl to her. It was in a location where her hair was thick and luxuriant, and where the missing tendril would not be noticeable. 'Yes,' she said. It felt like a vow.

He took a deep breath, then lifted the scissors from his lap. His hand shook slightly, but he isolated the curl and removed it with a careful motion. He kissed it reverently, before placing it in his watch pocket.

Juliana felt time stand still for an instant. In that moment, she took in the sight of him, perfectly framed against the lush trees beyond. The sun had emerged from behind the clouds and dappled them both in warm green light. She felt she would never forget this moment, or the happiness she felt. The dark shadows in their future seemed far, far away.

Chapter Eighteen

'One more thing, Captain.' Major Cooke still looked grave—as well he might. He and Harry had been analysing the latest information on Napoleon's forces and the numbers were, frankly, disheartening. The erstwhile Emperor had amassed a huge following and was currently working on his battle preparations. As were the British, the Prussians, Hanover, Brunswick and the Dutch. Across Europe, armies were in full preparation footing—organising stocks of food, tents, muskets, gunpowder, uniforms, shoes and, importantly, accurate maps. Harry and Major Cooke had spent the day and all evening calculating and recalculating the latest numbers—supplies received, further equipment that was on its way to the various camps and the remaining orders needing to be organised. They had to do all they could to ensure the army would be well supplied with all they needed.

It was now well past midnight and the Major had called for a bottle of port to help them through the final paperwork. Harry was tired, though worry prevented any risk of sleepiness. This was vital work, though tedious. Both men knew the importance of keeping their men armed, fed and sheltered. It could make all the difference between winning and losing.

'I signed the commission today for Lieutenant Evans's promotion—you did well recommending him.'

'Excellent news! I am delighted for him.' Harry could not resist a feeling of pride. He had seen Evans grow in skill and confidence during their two years serving together. He would make an excellent captain. He also felt a small pang of loss—he and Evans would not serve closely together in future.

'I have also discussed your own situation. I should inform you I have recommended you for Major, once you have completed your six years' service.'

Harry was touched. 'Thank you, sir.'

'Not at all, Captain—you have earned it. Reliable, intelligent, a natural leader of men. And you are courageous in battle—heart of a lion!'

Harry shook his head. 'Not so. I am a greater coward than you know.' He had to say it. The thought that he could be offered promotion under false colours greatly disturbed him.

'Nonsense!' Major Cooke brushed away his words,

unwilling to listen or accept Harry's assertion. 'You deserve it and will make a fine senior officer! But, I have more news for you. I have appointed you a new subaltern, as I know you will feel the loss of Lieutenant Evans.'

'Oh?' Harry was immediately interested. He hoped he would like the man—some junior officers were worse than useless.

'Yes—and here he is, with the port.' The young man who had been assisting them throughout the day, acting as secretary, runner and general aide, had returned with a large bottle of port. 'Thank you, Jem. Captain Fanton, may I present to you once again Ensign James Ford, who will assist you in managing your Company. He will travel with you on Monday, when you leave for Brussels.'

Harry shook the man's hand and said something appropriate. Inwardly, his heart sank. Jem, while a pleasant lad who was clearly eager to please, had seen little action and could certainly not be described as battle-ready. Harry foresaw he would spend much of his time in the build-up to the coming campaign trying to prepare a green youth for battle. Just for a second, he had a vision of Jem lying dead on a battlefield. His stomach clenched.

'Honoured to serve you, sir,' said Jem, his eyes shining. Harry suddenly felt old.

* * *

Exhausted and drained, Harry had no difficulties in falling asleep. The night watchman had been calling three o'clock when he had tiptoed into the house, admitted by an extremely sleepy footman. Harry thanked the man, knowing he would be expected to be on duty for breakfast as usual. He went straight to his chamber and, abandoning for once his soldier's habit of folding his clothes neatly as he removed them, he threw them all on to a chair, then climbed into bed, grateful for the blissful forgetfulness of sleep.

Within what seemed like moments though, he was awake again, drenched in sweat and convinced he was once more in that street in Badajoz. Unable to summon the strength to fight the memories, he lay like a corpse staring into the darkness as the recollections washed over him like a wave. He drowned in them...

Once again he was in Badajoz, that small Spanish town that had held out so long against the British siege. The French garrison had been taken, and Wellesley was victorious, but they had lost thousands of soldiers' lives in the assault. The common soldiers had drunk as much liquor as they could find and then the trouble had begun.

As dawn broke the officers had been called upon

to intervene, but when Harry had reached the scene what he found had held him transfixed with shock.

Harry closed his eyes now, accepting the inevitable.

Could he not have intervened to save that father from being murdered, blood from his neck wound spurting and flowing down three uneven steps to pool at his feet?

Could he not have prevented that young woman from being dragged by the hair into a nearby house? He saw again her white face, heard her screams mixed with the gleeful laughter of his berserking comrades as they continued their murderous, drunken assault on the families of Badajoz.

Standing in that dusty Spanish town, its walls finally breached, he had slowly understood that his comrades—British soldiers—had lost all control. They had murdered indiscriminately, their rage at the townspeople motivated by revenge. And not just murder. To his left, he had seen a small boy of about six being violently beaten by a redcoat. His agonised screams still filled Harry's consciousness.

On the day Harry had stood motionless, unable to move, think or even fully take in what was happening around him. He saw again the woman with the blue dress—the one he'd assumed was the boy's mother—attack the soldier with a kitchen knife.

She'd driven the knife through the soldier's back and straight into his heart. He'd slumped over the boy, his blood a slowly growing puddle in the dusty earth. The woman had started to remove the knife, then paused mid-action as another redcoat had brought his bayonet down on her neck with great force, cleaving her shoulder from her neck.

She'd fallen without a sound, arms outstretched. Woman, man and boy merged in a crumpled heap of blue fabric and red, red blood.

At the time, Harry had had no conscious idea of how long he'd stood there. Afterwards, he calculated that he had been frozen for no longer than a minute. Then his soldier's instincts had finally arisen. He had begun barking orders at the renegade soldiers, running towards the fray as he did so.

Running into the house, he had pulled the redcoat off the young woman and punched him—hard. The soldier had slumped to the floor. He had tried to apologise to the woman, but she'd run out, sobbing in fear and shock. He had followed and surveyed the scene again.

To his left, a British soldier had been kicking an elderly man who lay on the ground, desperately trying to protect his head. Harry had pulled him away. The soldier had turned with a snarl of fury, raising his bayonet as he did so.

'Aye, will you raise arms against your Captain?' he had asked. His disgust had been profound. This was one of his own men—one he had trained and supped with on many occasions. 'Get back to camp! *Now!*'

The man had slunk off, shuffling guiltily towards the main thoroughfare.

'Woo-hoo! The hunt is after you, my fine fox!'

Three redcoats had crossed in front of him, whooping and calling, in pursuit of an attractive young mother, her babe clasped in her arms, who had fled down an alleyway to his right.

'Stop right there!' Harry had roared.

They'd ignored him, intent on their chase. Harry had taken off after them and eventually succeeded in catching them in a small plaza. Thankfully, he had been assisted by two of his officer colleagues and they had managed to disarm the trio, who had been in a state of drunken bloodlust.

The woman had hidden under a farm cart at the edge of the plaza and, Harry had noticed, been beckoned into one of the buildings by an elderly lady, who had closed and locked her door again immediately. Shameful that the townspeople had needed to hide in fear of British soldiers!

Together, Harry and his colleagues had eventually gained control of the situation, though the sight of so many dead women, children and elderly had been sickening. And it still was. Three of his fellow officers had lost their lives, attacked by the rabid British soldiers.

As the clean-up and the floggings had begun Harry, exhausted, had found himself back in the same street.

Catching sight of a flash of blue, he had moved towards the dead mother. She'd lain where she had fallen, her pretty blue dress stained with blood. So much blood!

The soldier's body had lain prone on the ground beside her, the kitchen knife still protruding from his back. Harry had used his foot to move the man. There, beneath him, had lain the body of the child. His skin had been mottled with purpling and his eyes bloodshot and staring. He had suffocated from the weight of his dead attacker and his murdered mother.

Harry would never forget those eyes. *Why did you not save me?* they asked. *Why did you not even try?*

'I am sorry,' said Harry now, for the thousandth time. 'I am sorry.'

There was no escape from despair. Harry was as culpable as his men—more so, for had it not been his task, as their Captain, to control them? He might not have been able to save them all, but he certainly could have saved the boy. Why had he not checked on him?

He could pretend no longer. He did not belong here with civilised people. The evil in him was too much to bear. They—all of them—would be better if he were gone from their lives. And with the upcoming battle against the might of Napoleon's army, he was unlikely to survive anyway. At least if he were to die in battle, his life might have been worth something.

A small voice tried to persuade him. *They love you. They would want you to live.* Oh, but he was weak! When he thought of Juliana, of Adam, of Olivia, he did not think his heart could bear the pain. They thought him honourable and good. They had no idea of his true nature.

By morning, he had made his decision. As the darkness turned to grey and the first birds ventured a tentative chirp, he knew what he must do. With only a few days remaining until he left England, he must begin immediately. The evil that lived within him must be purged and the only atonement he could offer was his life. He must break with Juliana. He did not deserve such innocence in his life, and if he stayed with her he would taint her purity and corrupt her fierce, passionate heart.

Leaving her would take every ounce of strength

he had and he was also conscious of her keen mind. If she suspected the truth she would, he knew, never accept his decision. As well as strength, he would need all the guile and play-acting he could call on.

So he prayed, as he had never prayed before. He prayed he would be strong enough to do what must be done. He prayed her feelings were not so engaged as his after the short time as they had been together. She had not yet even said that she loved him.

Most of all, though, he prayed he would not break down and beg her to marry him.

Juliana swallowed hard. Now she was on her way, doubts assailed her. Was she doing the wrong thing? She clung to the safety strap as the cab rounded a corner at speed, the jarvey hurling abuse at a stray dog that had dared cross his path.

It's just because you're alone, she told herself. *Have courage.*

It was strange, when she came to think of it, how infrequently she was alone. Apart from in her chamber and on those odd occasions when Charlotte was called away and Juliana was left undisturbed in the morning room, her whole existence was in the company of others. Certainly she had never ventured out in London by herself before this.

Cavendish Square was an elegant, well-tended

plaza, with tall, imposing houses glowering over a pretty circular park. The cab came to a halt outside the house and the driver jumped down to open the door and lower the step for Juliana.

She bade him wait for her and mounted the steps to the mansion. A young footman opened the door, then froze when he saw her.

Taking advantage of his surprise, Juliana swept past him.

'You may inform General Hunter that Miss Milford wishes to speak to him,' she said imperiously, as if it was perfectly normal for a young unmarried woman to pay a social call on a man.

'Yes, miss.' The footman, recovering, bowed and led her to a small, beautifully furnished parlour. 'Please make yourself comfortable.'

Comfortable? Juliana felt anything but comfortable. She paced around the room, unable to sit or even think clearly. She was determined, indignant, angry and frightened all at once. Oh, how she wished she'd been able to speak to Harry about this! But he had spent all of yesterday at the War Office, so she hadn't seen him since the trip to Vauxhall the day before. She paused, smiling inwardly as she remembered Vauxhall. After their idyll in St James's Park she and Harry had travelled on to meet the others in perfect understanding, and Juliana had spent the day in a glow of happiness. Harry had been so attentive, his every look and gesture telling how much he cared for her. They had talked and walked together, and enjoyed the company of Mama, Charlotte and the others, but with eyes and hearts only for each other.

That was not the day to mention her plan to question General Hunter. It would have been too daunting a topic to consider in the middle of picnics and fireworks, and friendly, light-hearted conversation.

With only a few days left until their departure for France, Juliana knew she might never again have the chance to confront the corrupt General. Desperation had brought her to Cavendish Square.

'So it is true, then! I see you are every bit as foolhardy and impulsive as your mother!' The General stalked into the room, closing the door carefully behind him. 'What the devil do you mean, calling on me like this? Do you *wish* for tongues to wag?'

Bristling at the criticism of her mother, Juliana found her voice. 'I care not! I wish only to have the truth of my parentage confirmed and to tell you my opinion of you!'

Surprisingly, that drew a wry smile. He paused, eyeing her keenly. 'Pray, sit! I should be exceedingly interested to hear your opinion of me!'

She sat, then inwardly berated herself for obeying him. Something in his tone had compelled her, just when she needed to stand strong. *Ah, well.* Her feelings would become apparent through her words. He took a seat opposite her, resting his elbows on the arms of the gilded chair and steepling his fingers together.

She drew a deep breath.

'My opinion of you could not be lower! You behave as though you are honourable, and respectable, yet your actions have shown that the opposite is true. You have shown a cruelty and disregard for my mother that is unforgivable!'

He looked a little shocked. *Good.*

'Miss Milford—Juliana—I am not sure what you would have had me do. Abandon Elizabeth? Leave her to starve on the streets of Brussels? Yes, and you along with her? You owe your very life to me and I confess I am shocked by your ingratitude.'

'Ingratitude? *Ingratitude?*' She could barely contain herself. 'You seduced my mother, a woman many years younger than yourself, then you forced her into exile, far from friends and family, and you think I ought to be *grateful* because you spent a fraction of your wealth—' she gestured to their opulent surroundings '—assuaging your guilt? How dare you?'

His hands were gripping the arms of the chair.

She looked at the white knuckles, feeling a *frisson* of fear for the first time. His face was grey, his expression stormy. Then, abruptly and unexpectedly, he threw back his head and laughed.

She sat in bewilderment. Why would he laugh at such a moment?

A thought struck her—maybe he was insane!

He stood and she had to steel herself not to flinch as he approached. He walked past her chair, opening the door to hail the footman. 'Refreshments, please. Port. And tea for the lady.'

Returning to his seat, he eyed her levelly. 'I see Elizabeth has told you nothing of your origins— she always was chicken-hearted. It falls to me now to enlighten you.' His hand moved to his chin, one finger tapping his cheek. He leaned back. 'Permit me to tell you I am not in the habit of seducing girls who are young enough to be my daughter.' His tone dripped with wry humour.

She looked at him blankly, totally confused. 'I simply wish to know the truth.' Her voice quivered, so she lifted her chin in an act of brave defiance.

'Very well. I shall tell you the truth—though I am not sure you are ready to hear it.'

Chapter Nineteen

He paused, considering his words. 'I am not your father, Juliana. You *are* illegitimate—that part is true. But I am your *grandfather*. Elizabeth is my daughter—my only child. Her mother—your grandmother—died when she was very young. I could have disowned Elizabeth when she ran away with a handsome, empty-headed soldier, but I did not. By the time I found her, she was living in straitened circumstances in Brussels with you and surviving on the generosity of her friends. I could not abandon her, no matter what she had done.'

Juliana could barely take it in. 'What? My *grandfather*? But I thought—'

'Yes, it is abundantly clear to me what you thought!'

Oh, Lord! She had offered him the most terrible insult. Her face flooded with heat. 'I am so sorry, General Hunter! I made an assumption and I was wrong. I apologise for my words and for what I thought of you.'

He waved away her concerns. 'I accept your apology.' He chuckled. 'It is a new experience for me, being accused of seducing innocent girls! And I thought my life was now settled into a humdrum nothingness.'

Juliana's mind was afire. 'So—who is my father? Was there a John Milford?'

'Of course there was! That young puppy actually had the temerity to approach me, to ask if he could pay his addresses to Elizabeth. As if I would consider a minor title and a small estate adequate to compensate for the family's shameful background.'

'Wait—a *title*? I thought you said he was a soldier?'

'Pffft! The Milfords were not the sort of family I had in mind when planning for Elizabeth's marriage. And that boy—John Milford—full of fire and romance! He persuaded my weak daughter that a life following the Army was better than the safety of London. He had romantic notions of war and soldiering—many young fools do. They think of glory and heroism, and fail to realise their life will be filled with tedious waiting, muddy boots and moments of terror.'

'But—he was a respectable young man?'

'You might think so. His own parents forbade him from signing up and said he was too young to marry. It is the only thing we agreed on.'

'Are they still alive? Do I have family connections among the Milfords?'

'No. He was their only child and they are both dead now. The estate went to a distant cousin, I am told. It could have been yours, if Milford had actually married your mother!'

'Why did they not marry? Did he—was he just playing with Mama?'

'If it is any consolation, I believe he *intended* to marry her. The young fool had turned up at a church outside Dover, seeking marriage and without a special licence. Of course the priest sent him away with a flea in his ear! Idiot! From there, they went directly to France and he to battle, and he died soon after.'

'Why did you disapprove of him?'

'I knew little of him, but I certainly disapproved of his family—Papists, Jacobites and Whigs!'

She considered this. Her mind was whirling, trying to imagine Mama young and in love. 'Where did they meet?'

'Here, in London. Balls, and routs, and picnics—*pah*! My elderly cousin was supposed to be chaperoning Elizabeth, ensuring she would not be led astray. By the time I found out about her infatuation with Milford, it was too late. He had been wooing her, behind my back. A silly, weak girl, ready to fall for the first handsome buffoon who whispered love to her! She had her Season at twenty and rejected a perfectly suitable suitor.'

'She mentioned an "old man" to me—someone that she was being pressed to marry...'

He snorted.

'Old? He may have seemed so to her. He was but thirty-four—a man of property and sense, and willing to take on a vapourish chit with good breeding but no strength of character. Your mother should have accepted him.'

Juliana shook her head. 'She was right not to allow herself to be browbeaten by you!'

He matched her defiance, the expression on his stormy face identical to her own. 'Not so! I gave my opinion, certainly, and expressed the wish that, given time, she might reconsider. Of course I would not have forced her into marriage with someone she abhorred. What sort of father do you think me?'

'One whom Mama could so little trust that elopement seemed the better option!'

He recoiled, then closed his eyes briefly. When he opened them, the anguish there made her flinch. He spoke softly.

'I assumed they were bound for Gretna and travelled the Great North Road, where I could find no trace of them. I returned home, knowing her to be ruined.' He swallowed. 'Three weeks later, I received a letter from the priest who had been asked to marry them. He was known to young Milford, having served in their local parish two years before. The young chucklehead thought the priest would simply marry them, because Elizabeth had just turned twenty-one! That part of the Marriage Act which requires the reading of the banns, or a special licence, had escaped his notice. Of course the priest refused to do it—in fact, there was no legal way he *could* have done it!'

Juliana's head was spinning. Mama—her dear, sweet, frightened mama—had actually eloped, against the wishes of a father as fierce as General Hunter?

The General leaned back in his armchair. 'So, on they travelled, unmarried. Of course, when he died, it was I who had to take responsibility for Elizabeth and her infant. He had made no provision for them—selfish and foolish to the last. When I found her she was living in Brussels with a Dutch family who had befriended her. She did not wish to return to England—indeed, I also believed it was better for her to stay there.'

'You didn't exile her?'

'No. It was her choice in the end.' He pursed his lips. 'So, yes, I paid for your schooling and provided Elizabeth with an income these past twenty years. I confess I was shocked when I discovered she had returned to England—with her daughter in tow and without informing me.'

Juliana nodded slowly. 'I can understand that. You should know Mama did not wish to travel to England. That was my scheme, for my friend is now settled here.'

'Nevertheless, Elizabeth should have informed me. I would have counselled her to avoid London, and it was a mistake to launch you into society. Has she no sense? When word of your background begins to circulate—as it surely will—then they will shun you. You will receive the cut direct from people who conversed with you and invited you to their homes. They will be angry because they will feel they were tricked into treating you as an equal.'

She bowed her head. 'It is already happening.' Haltingly, she told him about the Wakelys and her suspicion that the Etheringtons had been spreading gossip.

'What! What! They think you are my illegitimate daughter?' He stood, clearly agitated, and began to pace around the room. '*Outrageous!* No one shall impugn you so! How dare they behave like this towards my daughter and my granddaughter!'

'Mama has decided we will return to Brussels in a few days.'

'Leave the field of battle because of a minor reverse? Chicken-hearted, as I said!'

Juliana shook her head. 'She is determined, not fearful. I have been unable to persuade her—indeed, I have no wish to. We will leave England on Wednesday as she wishes.'

He thought rapidly. 'Very well. I am forced to adopt a new tactic. We must brazen it out, show them that we have nothing to hide! Before you leave, I will accompany you on some of your social engagements and make it known I am pleased to receive my daughter and granddaughter.'

'But what of my illegitimacy?'

'We shall gloss over the details of your parents' marriage. Twenty years' exile for an elopement is punishment enough. People may chatter and speculate in private, but as long as they only meet you in public situations, then the *ton* can have no complaints. You can never be fully part of society, but you should not be subject to such insults!'

The door opened, admitting a young housemaid carrying a tea tray. Behind her, an imposing butler bore a bottle of port and a large glass, with an air of disinterested authority. Juliana noticed, however, how they both surreptitiously glanced at her. The speculation among the staff must be marked.

General Hunter noticed it, too. As Juliana took her first sip of tea and the servants made to leave, the General bade the butler remain.

Waiting until the door had closed behind the housemaid, he murmured laconically. 'Merson, no doubt you are wondering why I am entertaining a young lady in my parlour.'

'I should not presume to hold an opinion on such matters, sir,' Merson replied, though a gleam of speculation glinted in his eyes.

'My granddaughter, Miss Milford, is in town for a short visit. She will no doubt require suitable transport back to St James's Square.'

Merson bowed impassively. 'It is an honour, miss.'

'My pleasure.' Juliana beamed. It was starting to sink in that she had an actual *grandfather*! 'I shan't need transport, though—I asked the jarvey to wait.'

'A jarvey, eh?' The General's brows beetled together. 'I think not.' He nodded to Merson. 'Pay the jarvey and tell the groom to bring round my coach, please—the new one, with my insignia.'

'Very good, sir.' Bowing at each of them in turn, Merson withdrew.

The General rubbed his hands together gleefully. 'I

shall accompany you to St James's myself—though, perhaps we should call in Gunther's on the way. It is generally busy at this time of day. What do you think, eh? Shall we shock them all?'

Juliana twinkled at him. 'Oh, do let's! I only wish we could delay revealing the truth—now I know I am *not* your illegitimate daughter, I shall quite enjoy the reactions of those who think I am!'

He laughed and they sipped their drinks in perfect charity.

The day had finally come. Juliana gripped the rail. The sea wind whipped around her face and the creak and rush of the speedy packet mingled with the whoosh and susurration of the waves and the mournful calls of gulls. She licked her lips, tasting briny freshness which reflected the salty scent in the air.

She could just make out a dark line on the distant horizon. France. They had made good time—thank goodness!

The crossing to England, two months ago, had seen her distracted by her mother's illness, but otherwise excited at the prospect of visiting Charlotte, and exploring the England of her origins. This return journey saw her anxious, pensive and feeling much, much older.

She had answers to some of the questions that had plagued her—questions about who she was and the truth about her parentage. She had gained a grandfather—and already was feeling something like affection for the curmudgeonly old bully. She couldn't forgive him for being unkind to her mother, of course, although the situation was much more complex than her initial assumptions.

He had been as good as his word on Saturday and had squired her to Gunter's, where they had enjoyed ice-creams and conversed like old friends, under the interested eye of dozens of people. The next day he had accompanied her for a ride in Green Park, and yesterday he had even walked with her along Gracechurch Street, tipping his hat to the speculative gazers and introducing Juliana to those bold enough to demand an introduction.

The best moment of all had been when they'd bumped into Henrietta and Millicent outside a coffee house beside Bow Church. Henrietta, seeing them approach, had nudged Millicent hard in the ribs. Millicent, about to complain at this violent treatment, had instead belatedly spotted Juliana, her hand resting comfortably in the General's arm, and her eyes widened. She looked Juliana up and down insolently, a sneer marring her pretty features.

Ugly, thought Juliana. *She looks really ugly when she does that.*

The General had seen them, too. Patting Juliana's hand reassuringly, he stopped to address the two young ladies. They could hardly snub him, but pointedly ignored Juliana.

After an exchange of good days and enquiries after each other's health, General Hunter added, 'My health is just about to become a good deal worse.'

'Oh, really?' asked Millicent. 'Why so, General? For you look as fit and well as ever.'

'In body, perhaps. But I have become acquainted with my dear Juliana—' he threw her a warm look '—and now I am to lose her. She and Elizabeth are to travel home to Brussels before hostilities resume on the Continent.'

Henrietta and Millicent exchanged arch glances. *Why would the General force his acquaintance with his illegitimate daughter on them in broad daylight?* their expressions seemed to say.

Millicent scrunched her nose in disgust. 'I really am not interested in your private affairs, General, so if you will excuse us—'

'Of course you know my daughter, Elizabeth.' He spoke across her. They looked blankly at him, while inside Juliana was dancing with glee. He continued, a hint of exasperation now apparent. 'Mrs Milford? I believe you are acquainted with her?'

'Your—d-daughter?' Millicent was completely taken aback. Her mind slowly turned—Juliana could almost see its workings. 'So, Miss Milford is then your—?'

'My granddaughter, yes.' He spoke slowly, as if to a child.

'But—when you called in St James's Square— you never—I mean, nobody knew—everybody thought—' Millicent ground to a halt, the words drying up as her mind finally encompassed reality.

'Yes? Everybody thought what, exactly? Do, pray, continue.'

Ouch! thought Juliana. *I have been on the receiving end of that glare, that tone.*

She tried to feel sorry for Millicent, but found herself incapable of it.

Henrietta intervened, defiantly. 'Why was this not well known?'

'Sad to say my daughter and I were estranged.' Henrietta raised a sceptical eyebrow. 'It does happen in families, you know. Why, I heard of one such case, a year or so ago.' He adopted a thoughtful expression. 'I cannot quite recall all of the details, but there was, I believe, a bride whose own parents did not attend her wedding, amid talk of an elopement.'

Henrietta blushed fierily and practically dragged Millicent away, muttering about a pressing engagement. Millicent, clearly devastated by the General's happy news, complied.

'What was that about?' asked Juliana. 'An elopement?'

'Yes. Mr and Mrs Etherington are rumoured to have run away together—had you not known this?'

'No!' Juliana could not resist laughing a little. 'I am afraid I cannot imagine *anyone* agreeing to elope with Mr Etherington—or Henrietta, for that matter! Charlotte has been far too discreet—I will question her as soon as I am home.' A thought struck her. 'So, all the time Henrietta was judging me and Mama, she herself had—?'

He chuckled. 'Indeed. She can offer it, but she does not like to receive the same treatment.'

Juliana grinned now, enjoying the memory of Henrietta and Millicent's discomfort. General Hunter was a formidable man to have by one's side. A pity that she did not have time to get to know him better. He was smart, and fiery, and opinionated—*rather like me*, she thought ruefully. *And he is lonely*, she added, thinking of his beautiful, perfect, empty home—plenty of servants but little companionship.

She frowned. If only there'd been the opportunity to mend his relationship with his daughter. But her mother had resisted all attempts by Juliana even to discuss General Hunter. Mama knew, of course, that Juliana had been spending time with him in their last few days in London and surely she must suspect Juliana now knew the truth. But she had—cheerfully—refused to discuss the General and Juliana had eventually abandoned the attempt.

And so to the journey. They had set off yesterday, both crying at the goodbyes—it had been so hard to leave Charlotte, Adam, Olivia and Clara. Her mother had been quiet in the coach and Juliana had let her be, lost in her own thoughts.

On board, Mama had become ill again, inevitably. But this time, Juliana was ready for it. Harry had negotiated a tiny cabin, so her mother could suffer the indignities of seasickness in private, despite the demand for space amid the packed ranks of soldiers heading for war.

Harry.

Juliana frowned, finally acknowledging the gnawing worry inside her. Something was wrong.

He had been as urbane as ever, smiling and jesting with her mother and his sister, and superficially all had seemed well. But when Juliana had caught his eye, there had been—nothing. No spark, no warmth, no sense of connection. It was as though they were strangers.

She had thought she was imagining it at first. It was subtle, but marked—a strange coldness that was entirely perplexing. There were other changes, too. He had spent very little time at home since Vaux-hall, being constantly at the War Office or at his club. Last night had been the first time he had dined with them in days, it being his last night in England, too. He had been at his best—or his worst—during dinner, gently teasing Olivia, being charming to all the ladies and speaking of nothing. When his eyes briefly rested on Juliana his gaze had been uninter-ested, absent. It made her shiver again now just to remember it.

He had avoided her as much as possible on the journey, too. Instead of sharing the coach, he had de-cided to ride alongside them, and since they boarded he had spent his time in the company of the other officers.

Juliana had felt this sick tightness in her stomach and chest for nigh on three days now. Oh, she had tried to deny it. He was focusing on the upcoming battles, she had told herself. He was worrying about the terrible events he must face. He was preoccupied with military preparations. She must be patient, and supportive, and loving...

No. It would not do.

If he had wanted to, he could have made time for

her. Even a moment, here and there. He could have thrown her one of those warm looks—the ones that made her heart sing and her body tingle. The glances that let her know she was not alone, never alone.

His evasiveness was subtle and masterfully done. Where once he had contrived to sit near her, to walk beside her and to seek her opinion, now all was changed. She was one of many, no longer favoured. She had told him of her visit to Cavendish Square, and her reunion with her grandfather, as soon as she had returned to the house. He had been properly astonished, asking her questions and exclaiming at her revelations. Even then, though, he had used his astonishment as a shield against true intimacy. He was all amazement—he could not stay, being promised to a prior engagement, but he would think about it all day, for sure.

Then he was gone, leaving Juliana with a mix of puzzlement and disappointment. Later, the news, revealed by his valet to Priddy. He was out driving Miss Millicent Etherington in the phaeton.

Pain in her right hand brought Juliana back to the present. Her knuckles were white where she was clasping the rail too tightly. She let go, her hand briefly a frozen claw, paralysed by the intensity of her grip. Opening her fingers carefully, she gazed down at her hand in abstraction.

She could no longer deny it. Harry had changed his mind. He no longer loved her. Fear, swirling through her body, froze her thoughts. *No! It could not be!* Harry was true. Was loving. Loved her. As she loved him. They shared a special bond. Something unique.

The doubts persisted. Was she deluding herself? She must know!

She turned. As ever, having made her mind up, she was determined to act immediately. With Mama safely below deck, this might be her last opportunity to question him. She stalked confidently aft, her gait adapting to the sway and pitch of the ship. She had spotted Harry's new aide-de-camp earlier, sitting with a group of junior officers on a pile of gnarled ropes.

'Jem?'

He jumped up, eager to please. 'Miss Milford! How may I be of assistance?'

She looked at him, his innocent trusting face, and saw herself. Was she also too trusting?

'I need to speak with Captain Fanton.'

'Of course! I shall inform him this instant!'

She waited, trying to calm her tumultuous thoughts. When Harry came, she could suggest they walk forward—there was a gap amidships where they might converse without being overheard. With this wind, and the increasing numbers of gulls mewing above them, it should not be difficult.

'Miss Milford!' It was Jem. 'I regret…er… Captain Fanton is…is unable to speak with you at present.' His gaze dropped away under Juliana's shocked reaction. 'He bids me tell you he, that is to say—Major Cooke has need of him at the present time.'

Juliana swallowed. Jem was clearly lying and feeling uncomfortable about it. *Harry did not wish to speak to her!* She could barely think, but murmured something appropriate to Jem, who disappeared gratefully.

She walked slowly towards the bow as the shock began to sink in. Harry had sent Jem to lie to her, in order to avoid a conversation with her. As though she was nothing to him.

Her fears were all confirmed. Pain, as if from a needle in her chest, pierced her. He was determined to avoid her. *Why?* her heart made the cry. What had changed?

It must be his worries about the coming war. Soldiers had to act with courage despite their inner qualms. Did he seek to spare her from grief if he died? Was he acting from some perverse sense of honour?

Her gut twisted. She was already feeling that grief. The loss of him—the very notion of it—had her reeling. She already knew he might die. But he was not yet in battle. Why should he take away these last days from them?

She *must* speak with him, make him see sense.

Moving swiftly, she made her way through the narrow doorway and down the steep steps to the cabins below decks, making her way down the dimly lit corridor to the large cabin reserved for Major Cooke's continuous meetings.

Scratching lightly at the door, she waited until the Major bade her enter. He was alone, as expected.

'Miss Milford! A pleasure to see you, my dear! Do, please, be seated. May I offer you refreshments?'

She sat, but declined his hospitality, explaining she was seeking Captain Fanton.

'Ah, yes, Fanton has been assisting you and your mother with your travel arrangements, has he not? Well, he is not here, as you see. I will summon him for you, though.'

Before she could stop him, he had rung one of the bell ropes on the wall of the cabin. Juliana bit her lip. She had wanted to discover Harry's whereabouts, rather than have him summoned to her!

'How is your dear mother? I understand the sea does not agree with her?'

'She is sleeping, thankfully. But we will be in port soon and I wish to ensure she can go directly to an inn to rest.' This was true, but she was more than capable of finding an inn herself, without Harry's help.

The Major sat and they conversed politely for some minutes. Then, finally, the knock came. Juliana's stomach turned over. 'Enter!' bade Major Cooke. The door opened and Harry stepped inside.

Chapter Twenty

He saw her immediately, of course. For an instant, his eyes blazed—with what emotion, she could not tell. Then the mask reasserted itself and he stepped forward, all smiles and charm.

'Miss Milford! I had just been seeking you.'

No, you hadn't, she thought.

'Oh, had you?' she asked innocently, her head tilted to one side. 'I understood from Jem that you were here, with Major Cooke.'

'And here I am! Perhaps Jem misunderstood before.'

'Perhaps.' She smiled frozenly at him, trying to mask her inner turmoil. They both knew what was really happening here. She turned to the Major. 'Major Cooke, thank you for finding Captain Fanton for me. We shall leave you now, as I know you will have much to do.'

'Oh, no! Pray, Miss Milford, make use of this

cabin for your discussion. I wish to have a walk on deck before we berth.'

Harry looked nonplussed. 'Sir—never say we have evicted you from your own cabin! Miss Milford can have nothing to say to me that you cannot also hear!'

Coward! thought Juliana. Her eyes flashed fire at him. He clearly took her meaning, but was defeated by the Major's determination. 'No, no, I insist, Captain! And I also charge you to chaperon Mrs Milford and her daughter to Brussels. You must accompany them all the way there—for I should not like it to be on my conscience if anything were to befall them.'

'But, sir, I assumed my place would be with you on the journey—we still have much planning to do!'

'I will include you in my daily dispatches. You will likely move faster than us anyway and I shall need you to update Wellington as soon as you get to Brussels.'

'Yes, sir.' Harry looked resigned, Juliana noted, but a muscle twitched along his jaw.

The Major bustled out, asking Juliana to pass all good wishes to Mrs Milford and bidding Harry again to do all he could to ensure the comfort and safety of the two ladies on their journey to Brussels.

There was a strained silence for a few seconds.

Then Juliana ventured, 'Harry, I wished to be sure you are well.'

'I am perfectly well,' he confirmed courteously, 'though it will be dashed inconvenient to leave Major Cooke and rely on dispatches—if you don't mind my frankness.' He fidgeted absent-mindedly with a button on his sleeve, frowning at it as if it offended him.

That was Juliana's cue. She was expected to reassure him politely. But she had often done the unexpected. Her heart melted as she studied his face, so familiar to her now. Then he looked up and directly at her, and the emptiness in his gaze chilled her to the bone.

She had to reach him. 'Harry, these past days, you have seemed…distant. I am sure you have been worrying about what lies ahead, but you do not need to be so cold towards me. I am here to support you, to make things easier for you in whatever way I can.'

'You will make things easier if you end this conversation. *Now.*' His tone was hard, implacable. She looked into his blue eyes—those eyes that had once softened with love for her. Now they were cold, hard and empty. He held himself rigid, as if on parade, his face emotionless and his expression ice cold. Desperate to reach him, Juliana placed a hand on his arm.

'Harry, please listen to me!'

Pointedly, he removed her hand. 'Madam, you presume too much. I made you no promises.'

Juliana felt as though she might faint. 'What?' she asked, dazed. *'What?'* She brought her hand to her mouth. She could *feel* the blood draining from her face.

'I will accompany you and your mother to Brussels, as ordered by my senior officer. But my fate and my preparations are none of your concern. Now, if you will excuse me…' He bowed sharply, turned on his heel and left. The door swung closed behind him, shutting with an audible, final click.

Juliana gripped the Major's table in shock. How long she stood there, unseeing, she could not afterwards recall. Harry's cruel words rang in her ears, while the cold look in his eyes was seared into her memory. Slowly, she moved, making her way along the corridor, up the narrow stairs and out on to the deck. It was now raining. She knew she should lift her hood to protect her bonnet, but somehow nothing mattered. She stumbled forward to the edge and gripped the wooden rail with both hands, gazing at the swirling foam and swelling waves below.

She laughed shortly, uncaring what those nearby thought of her. *She was a fool!* And he had played her, like a virtuoso played the violin, drawing every last drop of sweetness and emotion before stopping, leaving notes hanging in the air and the audience bereft. A master, in total command of the situation.

Of course she should have known better. She, who had seen what he was from their very first meeting. Her hackles had been up that first day in Dover, bristling like a hound scenting danger. She had *known*! Yet she had allowed him to persuade her of his good faith, had believed his flirtation to be genuine. How many women had he broken with his games? For he had ensured her heart was truly his before drawing back. No mere flirtation would do. Harry had pursued her and persuaded her, and convinced her that his act was real. At least on stage the villains made themselves obvious by costume, and mask and demeanour. Harry took on the airs of an honourable man, all the while concealing his black heart.

As the realisation sank in, Juliana's anger rose. Here, by her side, her true enemy had walked. When she thought of her own behaviour—smiling and sharing her deepest thoughts and fears with him, allowing him to kiss her... Oh, how she wished someone had shaken her! *Look!* they should have said. *See him—the true Harry!*

What had he said to Olivia, when she had wanted to depress Mr Nightingale's aspirations? That Olivia could rid herself of her admirer while avoiding dramas? That was Harry in action—a master of the subtle withdrawal. All of the changes of the past days fitted entirely with his advice to Olivia. He was practised in the art of rejection and it cut her as surely as if he had stabbed a knife into her heart.

At least Olivia had treated Mr Nightingale with kindness. She had not deliberately led him on, but had simply failed at first to understand her own heart. Harry had no such excuse. A practised philanderer, he had simply taken his fill of Juliana's company, won her round, then walked away.

At least she had not shared his bed! And, to be fair, he had made no serious attempt to seduce her. Remembering the night she had unwittingly entered his chamber, she shuddered. Anything might have happened! But even Harry, depraved as he was, had clearly drawn the line at seducing his sister-in-law's friend while she was a guest in their home.

Suddenly, her mama's reckless actions made a little more sense. At almost the same age as Juliana was now, she had eloped, crossing to France in a packet probably similar to this one, because she had believed herself to be in love. A year later she was mother to an infant, with no man and no prospects, relying on the kindness of strangers.

Would I have eloped with Harry, if he had asked me? Juliana gritted her teeth.

Poor deluded fool that she was, she could not be sure of anything. Would she have shared his bed, risking her reputation and her future? She could not say. The cool rain streamed down her face. She welcomed it, as it hid the weakness of her hot tears.

One thing was clear. She would not, *could* not judge dear Mama for her choices all those years ago. And her mother had always maintained John Milford had loved her. At least she had had that.

Juliana had not that comfort. Where she had given her heart, guilelessly and trustingly, Harry had hidden his intent behind a mask of smiles, a façade of warmth and caring. His false colours had deceived her. No more.

Juliana dreamed…

She steps through the door into a long hallway. There he is! He smiles and comes towards her, arms opening wide. She moves towards him, waiting to feel those strong arms closing around her, sense his warmth, hear his heart beating.

At the last instant he sidesteps, drops his arms to his sides and says, 'I am only jesting!' Then they are walking through the hallway, not touching, not together.

The sense of loss overwhelms her. She looks at his

profile. He is oblivious, impassive, uncaring. The pain washes over her...

She woke, her face wet with tears. Where was she? The bedroom was unfamiliar in the soft dawn light. She raised her head from the wet pillow, then sank back down again. Brussels. Home. She turned over.

Another bad night. Sleep eluded her every night, as her mind was racked with pain. She tended to fall asleep eventually, sometimes hearing the bell-ringers call three, or even four, before oblivion claimed her. And always, she woke before dawn, swamped by grief and loss, and that tight knot of injustice.

The journey to Brussels had been every bit as painful as she had anticipated. Harry had been distant, polite and cold. Even her mother had noticed it, but had put it down—as Juliana previously had—to natural concern about the upcoming battles. It had been a relief when he had deposited them in their quiet house in the Rue de Brabant, disappearing off to meet with his Army colleagues. Juliana had turned quickly, not wanting to watch him walk away.

Mrs Milford showed no anxiety about being back in Brussels—despite the fact there was every possibility that Napoleon and his huge army would be on the march within weeks. Their servant, Sandrine, had made all ready for them and, Juliana's mother declared, it was a relief to be back where she could be at ease.

Mrs Milford had quickly settled back into her old life, receiving visits from all her old friends, who were mostly of the lesser nobility and gentry—from France, England, Prussia, the Netherlands and even Italy. Madame Vastine, a plump, middle-aged matron, had taken them both under her wing, assuring them even if 'that awful Napoleon' was victorious, she would ensure they would be safe. Juliana did not share her confidence.

'We will have much to do,' she said, 'if they join battle anywhere near Brussels, for they will bring the wounded here.'

She explained she was assisting at the local convent hospital, in order to prepare for the work of tending the wounded.

'Is this just for the French?' asked Mama. Juliana, still in a haze of loss, could barely bring herself to be interested.

'*Mais non!* The sisters tend to all God's children, no matter their uniform! These heathens try to take *le bon Dieu* out of France, but they cannot remove Him from our hearts!' She looked at Juliana keenly. 'Mademoiselle Milford, I would appreciate your assistance at *l'hôpital* tomorrow, if you are not otherwise engaged.'

'Oh, yes, do go, Juliana! For I will be busy myself—all day.' Mrs Milford looked mischievous and mysterious as she said it. Juliana found she had not the energy to probe Mama.

And so she found herself as the newest recruit in the convent hospital. As May turned to June and training was increased, the hospital became busier with soldiers accidentally injured during the preparations for the real war that everyone expected to come sooner rather than later. In a short time, Juliana grew adept at bathing and bandaging wounds, mopping fevered brows and feeding and comforting the wounded. She resisted the more gruesome duties—like holding men down while a surgeon sawed off an infected limb—and left others to care for those who were clearly dying. She knew she had not the strength to deal with tragedy just now, as every soldier who came in was Harry, and every soldier who yelled in pain was Harry, and every soldier who died was Harry. Still, her sleep improved, if only through exhaustion.

Madame Vastine and the Sisters were grateful for her assistance nevertheless. Juliana was grateful, too. Grateful to have something to occupy her mind and her hands. Grateful to feel she had purpose. Grateful not to be sitting in a drawing room, conversing about the war, while inside her heart was breaking. Napoleon was moving north. Brussels was in his path. Yet nothing mattered, except that she had not seen Harry for four whole weeks.

She veered from pain to anger and back again, but the most destructive emotion of all was hope. It tore her apart as she imagined him coming to her, smiling with his eyes and taking her in his arms…

'Juliana! You are wool-gathering again!' Mrs Milford's voice pierced Juliana's reverie. 'Where is my blue fan? I am sure I saw it just yesterday. I wish to bring it with me to the ball tonight, as this humidity will be the death of me in a crowded ballroom.'

'I know exactly where it is, Mama.' Juliana crossed to the dresser and opened the second drawer. There it was, nestled on top of Mama's letters and papers.

'What are you doing there? Come away from there!' Mama's voice was unusually sharp.

'I have your fan.' Juliana handed it to her, a little puzzled. Her mother was not normally so sensitive. Perhaps the pre-battle fever was affecting her as well. 'You look beautiful, Mama.'

Her mother kissed her. 'As do you, my darling Juliana. I do adore that shade of lilac on you.'

Juliana glanced in the mirror. It did become her. She loved this dress—a beautiful lilac silk with intricate embroidery on the bodice and along the hemline. Sandrine had dressed her hair in a classic Grecian knot, side curls perfectly placed to frame her face. Her only jewellery was a strand of pearls but, with her long evening gloves, dancing slippers and delicate fan, she certainly did not feel under-dressed. The Duchess of Richmond's ball had been the talk of Brussels for weeks and Juliana had been unable to resist imagining seeing Harry there. If Harry could see her tonight, at her finest, surely he—

'Now, Juliana, you must enjoy the ball tonight! That is an order from your mama! Yes, do not think I have not noticed you are troubled.' Her mother gripped her hand lightly. 'Dance with lots of handsome soldiers and let us all forget that war will likely be upon us by the end of the week.'

Juliana swallowed. No, she could not talk to anyone about what had occurred between her and Harry, not even Mama. 'Are you sure we will not be criticised for attending? The Duchess may not be pleased to know that a—that I am at her ball.'

Although they still had not talked of her mother's past, she did not deny Juliana's concerns. 'Nonsense! This is not London, with its high sticklers! It will be perfectly fine, you'll see.'

* * *

And so it proved. The Duchess's ball was thronged with all of Brussels society—including almost all the Army officers. Juliana's heart skipped a beat each time she saw a young soldier, for fear—or hope—that it might be Harry. They wore their red coats with knee breeches and dancing slippers, at the Duchess's behest—she had decreed they were to show defiance against Napoleon's approach. The Duke of Wellington was there, having calm conversations with his associates, and looking more relaxed than many of the non-military men, who, despite the Duchess's strictures, wore expressions ranging from the morose to the harried. The Gordon Highlanders danced some thrilling reels and the atmosphere was one of febrile celebration.

Brussels was filled with royalty, military and society families, in gay defiance of Napoleon's pretensions. Parties and balls were commonplace, but tonight, the Duchess of Richmond had outdone herself. Despite the thunderstorms and heavy rain, which might have caused her some anxiety, everyone came and the ballroom was thronged in what their hostess would be delighted to call a 'sad crush'.

Juliana danced twice, briefly forgetting her woes in the thrill of the steps. Oh, how she loved to dance!

This was truly the first moment she had been distracted from the pain of Harry's betrayal. She moved through the figure: forward, back, now turn, and round again…her mind focused only on getting it right, and, briefly, fleetingly, she received respite from pain.

Harry saw her instantly. She was twirling around with a captain of Dragoons whom he knew slightly. He could sense her exhilaration in the energy and accuracy with which she moved through the dance and—there—the enjoyment on her beautiful face. He shrank back against a pillar, anxious to avoid her seeing him. He drank in every inch of her, every instant. He dared to hope that perhaps he had been right and only her pride, not her heart, had suffered.

Nonetheless, guilt washed over him as he recalled his last sight of her, alighting from the carriage outside her Brussels home in the Rue de Brabant, her face pale and drawn. He had thrown himself into his duties, volunteering for every dispatch, every task that would take him out of Brussels. The men were currently on the march, along the road towards Charleroi, where it was rumoured Napoleon might attack. He had been given a horse and charged with reporting to Headquarters. This he had done and, after food, a few hours' sleep and a bath, could not resist the ball and perhaps his last-ever glimpse of the woman he loved.

Guilt followed him everywhere he went. He imagined her distress, felt it in every breath he took, every task he tried to complete. Every minute of every day. He would never forgive himself for any hurt he had caused her. He welcomed the guilt, wrapped himself in it as if it were a cloak. It went perfectly with his self-loathing.

His love for her was as strong as ever, and it killed him to think he might have caused her to feel pain. In these last days of his life, he was comforted by one thought. At the end, he was glad to have finally known love.

Mama had been right. The humidity tonight was oppressive and, after a particularly lively country dance, Juliana sought the sanctuary of the terrace. Low clouds were gathering again, threatening to spoil the evening with yet more rain, but at least there might be a breath of breeze outside.

Harry wasn't here. Juliana's shoulders slumped as she acknowledged the forlorn hope she'd held—that he would see her in this dress, with her hair expertly styled, and that he would—what? Have a sudden change of heart? She shook her head, annoyed with her own weakness. He was avoiding her. Of course he wouldn't come to the ball.

The terrace was brightly lit and, apart from three young ladies grouped together at the far end, Juliana seemed to have the terrace to herself. There was a seat to her right and she moved towards it, almost colliding with someone large coming from the opposite direction.

'Oh! Pardon me!'

'Excuse me!'

'Juliana!' Harry's face was lit by the three lanterns behind her, so she saw his unguarded expression clearly, unmistakably. *Longing.* A look in his eyes of such deep yearning, and love, and sadness, that it stopped her in her tracks.

Chapter Twenty-One

He still loved her! She could see it. Moved beyond
measure, and acting purely on instinct, she launched
herself forward and pressed her lips to his. For an
instant she thought he might resist, then his arms
came around her and his mouth responded to hers.
They kissed ferociously, then tenderly. She tried
to summon awareness—not because other people
might see them, but because she wanted to *remember.* She wanted to experience every feeling, in her
body and in her heart, in such a way that she would
never, ever forget this moment.

All too soon, he pushed her away. Raking his
fingers through his hair and glancing at the now
giggling girls, he led Juliana off the terrace to the
gardens below.

Here, the light was kinder—occasional torches
and a little starlight from the breaks in the clouds. It
wrapped them in semi-darkness and took them away

from prying eyes. Harry seemed to be struggling to speak. Juliana was dazed, too, but in a dreamy, ecstatic way. His hand in hers was warm and solid, and her only anchor.

'Juliana!' His voice was husky. 'This cannot be! I cannot—' He dropped her hand and stalked a few paces to the side. 'Can't you see? I am unworthy, evil, unsuitable for you!'

What was this? *Evil?* What on earth was he talking about? Taking a deep breath, for it was possible he was on the verge of disclosing his most private thoughts to her, she said shakily, 'I do not understand, Harry. Why would you be unworthy?'

He shook his head. 'Everyone thinks I am well, that I am happy. The amiable Captain Fanton!' He laughed hollowly. The sound was chilling. 'I know how to make friends, how to charm my colleagues and the ladies, how to be liked. But the truth is, I am not him. I am Harry. And Harry is a coward, a disgusting, foul coward.' She gasped and would have spoken, but he was determined to continue.

'Since Badajoz, I have held this knowledge within me. What happened there torments me. When they speak of hell on Sundays, I hear it. I *know* it. I have been there. I go back there all the time. The things I have done… The things I have seen… The fear that makes me want to run from battle… The cowardice that is part of my soul... I am darkness. I fear sucking the life and the light out of those around me.' He shook his head. 'So I stay nowhere. I move constantly. I have a hundred friends, but no wife.' His voice cracked with emotion. 'I can never marry. How could I ask an innocent, sweet maiden to share her life with a *monster* like me?'

He sank to the ground, wrapping his arms around his knees. His whole body was shaking. He looked up at her.

'I look at you and I see light, and life, and beauty. And I want nothing more than to love you, to pull you close, to ask you to help me. But I will not do it! For it would destroy you, and how could I live with myself knowing I had harmed the woman I— the woman I—'

He bent his head, his words disappearing into muffled sobs. Juliana knelt beside him, uncaring of her silk dress on the damp grass. 'Harry! Harry! Listen to me!'

No response. So she did the only thing she could. She wrapped her arms around him and held him while he cried. After a long, long time, his struggles eased and he quietened. Finally, he raised his head. What she saw in his eyes almost killed her.

'Tell me,' she said softly.

And he did. All of it. What had happened after

the siege of Badajoz. How he felt responsible for not saving everyone—particularly that one small boy. She listened gravely, intently, her head tilted to one side. And all the time she gripped his hand, anchoring him to her.

Finally, he stopped. 'So now you know.'

'Yes. Thank you for telling me finally.' She shook her head slowly, reflectively, as his words sank in. Had he been carrying this burden all the time they were together—even the times when she thought they had both been so happy? 'You ought to have told me before.'

He shook his head. 'I was a coward in that, too. I wished only to hide the truth, to hide myself from you. But I am beaten down now. I have nothing left. You might as well know.' He gripped her hand. 'Do you see?' he demanded, his gaze filled with fierceness and despair. 'Do you see now what a weakling I am? What a craven fool?'

'No. I do not see that.' Her voice was sure and steady.

He looked at her blankly. 'Juliana, I beg you, please go and leave me to recover my wits. I have told you everything. You can want nothing more to do with me.'

Not for an instant did Juliana consider leaving his

side. 'No. I have listened to you and I am still here, still holding your hand.'

He glanced down at their clasped hands, then back to her face. His expression was full of confusion. 'Why?' he said huskily. 'Why are you still here? Is it—is it pity?'

'No!'

Now. This was her chance to speak. She might never have another. She prayed for the right words, though all she could do was to speak from her heart and hope.

'Thank you for telling me everything. But, know this. When I stay with you, it is not your choice. It is *my* choice. And I choose you. *I choose you*, even though you believe yourself to be weak, or cowardly, or broken. For I know your true heart. And I am not deceived—though you tried hard to deceive me.' She took a deep breath. 'I love you, Harry.'

A look of confusion, mixed with amazement, dawned on his face. 'Truly?' His voice was almost a whisper. 'You see me—like this, you know the truth—yet you do not spurn me?'

Juliana almost laughed as joy and relief welled up inside her. Was this it? Was this the twisted logic that had caused him to reject her? He had actually thought this would change things between them!

'Of course I do not spurn you! Indeed, I imagine many soldiers feel as you do tonight. They just hide it.'

He looked at her warily. 'Do you understand what you are saying? Did you understand what I told you just now—about Badajoz?

'Of course I did! I am not completely mutton-headed, you know!'

'Then—why—how can you choose a broken coward? You, who could have any man you wanted!'

'But I do not want any other man. There is only you. So I suppose you will have to make the best of it.' Her manner was matter of fact, but her heart was still pounding.

Her prosaic tone finally seemed to be his undoing. 'Oh, Juliana! Juliana!' He reached for her, covering her face with kisses. 'I love you! You have no idea how I love you!'

'I believe I do,' she said drily, some moments later. 'Though I wish you could have been more honest with me. You were so cruel on the ship.'

'I know.' He wiped away a tear from her face and licked it from his finger. 'I saw no other solution. I am not worthy of you. I know that. But tonight, I am so weak as to let you see it.'

She shook her head, denying his self-judgement.

'Now that I know the truth, be warned. I will not let you pretend again that you do not care.'

'You have me. But, Juliana, I mean what I said. Should I survive the upcoming battles, I cannot marry you.'

'Because of my illegitimacy?'

'No! Never!' He held both her hands, speaking fiercely. 'It is because, despite your words tonight, I would not saddle you with a coward for a husband. I will not be moved on this.'

Her heart sank. What strange reasoning was this? And why would he dismiss her base birth with such little consideration? No matter what he said, her illegitimacy remained a huge barrier to any thoughts of a future together. Looking at his stubborn expression, she decided to leave it—for now. Tonight, he loved her. That was enough.

They sat for a full hour, kissing, murmuring words of love and talking of the pain they had both been feeling since their estrangement. She was content that his motives, though clearly misguided, at least were borne out of love and a desire to spare her.

Suddenly, both stilled and turned their heads towards the ballroom. Something was amiss! The music had stopped mid-tune and there were raised voices coming through the open terrace doors. Harry stood, offering her his hand, and together they hurried back inside. As they walked, the first heavy drops of rain began to fall.

Blinking at the bright light, Juliana took a moment to take in the chaos. Wellington was disappearing out of the ballroom and into a private parlour, his senior officers following. Some women were crying, while older gentlemen were standing around muttering and looking grave. And the soldiers! They were milling around, grouping together, searching for comrades. Evans—now Captain Evans, Juliana remembered—approached them in haste.

'There you are, Harry! It's on! Napoleon is on the move. He has crossed the border and battle is to be joined today. We are to be at Quatre-Bras with our men by three o'clock!'

'What! Three o'clock? But that's less than two hours from now!'

'I know. We're going to war in our evening dress! The horses are being brought here. Officers are wanted in the parlour in ten minutes—we've to bid our farewells to our…er…loved ones.'

Farewell! This was it, then. They looked at each other, conscious they could not kiss here, in full view. Evans, belatedly sensing the charged air between them, muttered something about the parlour and made a hasty retreat. Harry gazed into Juliana's eyes and his look was the opposite of the coldness she had seen there recently.

Taking her hand, he raised it reverently to his lips. 'I love you,' he murmured.

'I love you, too,' she replied, her voice almost a whisper.

He stepped back, bowed smartly and was gone.

Friday 16th June, 1815

Dawn was breaking. The rain had eased a little, thankfully, but the road was a muddy swamp in places. Harry marched his men along, knowing many of them would be dead by sunset. The second battalion was one of the few which had fought the French in the Peninsula, so Harry knew they would be central to the Duke's plans.

Wellington had given precise orders about the deployment of each unit, as he always did. He thought about every single aspect and detail, and had a huge team of aides-de-camp continually issuing specific instructions. Napoleon had crossed the border a day earlier than expected, and the Prince of Orange, with his small unit, was the only force currently defending the strategic crossroads at Quatre-Bras.

Harry knew nothing was certain today. Napoleon had them outnumbered and General Blücher's Prussian army was many miles away, facing the other part of the French Army at Ligny. If they could hold the crossroads, it would be easier for the two Armies to join together later to face the French as a single force. Still, it was not for him to think of tactics, or strategy. His role was to play his part as best he could. Helping defend the crossroads would stop the French from marching on Brussels, where his Juliana waited. That was simple and clear. For the first time, he had someone to fight for.

Juliana finally lay down mid-morning. With Mama, she had watched from an upper window in the house as the army filed past, with tramping feet and banging drums—a process which took nearly four hours. The people of Brussels had lined the streets, knowing their fate could also be settled this day. Juliana struggled to imagine what Harry was travelling towards. She pictured him as she had seen him last, looking noble and serene, no sign of the turmoil he had allowed her to witness in the gardens last night. Would it be the last time she saw him alive? The Duke of Wellington had been in a confident mood, apparently telling people he would be back in Brussels in time for dinner with the job done. Juliana, remembering the grim determination in Harry's eyes, could not believe it.

* * *

She had slept fitfully and woke in the early afternoon. There would be no news yet, but she could not stop herself from going to find her mother to confirm it.

Mrs Milford was in the front parlour with three of her friends, all clucking and fussing with vague anxiety. She looked relieved to see Juliana, reaching out her hand and pulling her daughter into a brief embrace. Madame Vastine had been to the convent. The nuns were working hard, preparing for the onslaught that would happen later. They were erecting tents at the Louvain Gate and the Namur Gate for the wounded and had appealed for blankets, bandages and pillows. Juliana dared not think about it.

And so the afternoon passed and the sun began to sink lower in the sky. They had conflicting reports all day—the Allies were holding fast at Quatre-Bras, but the Prussians had come under severe pressure at Ligny. No one could tell who would prevail. But all Juliana could think of was Harry.

'We did it, sir!' Jem's eyes gleamed with relief and pride as they watched the French pull back from Quatre-Bras. They had arrived in time to support the Prince of Orange and his small force—strangely, the French had made no serious attack until after the Allied reinforcements had arrived. They both sank down on to the damp ground with relief, too tired to do much more. After a brief rest, Harry sought out Major Cooke.

The Major was in sombre mood, but came forward to shake Harry's hand as soon as he spied him. 'Well done, lad. Your men fought like lions all day.'

'Thank you, sir. Have we further orders?'

'It's not good, Fanton. Although we held the line here at Quatre-Bras, Blücher and the Prussians were pushed back at Ligny. The Duke wants us to pull back tomorrow to a stronger position. We are too far ahead of Blücher here and we will surely need the Prussians.'

Harry frowned. Had their efforts been for nothing? 'We are abandoning the crossroads?'

'We are indeed pulling back, but make no mistake, this was an important victory. Holding the French back at the crossroads means Wellington, not Napoleon, will choose the battleground. He has scouted the area previously and has a good idea of the land around here.'

He unrolled a map. 'The march begins tonight. We are to make our stand here.' With his finger, he indicated the area below a small village south of Brussels. Waterloo.

Saturday 17th June, 1815

The next day, a strange atmosphere pervaded Brussels. Juliana was told by at least three people that the British and Dutch had won the battle yesterday and held the crossroads at Quatre-Bras, though the Duke of Brunswick had been killed, and a great many others, and the Prussians had been pushed back at Ligny. The Highlanders had been hard hit. Juliana wept when she remembered the strong young men who had played the pipes and danced the reels at the Duchess's ball. She had enquired after Harry and been told he had survived the engagement unscathed. He was on the march, with his men, to a new location. Her relief was short-lived, as she now had to worry about his next engagement.

Juliana, her mother and Madame Vastine spent the day giving aid to the wounded. Many hundreds had arrived in carts and wagons. The tents at the gates had proved insufficient to house them and the parks were now full of small tents and awnings, sheltering the injured from the hot sun and heavy showers. Juliana's day passed in a blur of lint, slings and bandages. She saw two men die while she held their hands, and helped hold another down while a surgeon dug out a musket ball from his thigh. After the surgeons were done with them, the men were loaded back on to wagons and brought to local houses to be billeted. The townspeople had opened their doors and their hearts to those defending the city, and welcomed in soldiers from England, Prussia, Portugal, Brunswick, Hanover, Scotland, Spain, Austria and Dutch Belgium, vowing to give them every succour as they healed.

Her mother had already asked Sandrine to prepare their small house for the wounded, and Sandrine had vowed to procure everything that was necessary. Juliana had offered her own room—she would sleep with Mama in her mother's bed, as she had done when she was a child. Sandrine had stripped back Juliana's bed and added a pallet on the floor—she was sure Juliana's small room could accommodate two wounded men. They all knew battle would be joined again, and soon.

Many of the society families had now, belatedly, realised the danger and the Antwerp road was busy with an exodus of those with the money and means to flee. Juliana and her mother had no carriage, nor had they the money to pay the extortionate amounts that buying one would cost in this crisis.

Her mother was phlegmatic about it. 'I do not wish to leave, Juliana. We will do more good if we stay to help.' Juliana did not argue overmuch; though she would have preferred to know her mother was safe, she herself had no intention of leaving Brussels until

Harry's fate was known. She fell into bed, worn out and numb, but still sent a fervent prayer for her love before falling into a fitful sleep.

Harry spent the day on the march, through heavy rain. He and his men traversed farmland, low hills and country lanes which were more like muddy streams than roads. From time to time they discovered fields of grain and stopped briefly to gather supplies.

The French Army was also on the move, following, but with no orders to attack. Both Wellington and Napoleon were content, it seemed, to move the battle to a new location. At times the French advance was surprisingly close to the Allied rear. Once, gathering grain in a field, Harry surprised a French soldier on the same mission. The man wore the distinctive uniform and shako of a French line regiment. When Harry came upon him, the Frenchman was bent to the task of stripping grain from a long stalk. The Frenchman raised his head, surprised, then, after a moment's pause, went back to his task. Harry kept walking, quickly stripped a couple of plants, pocketed the grain, then left.

Returning to the main body of men, Harry reflected on the strangeness of war. Today, they had the same concerns—hunger, tiredness and walking in this damnable rain. Tomorrow, one might kill the other. Had the man a sweetheart, like himself?

This led his thoughts to Juliana, for the thousandth time that day. His chest swelled as he thought of her—her fiery, passionate nature, and the miracle that she could love a man as broken as he. He squared his shoulders. Suddenly the road had become easier, the rain less cold, and the march more purposeful.

Sunday 18th June, 1815

The area south of Waterloo suited Wellington's purpose very well. The undulating countryside would allow him to fight from a ridge punctuated by three fortified farms and hide the bulk of his army behind it, so the French would not see where his forces were massed at any time. They could move easily from line to square formations, depending on whether they faced infantry or cavalry, and there was a sunken road behind the ridge which would assist with communications.

Harry's battalion, the second, was sent to the centre, less than a mile from the farm at La Haye Sainte, along with the King's German Legion and two other units. On receiving the orders, Harry nodded grimly. Wellington trusted them to hold this key position; the entire outcome might rely on them.

They had spent all day and most of the night marching, without food or rest, to get to their position. The countryside was farmland, with rye growing taller than a man in places. As the army passed, what was not foraged was trampled underfoot. The rain had not helped matters; they were all cold, tired and hungry. Yet they each knew their duty. Harry glanced at Jem, who was still by his side. Gone was the confidence and joy of a few days ago; Jem was subdued and silent, the rain dripping off his hat and running down his shoulder belt like tears. Harry wondered where Juliana was right now, what she was doing. He hoped she was sleeping soundly. He hoped she would remain safe.

'Get some rest,' he ordered, though the men were already bivouacking, not needing to be told. Having relieved himself and swigged some water, he lay down, uncaring of the rain, wrapped his greatcoat over himself as best he could and slept instantly.

A moment later, or so it seemed, the wake-up was sounded—trumpets, bugles and drums calling the men to rise and prepare, all along the lines. Five o'clock and the sun was just above the horizon. His teeth chattering, Harry gratefully accepted the double ration of gin which was being issued to everyone. It gave him the illusion of warmth as it slid down his throat. At least the rain had stopped.

He shook out his greatcoat and hung it on a nearby bush, hoping the sun's rays would dry it a little before battle was joined. Jem, always his shadow, copied him without speaking. They moved towards the campfire, and a simple breakfast of mixed-grain stirabout, which was at least warm and filling. The ground was saturated and Harry's boots made a squelching sound as he moved across the ridge, trying to pick his way through the soft landscape via the remaining tussocks of grass. After eating, he checked his musket, retrieved his still-damp coat and took his place in the formation. Now, they waited.

Sunday Mass in Brussels and the churches had never been so full. Juliana, like hundreds of others, prayed as she had never prayed before. The guns had not yet started their death sounds, but it could not be long now. Everyone knew that both armies had spent yesterday moving into position; today, battle would be joined. She closed her eyes, allowing the reassuring rhythm of Latin prayers to wash over her, and pictured Harry. Pictured him healthy and well, and smiling at her mischievously.

Please bring him back to me, she entreated silently. *Please keep him safe.*

Chapter Twenty-Two

Harry was exhausted. Since battle was joined in the late morning, he and his men had been involved in a continuous fight to help hold the line near La Haye Sainte. His hearing dulled from the continuous boom of cannon fire and his musket arm tense and sore, Harry nevertheless focused on staying alert and protecting his men, barking orders continually. He was particularly aware of Jem and repeatedly charged the young man to be careful.

With a brief moment's respite, he glanced at the boy. For all his years, he seemed a boy to Harry—he was not much older than Olivia. Jem was reloading his musket for the hundredth time that afternoon, ready for the next assault. It was becoming more and more difficult to defend the stronghold, as wave after wave of French cavalry attacked. Harry and his men were behind the ridge, withstanding alternating waves of cannonade and cavalry attacks. They would lie flat when their own artillerymen fired on the advancing French cavalry, then, at a crucial moment, the command would come to the infantrymen: 'Prepare to receive cavalry!' On hearing it, they would race to form into squares, four men deep, while the artillery would fall in behind. The front row would drop to their knees, bayonets raised, while the lines behind fired round after round on the French cavalry, the men behind reloading continually. In between, when the cavalry fell back, the French cannons boomed, and their own, and men fell all around them.

Suddenly, an aide-de-camp rode through with fresh orders. 'Fall back! Fall back slowly behind the ridge!'

Harry's heart sank. Was this it, then, the beginning of a retreat that would see them overrun? No matter. His job was to follow orders. He must ensure his men did not panic, but moved back carefully, supporting each other and not allowing any part of the line to be breached. They moved out of their square and began retreating.

It happened so quickly he almost missed it. A small group of French horsemen, ahead of their comrades, suddenly appeared in a running attack, muskets at the ready.

To Harry's left, a soldier fell, hit. He raised his

own gun and fired, as did Jem, to his right. Then the cavalrymen were upon them. Raising his bayonet, he managed to stab one man in the throat, then, not waiting for him to fall, Harry turned immediately to help Jem.

He was too late. A French horse—a beautiful bay creature—took a hit from a musket ball, stumbled in the mud and fell, rolling on top of Jem, who disappeared from view. The horse struggled in the mud for a few seconds, then expired. The rider scrambled away, unhurt, and immediately engaged with a group of British fighters on Harry's right. Harry swung at the Frenchman in front of him, managing to land a blow on the man's fighting arm. The soldier twisted away and he and Harry fought hand to hand, the sound of clashing metal echoed by a dozen other fights happening all around them. Harry twisted, ducked and saw his chance. His bayonet pierced warm flesh. The French soldier grunted in surprise, then fell forward, bleeding profusely. He did not rise again.

Jem! Harry staggered forward to the dead horse. He could see Jem's arm protruding from beneath the creature. The hand was flailing wildly. He was alive! Harry sank to his knees. Jem was trapped from the chest down, the weight of the horse pressing on his lungs and preventing him from taking a breath. His face was purple, his lips blue and his eyes were desperate and bloodshot.

In an instant Harry was back at Badajoz, the dead boy's bloodshot eyes staring at him accusingly.

No! This time, he would not fail. Impossible to move the horse, but the soft mud gave him an idea. Moving round to grasp Jem by the shoulders, he pulled with all his might. The deep mud gave way beneath him and he slipped away, unable to brace himself to apply enough force to pull Jem out. He tried again, aware that Jem had stopped struggling and was now passed out.

Strangely, it made it easier to achieve a better grip. Oblivious to the sounds of battle all around, he pulled and pulled, and pulled again. And then it happened—with a gloopy pop, Jem's limp body moved through the deep mud and released itself against Harry's chest, knocking him off balance. Quickly, he scrambled round to check if Jem was breathing. He leaned down. There! The faintest hint of air against his cheek.

'Vive l'Empereur!' Instinctively, hearing the war cry, Harry twisted round, raising his weapon as he did so. It was enough to deflect the blow that would have cleaved his head in two, but not enough to stop the blade of the French sword hitting his head with full force. As he lost consciousness, Harry knew he

was lost. The French soldier would finish the job within seconds. He was a dead man. Dimly, he conjured up an image of his Juliana. His heart ached with a fierce pride that she had loved him, coupled with sadness about the shared life they would never live.

Juliana, he thought, as the blackness closed in. *I love you.*

Around ten o'clock in the evening, the sounds of the guns finally dwindled, then stopped altogether. Juliana and Mama stood, picked up their shawls and went outside. The last light had not quite left the sky, and the town lanterns were just being lit. In that twilight state between day and night, light and darkness, Juliana moved with her mother towards the Place Royale. Soon they would know. Who had prevailed? Who had won the day?

Everywhere they went, confusion reigned. The Allies had prevailed. No, the French had won and were advancing on the city! Confusion gave way to fear, as the townspeople, panicking, returned to their homes and barricaded themselves in. The posters and prints mocking Napoleon, which they had proudly displayed in their windows, were hastily removed.

There was nothing they could do but return home

and wait. Juliana lay down, but could not sleep. Was Harry alive? Would he come back to her?

Monday 19th June, 1815

Dawn finally came and good news with it. The French were routed! It had been a close-run thing, but the Allies were victorious! The bell-ringers hurried to their towers, and soon the sounds of jubilation rang throughout Brussels.

Strangers hugged each other. Wine, beer and champagne was shared, and somewhere a fiddler began to play. Juliana and Mama wandered through the streets, enjoying the relief and the celebrations, yet Juliana could not be easy. Just because the Allies had won did not mean Harry had survived. Until she saw him, until she could put her arms around him and feel his warmth, she could not truly celebrate. Instead, she put an arm around her mother, who looked tired.

'Let us go home to rest, Mama. The wounded will begin arriving soon.'

Juliana stopped to mop her brow. Although it was not yet nine in the morning, the sun was strong. So many injured soldiers! Another wound to bandage, more broth to feed someone, a sip of water for this one in a fever. She moved among the casualties, helping where she could, continually searching. Searching for Harry. She overheard snatches of conversation as she went.

'—and then we broke for the woods, but by the time they reached us, we'd regrouped. We showed them what for!'

'Wellington is still in Waterloo, writing dispatches. Won't leave the battlefield and come back to Brussels 'til it's done…'

'I'm the only one left of my unit. Cannons got us when we were exposed on the ridge. Don't know why I'm still alive…'

Juliana had risen early and gone to the convent, even as more details of Wellington and Blücher's near-impossible victory had filtered through. Blücher had marched his Prussian army to Wellington's assistance in time and Napoleon had been unable to stand before their combined force. The Emperor turned tail by nine o'clock in the evening and the French forces were now retreating towards Paris.

As the wounded began arriving, Juliana started looking for Harry, even as she helped the nuns and the doctors tend to the injured. One of the first men she recognised was Evans, who had suffered a broken arm and a nasty slash on his hand from a sabre.

He was jubilant with victory, but had no news of Harry.

'Depend upon it,' he opined gleefully, 'he will walk in here with a smile on his face and not a mark on him!'

Juliana did not share his confidence. She could not shake the memory of her mama's remorse that she had not been there to care for her father. His infected wound had apparently taken a week to kill him—a week when he was being cared for by well-meaning strangers. Her mother had said she would always wonder if she could have saved him. Juliana did not wish to experience the same regret.

It was twelve hours since the battle had been won, and the sun was blazing down on the Warandepark. The injured were suffering in the airless tents, but there was nowhere else to bring them until they had been cared for. The heat was intense. Juliana walked past the octagonal pond—transformed today by a circle of tents all around. She bent her head and entered the next tent, immediately scanning the wounded men, all laid out on pallets on the floor.

'Miss Milford! Miss!'

The voice was male, cracked and faint. *Could it be Harry?* Juliana quickly turned, locating the soldier who had recognised her. He was covered in mud like many of the wounded and was too small to be Harry. Her heart sank.

'Miss Milford!' He reached up to her, his eyes bloodshot and frantic.

'Jem!' She sank down beside him, taking his hand and automatically scanning his body for signs of injury. His left leg looked nasty—a broken bone visible through an open wound. Someone had set and splinted it with what looked like a tree limb, but the wound had not been dressed.

She reached into her basket for some bandages and set to work, passing the bandages awkwardly through the gap between the leg and the crooked splint. Now she had finally found someone who might know Harry's fate, she was frightened to ask. Jem flinched. Biting her lip, she concentrated, gently wrapping the clean bandages around his leg. He exhaled, then gripped her arm. 'Miss Milford! You must listen—it's about the Captain!'

Time seemed to stand still. Here it was. What was his news? She finished tying off the bandage, then looked at him. 'Tell me.'

'When they took me from the battlefield—they thought he was dead, so they left him. But he was breathing! I swear it! They would not listen, and I was the last man put into the cart that time.'

The world seemed to rock a little. She put a hand

on the ground beside Jem's pallet. 'What are you saying? That H—that Captain Fanton is alive, lying on the battlefield?'

He nodded. 'It's possible. He may be dead by now. This must have been two hours ago. He—he saved my life, pulled me out from under a dead horse. He must have been hit while doing it because there he was, beside the horse, when I came round.' His eyes became unfocused. 'Beautiful creature. Bay. Such a waste.' His grip on her arm tightened. 'If they didn't go straight back for him, he might not be found.'

'Where? Where is he?' Juliana spoke sharply.

He frowned. 'I cannot recall exactly. Not more than a mile from the farmhouse at La Haye Sainte, I think.'

'I have no idea where that is. Can you take me there?'

'They won't let me go.' He gestured towards his leg. 'They've told me I'm staying here in the heat, until they find somewhere to billet me. Could be hours yet. You will not be allowed to go the battlefield, Miss Milford. The carts are only taking those who have been officially assigned to collecting the wounded. You could check the carts as they come into the city.'

'But what if they don't bring him on time?' Juliana frantically considered the problem.

'I am sorry, miss. You will have to wait.' Jem's voice was weak and resigned.

'We shall see about that!' She straightened her spine. 'When someone tells me I *must* do something, it immediately creates in me the desire to do the exact opposite! It is one of my greatest flaws, I know, but on a day like today it may turn out to be a strength.'

Juliana considered. Jem watched her warily. Somehow, she had to get to the battlefield. She glanced at Jem, who looked distressed and ill. She could not just leave him here! So she needed a plan that would solve both problems.

Looking around, she considered the bustling chaos, nodding thoughtfully as the germ of an idea came to her. She checked it over in her mind, looking for weak spots. There were a few and she would need to be brazen to carry it off.

For you, Harry, she murmured under her breath. *I can do this!*

She squeezed Jem's shoulder and rose decisively.

Moving assuredly through the disorder, she made her way to the supplies tent. Filling her basket with everything she thought she might need, she then walked confidently to the back, where the runners waited, sipping refreshments between runs.

'You there!' She chose two very young men, hoping they would be less likely to question her. 'I've been ordered to move a soldier to another location. I'll need a cart!'

'All the carts are going straight back to the battle-field, miss. They're still bringing back the wounded.'

Perfect! thought Juliana. She shrugged. 'I suppose one will have to be slightly delayed. This man has passed on information that is needed. I am to be brought to a place called Waterloo.' She feigned innocence, as if she had no idea of the significance of Waterloo and the fact that Wellington himself was billeted there.

'Waterloo!' The soldiers exchanged glances, suddenly interested. 'Of course! Whatever we can do to assist!' One bustled off to find a cart, while the other accompanied Juliana back to the tent where Jem lay.

'It's him,' said Juliana, pointing in a uninterested way at Jem. 'He has information that should be told at Waterloo and I am to ensure he is properly cared for—' she lowered her voice '—to ensure he does not expire in the meantime.'

Jem looked more than a little surprised to discover he was now an important—and dying—informant, but thankfully said nothing to contradict her tale. Within ten minutes he had been placed in the back of a sturdy farm cart, Juliana beside him, with her basket and, of all things, a parasol she had purloined from one of the other ladies who were ministering to the sick. She angled it as best she could to shield poor Jem from the hot sun.

The two soldiers who had assisted her in getting Jem into the cart now saluted in farewell. Juliana raised her hand, relieved her ruse had worked so well so far. She eyed the back of the Flemish driver's head speculatively. She had listened carefully as the soldiers had instructed him. Thankfully, they had been fairly vague.

'Hello. Do you speak English?' The man half-turned at her words, then shrugged. *'Français?'*

'Oui,' he indicated gruffly.

Good. In French, she instructed him to go via the Rue de Brabant, then turned back to Jem, asking him for the name of the place he had last seen Harry. 'Is it near Waterloo?'

'La Haye Sainte. It's around four miles further on, near the centre of the ridge where the battle was fought.'

The centre! Trust Harry to end up in the thick of things!

'We will be going to La Haye Sainte,' she told the driver assuredly, 'after we billet this soldier in the Rue de Brabant.' For a second, she wondered if the driver might question or challenge her. His eyes narrowed as he pondered her words. Did he care enough to make a fuss about bringing an unaccompanied lady to the field? Then he shrugged, yawned and scratched his stomach. Juliana closed her eyes briefly in relief, then began plying Jem with questions, looking for every detail that might help her find Harry.

On arriving home, she helped the driver and Sandrine lift Jem to the bedroom, while her mother clucked and fussed in the background. The driver was plied with bread, cold meat and ale, which he accepted gratefully. While he was distracted, Juliana whispered her plans to Mama, who squawked in distress, taking both her hands.

'Julie-Annie! Must you do this?' Mama looked carefully into her eyes and flinched from what she found there. 'I see you must.' She nodded, squaring her shoulders. Juliana was conscious of a feeling of relief—her mother's newfound strength made this so much easier. 'Be safe, child.' They embraced briefly, then Juliana pulled away, intent on her mission.

Juliana climbed into the cart, beside the driver, and he clicked the horse to go. An hour had passed since Jem had spoken to her—three hours, then, since Harry had been left on the field of battle. Frustrating though it was not to have been able to order a carriage to go to him *instantly*, at least her plan so far was working.

Could she really do this? Deliberately go to a battlefield, where it was rumoured forty thousand men died yesterday? Go alone, without protection, relying on the discipline of the soldiers who would be organising the burials and the removal of the wounded?

Yes. And yes. And *yes*. As Mama had said, she *must*. She could not wait in Brussels, simply hoping and praying, when perhaps Harry might be dying under a hot sun and she could save him.

Now there was nothing to do but wait and wonder, and hope, while the cart lumbered down the crowded road and the sun shone mercilessly, and birds twittered and swooped as if such events were commonplace. They passed dozens of carts, heading back to Brussels with the wounded. Ahead, another empty vehicle, off to gather another human cargo. Thankfully, the road took them through the Forest of Soignes, giving blessed temporary relief from the heat.

The village of Waterloo was thronged with soldiers. They stood in groups, or rested under trees. Those who were awake seemed light-hearted, now they knew the battle—and the war—was won. Juliana wondered if she would catch sight of the Duke of Wellington, who had won the victory, but he was nowhere to be seen.

'Ici?' asked the driver, asking if Juliana wanted to stop.

'Non,' she responded. 'La Haye Sainte.'

Her heart thumped loudly. Would the driver challenge her? He eyed her keenly for a second, then nodded. The cart lumbered on, continuing southwards on the Charleroi road. Juliana released the breath she had been holding.

A few miles further on, and with the road deteriorating, the cart abruptly stopped. 'La Haye Sainte,' said the laconic driver, indicating with his right arm a farmhouse on the ridge above. Ahead, the road had disappeared entirely beneath deep ruts. Juliana nodded. He could go no further. Already they were being approached by two soldiers, carrying a wounded man between them. They deposited him in the cart wordlessly, then turned and began to trudge back up the ridge.

They ignored Juliana completely.

'I can do this,' she muttered. Even to herself, it sounded like a vow. After retying her straw bonnet, she thanked the driver, then shuffled across and jumped lightly down from the cart. The driver began turning the cart for the journey back to Brussels with his new passengers—for more wounded men were now being carried or helped towards it. Hefting her basket, Juliana began to trudge through the mud towards the buildings.

Within just a few paces her progress had slowed. The mud was deep, clingy and greedy. The sun had created a thin hardened crust on the top, but her kid boots sank straight through with every step. It was ankle deep in places. Juliana's petticoat and her white cotton dress—which had been clean and crisp this morning—were already heavily stained with mud right along the bottom. How on earth had the army fought in this? She left the path and walked up the grassy bank alongside. Here the ground was soft, but passable.

As she walked laboriously closer to the farmhouse, she began to see the fallen. Men, horses and weapons were sprawled randomly all around. Soldiers from both sides were displayed, gruesome evidence of the causes of their deaths clear to see. And the stench! Blood, excrement and mud.

Juliana's stomach heaved as she almost stepped on a dead French soldier, his chest sliced open and his eyes staring vacantly at the blue sky above. She leaned over and lost the meagre contents of her stomach, being careful not to splash any on the dead soldier. What a strange courtesy! The man did not care now. She tried *not* to think about discovering Harry in a similar state.

She spent the next hour checking along the sunken road behind the farmhouse, a half-mile in each direction. The tall hedges and her parasol gave her some respite, but still, the heat followed her like a curse. The dead were everywhere and the living, moving among them. There were women and Allied soldiers, checking for anyone still alive, removing equipment, uniforms and other possessions that might prove useful, and moving the Allied dead to trenches for mass burial. The French bodies were being burned. One woman was applying pliers to the mouths of the dead and pocketing the bloody teeth she pulled. Juliana shuddered.

What if Harry was there, amid the dead, or buried already? The trenches were being filled in with clay and debris, new ones being dug as the old ones were populated.

She moved slowly along the road, steeling herself to look at every man lying there, every face, to miss no one, to stay until she found him. The midday sun beat down relentlessly. After an hour it began to become almost rhythmic—step, lift boots from cling-ing mud, check dead soldier.

Not Harry. Not Harry. Not Harry.

Having exhausted the road, she came back to the farm and made a systematic search there. One of the buildings had burned down, the ashes still glow-ing red and emitting a small plume of white smoke. There was a pretty garden on one side and an or-chard on the other. Juliana could see clearly how beautiful a place it had been, before yesterday. She knew from Jem's words that Harry had not fought in the farmhouse itself, but there was the possibil-ity he had been moved here afterwards.

No. He was not here.

She stopped for a moment to fill her flask with water in the farmhouse well, in the corner of the garden. The farmyard was busy with soldiers and women, and the wounded, and piles of supplies were being sorted in one corner. She asked for a second flask and was given it, so filled that, too. With a quick thanks to the woman who had given it to her, she left through the other side of the farmyard and towards the main battlefield. Cresting the ridge, and slightly out of breath, she stood still in shock.

As far as the eye could see—three miles at least—the land was a sea of reddish-brown mud. Here and there were trees and hedges that had survived the battle, but everything else had disintegrated into ochre clay. The landscape was dotted with abandoned artillery, dead horses and bodies. Her eye swept over them all, as the enormity of the task ahead sank in. How was she to possibly find him among all of this?

She squared her shoulders. Men had fought here, yesterday, and kept fighting, even when they believed they could not prevail. She could do no less.

And so she began. Forward and back along the uneven *chaussée*, using trees and hedges as landmarks, checking every single body she found. Not Harry.

Occasionally, she discovered a wounded man, still alive. British, French, Prussian—she did not care. Each time, she called for help to the others. Some, like her, seemed to be searching for someone in particular. Others, in uniform, were systematically removing the wounded to the carts. At least she was able to rescue some men, then. Someone's brother. Someone's son. Someone's love.

She was not to know that, afterwards, some of those men would speak of the Angel of the battlefield, the beauty in white who found them and called for help, and saved them.

On she walked, and on some more. She went back and forth, systematically covering every inch of ground within a half-mile of the farmhouse. She filled her flasks seven times at the farm, then left again, intent on her quest. The mud on her dress was now at knee level, she noted absently, and the basket was three times as heavy as it had been.

Her arms burned from the sun, her back, knees and feet ached, and her head pounded. Still she had not found him. At least the heat of the sun was decreasing now. She stopped, looking westwards. The sun had lowered—she guessed it must now be seven or eight o'clock in the evening. She had been searching for almost nine hours! Sighing, she made a decision. She would have to rest. Just for a few moments. Slowly, she made her way down the ridge, to sit under an oak tree that stood, silent and strong, amid the carnage.

After drinking, she closed her eyes and tried to recall every detail of what Jem had told her. It seemed likely—now she knew the area better—that he was probably in the area behind the farmhouse, where she had first searched, rather than on the main battlefield.

Of course, Jem's memory was unclear, as Harry had rescued him from being crushed by a horse. What had he said? How the horse had crushed him and Harry had been pulling him out when he had fainted from lack of air. And when he had awoken, with the battle over and confusion all around, they had pulled him away and carried him upwards to a cart without listening to his ravings about the Captain.

Juliana caught her breath. He had said it was a *bay* horse! Pessimism turned to excitement. She now knew she was looking for a large bay horse, probably behind the farmhouse and on a slight hill. Oh, why had she not remembered it before?

'Thank you, Jem!' she whispered.

With hope renewed, she ignored the protest of her sunburned arms and aching limbs. Hurrying as best she could, she moved directly towards the farmhouse, scanning all around for dead horses with bay colouring.

The first three proved fruitless—no one lying anywhere near—but then—

She knew, as soon as she saw it, that this was the one. The horse lay stiffly on an incline, its limbs half-submerged in the clinging mud and its position such that her eye had passed over it earlier. Now that she knew what she was looking for, she saw there was a small area of ground *behind* the horse where she definitely hadn't searched before. It was entirely possible for someone to be lying there, hidden from view.

She raced up the incline as fast as the mud would

allow, her heart racing with mingled fear and excitement.

And there he was. Lying on his back, one hand resting on his chest. His face and head were covered with blood and dirt, and she could not tell by looking if he was alive. She sank down beside him and gently touched his face.

'Harry!'

Chapter Twenty-Three

So this is death. Thus far it is remarkably easy. The pain is gone, but his mind is awhirl with random thoughts, images and memories. He swoops through the sky of his mind like a swallow in flight, whirling and dipping through the space. Suddenly, though, his focus becomes clearer. He sees a flash of blue and follows it, darting like an arrow towards the scene. He lands, settles and looks around.

The dusty street in Badajoz looks the same, except this time it is empty of people, blood and horror. A door stands open to his right and the woman is there, wearing the same blue dress she wore on the day she died. She looks at the kitchen knife in her hand. It glints silver and clean in the sunlight. She looks at it, then places it on the sill.

'Fabián Galdós de Marcos!' she calls to someone in the house behind her. 'Come outside! He is here!'

She's speaking Spanish, Harry thinks, *and yet I understand every word.*

The boy is there, smiling shyly at Harry. Without looking, he reaches up to his mama and she takes his hand. 'Fabián, tell him,' she urges the child softly.

'It was not your fault,' says the boy, looking at him with clear eyes and healthy, glowing skin. 'You are not to blame.'

His mama nods. 'You did all you could, soldier. You are absolved.' She moves her hand like a blade, moving downwards, then up and across in the shape of a cross. 'Ego te absolvo a peccatis tuis in nomine Patris, et Filii, et Spiritus Sancti.'

Latin, thinks Harry. As she says the words he feels a lightness coming over him and a peace such as he has never known. Fabián and his mama smile.

'Your soldiering days are done now,' she says. 'You have another calling.'

'Harry!'

The voice is familiar. He looks around in confusion. No one is there.

'Harry! Come back!'

It is compelling. He has to follow. Badajoz fades, though he senses its eternal peace within him. He moves towards the voice...

'Harry! Oh, Harry, please wake up! Please come back!' Juliana raised her head from his chest, overcome. His heart was beating! Her voice cracked as she searched his face for any sign that he could hear her. There was a bad-looking wound on his head, but, apart from that, he seemed intact. She had swept his arms and legs with gentle hands, and checked his torso for any signs of a wound. Nothing. Just the injury to his head. She gently ran her hand over his ribs, seeking unseen injuries. She paused as her hand sensed something strange on his chest—a small lump on his breastbone. What on earth was it? Could it be a break in the bone? If so, it could be serious—his heart or lungs could be damaged. Quickly she loosened his clothing, and separated his shirt to view the injury better. Scanning down his smooth skin, she caught her breath.

It wasn't an injury. It was a small leather pouch, suspended round his neck by a thin leather strip. With shaking hands, she carefully opened it. Inside was a glossy dark curl, gleaming in the sunlight as it had the day he cut it from her head.

'Oh, Harry,' she cried. She could almost *feel* her heart breaking. 'Please live. Please.'

Carefully replacing the lock of hair, she looked more carefully at the deep gash to the side of his head. She could see the bone of his skull beneath, though, thankfully, the bone itself looked unbroken. It was still frightening. Since arriving back in

Brussels, she had seen too many soldiers die after innocuous-looking wounds to the head. The longer they slept the worse it tended to be. And Harry had been passed out for a full day. Was this to be Harry's fate? Against almost impossible odds, she had found him and he was alive. Was he now to be lost to her after all?

What could she do for him? Taking a flask from her basket, she dribbled a little water into his mouth. Nothing. No response. She wiped the spilled water away from his lips, noting as she did so that his face was covered in blood, mud and soot. She spilled some of the precious water on to a clean handkerchief and gently sponged the blood and grime from his beloved face. There! Now he looked like himself again—although his face was badly sunburned.

She rested back on her heels. In a moment she would call for help and they would come and carry him to a wagon, and she would bring him home. For now, she just wanted to try, one last time, to see if she could awaken him. Moving carefully, she lay down beside him. Lifting his left arm away from his body, she snuggled close and rested her head on his shoulder, her left hand over his heart. She stayed like that for a few minutes, lying with him under a paling evening sky, the dead of Waterloo all around.

'Harry!' she pleaded softly. 'Come back!'

Then, the miracle. His arm closed around her and he moved his head a little. She immediately raised herself up—just in time to see his eyes open.

'Harry!' she whispered. Her mind could not produce any other words in that moment.

He looked at her hazily. 'Juliana?' His voice was hoarse.

She laughed, joy filling her. 'Yes! All is well.'

'I know.' His grip tightened and he murmured her name again, reverently. She could wait no longer, but pressed her lips gently to his. He responded and they kissed slowly and gently. Her eyelashes fluttered closed as she savoured the feeling of his warm lips beneath hers. She had wondered if she would ever again feel this sensation.

After a long moment, she sat back, to see him better. His eyes softened with love as they locked gazes. She should say something, she knew. He would probably be wondering how bad his injuries were. She had comforted men earlier today who had awoken to find that a limb had been amputated, or that they had lost an eye.

'You are injured, but you are going to be well.' Her voice trembled. 'You have all your limbs and—it seems—your faculties.'

They grinned foolishly at each other. Then, as if thinking of it for the first time, he muttered, 'Where the devil am I? And—ouch! What the deuce happened to my head?' He winced slightly as his fingers found the wound. She grimaced in sympathy, but he eyed her roguishly. 'Did you hit me with a spade again?'

Now she did laugh and he joined her. All truly was well.

Harry's recovery was rapid. The wound healed cleanly, though the scar was deep. Luckily, he suffered no fever and his mind had been unaffected by the blow to the head. Under Juliana's tender ministrations and with regular visits from Dr Hume, he was cosseted, fed and cared for, until, after two weeks, he declared he could stand no more of it and demanded his clothes.

Her mother would have argued, but Juliana, seeing how he chafed for his freedom, agreed to it. She asked Peter—the new manservant they'd employed to help look after Harry and Jem—to bring Harry's uniform, which had of course been washed and pressed. Jem, watching forlornly from the bed, asked if he might be allowed to get up, too, but this was met with a firm denial from Mrs Milford.

'Now, Jem, you know the doctor said you are to put no weight on that leg for another three weeks!

Do you want to set back your recovery?' she demanded, hands on hips.

'No, of course not, Mrs Milford.' Jem subsided, chastened, but Harry leaned over the bed to gently cuff his friend's shoulder.

'Never fear, Jem, I am not abandoning you. I will return later for today's chess game. Now, ladies, if you will excuse me, I shall contrive to don my uniform!'

Juliana, smiling at Harry's evident glee, was last to leave. She met Harry's gaze and smiled at his mischievous wink in her direction. She was glad he was so well recovered and, she admitted, surprised they'd managed to keep him from leaving the bedroom before now.

Jem had been a great help, she knew, as the two soldiers had entertained each other for much of the time, with chess and cards, and light-hearted conversation. At times, they had talked of more important issues, too—she had twice joined them when they were recalling aspects of the battle. Harry was gently helping Jem make sense of it all, she thought. She was pleased they had trusted her enough to keep talking when she entered and she had sat quietly, listening to the careful way they were exploring the subject.

Having them both in the same room had been a

godsend. Harry had insisted on sleeping on the pallet, though Jem had wanted to give up his comfortable bed to his Captain. 'No, lad,' Harry had said firmly, 'you need it for that leg of yours.'

Major Cooke had visited, before he left for Paris. 'You are both on leave, indefinitely,' he had instructed, after enquiring after their health and praising them both for their efforts in battle.

Harry had asked to speak to him privately, if possible, but, since the doctor had forbidden him from leaving his bed, the best they could contrive was for Juliana to engage in conversation with Jem, while the Major had lowered himself to sit by Harry's pallet, where they had conversed in low tones.

Juliana couldn't help overhearing expressions of surprise from the Major, and, as he left, he had begged Harry to 'reconsider'.

Reconsider what? she wondered. A worrying idea had soon come to her.

She and Harry had, naturally, not had the opportunity for private conversation since he had been helped from the battlefield by two burly infantrymen, but she would never forget the journey back to Brussels, his head warm and heavy in her lap, and his hand in hers. After a while, they both realised that one hand was not enough and he had raised his other hand so she could hold that, too.

Since then, they had communicated constantly using their eyes, and smiles, and as much touch as they could manage in company. This included Juliana straightening Harry's pillows very frequently and checking his wound a lot, and, on occasion, some blatant hand-holding. Her mother and Jem had indulged them, although Jem was once heard to wonder plaintively why no one ever fixed *his* pillows. At this, Juliana blushed furiously while Harry threw a pillow at him, laughing.

Juliana was once more secure in Harry's love for her and misunderstandings were, she hoped, at an end. But she could not forget that, on the night before the battle, at the ball, he had told her that he could not marry her. He had said it was due to his own cowardice, but Juliana had seen no signs of self-loathing in him since Waterloo. She knew, though, more than most people, that Harry was a master at hiding his true feelings when he wished to.

She longed to be his wife—to call him 'Husband' and share his bed and his life. But, until he declared himself, she could not know if that would ever happen. And now she had a new worry. What if Harry had told Major Cooke that he intended to marry her and Major Cooke had advised against it?

Living in Brussels, in the aftermath of the greatest battle ever fought, it was easy to forget society's rules. She was not a suitable wife for one who was brother to an earl and a rising star in the Army. That had not changed, no matter how much harmony now existed between her and Harry. He had tried to dismiss her fears, that night at the ball on the eve of battle, but now they had returned in full force.

She was excited that he was up and about, for it would hopefully allow them more opportunities for private speech. However, it also brought closer the time when he would, necessarily, leave them. If he was well enough to be up and about, he would soon move to a hotel or rented lodgings, and from there he would travel to Paris with the Army or home to England.

She hurried to her room and called Sandrine. For some reason, she wished to change her dress, now Harry was up. Sandrine helped her don her new gown—a beautiful muslin in a warm lemon, which seemed to make her skin glow with health. She was unaware that happiness was shining out of her and adding to her natural beauty. Sandrine complimented her as she tidied her hair, but Juliana could not listen properly. She knew only that Harry would admire her in this dress and with her hair well dressed and glossy. She almost skipped her way to the parlour.

He was already there, conversing with her mama, and looking stunning in his regimentals. His handsome face was still slightly tanned from the sunburn of Waterloo, though it had faded significantly during his time indoors. He looked up when she entered, with a gaze of such warmth that her breath caught in her throat.

'Well!' murmured Mama, with a twinkle. 'I find myself definitely *de trop*, so I shall go and speak to Jem.' She nodded significantly at Harry, who gave her a speaking look in return. What was this? What had they been discussing?

She was soon to find out. As soon as the door closed behind Mama, Harry turned to her and enfolded her in his arms, and they kissed with all the ferocity of the forced abstinence of the past weeks.

Eventually, they paused for breath. Juliana was seated in his lap—a novel and not unpleasant experience—but, disappointingly, he lifted her and placed her beside him on the sofa.

'No,' he said firmly when she protested, 'I understand, my love. Believe me, I feel the same frustration, but I must speak with you, and I cannot do that when your…er…anatomy is pressing on my lap.'

She gurgled at his description and blushed at the same time.

'Very well.' She folded her hands together in her lap and adopted a demure expression. He groaned and she looked at him innocently. 'What?'

With a visible effort, he restrained himself from embracing her again. His demeanour grew serious.

'When I spoke to you before the battle, I told you I could not marry you. That you deserved better than a weak coward for a husband.'

'And I told you,' she interrupted, 'it was not *your* choice.'

He shook his head. 'It was amazing to me then, and is still impossible for me to understand, why you should be so strong, so brave and so dashed *stubborn* to want to take me regardless!'

'You know already I am stubborn,' she said pertly. 'Occasionally that will work to your advantage.' He looked startled, then threw his head back and laughed.

'You are a diamond!' he declared. 'A rare find—and I know you will test me.'

'We shall test each other,' she agreed, 'when we are married.'

His eyes narrowed. 'It is customary,' he drawled, 'for a lady to *wait* for a proposal from a gentleman.'

'Well, do get on with it, then! For I have been waiting since Waterloo!'

He smiled at the twinkle in her eyes, then stood. What was he about? Her heart missed a beat when he knelt before her, his demeanour intent.

'Juliana.' He took her hands in his and his eyes locked with hers. 'I have been a coward, a deceiver and a weakling. In my foolishness, I have hurt you. I have little to offer you, save a heart filled with love for you. It seems impossible to think that you might have me, but I will ask nevertheless. Will you marry me?'

'Gladly! With all my heart!'

His eyes blazed, reflecting the fire in her own soul. They did not kiss—the moment was too intense even for kissing—but instead they clasped each other close, revelling in the sensation of two heartbeats and a shared future. After a long moment they separated enough to look, and smile, then, finally, to enjoy a long, slow kiss.

'I love you, Juliana.' It sounded like a vow.

'And I love you, Harry.'

Finally, she thought, *things are how they should be. Finally.*

Chapter Twenty-Four

They talked then of his dream at Waterloo, and how he felt healed of the wound to his spirit he had carried since Badajoz. Juliana had never felt closer to him than she did in that moment.

After a while she knew she must speak. She had to know if he was sure about the wisdom of marrying her. 'Harry, there is something I must ask you.'

He brushed a tendril of hair away from her face, and followed it with a feather-light kiss on her cheek. Resisting the urge to touch the spot where his lips had rested, she instead steeled herself to ask about the thing that was worrying her.

'Did Major Cooke caution you against marrying me?'

'No! Of course not! Why would you even think such a thing?'

She explained what she had overheard. He frowned. 'Yes, I do need to tell you about that conversation. You should know everything, before you finally decide if you will have me.'

'But I have already decided!'

'You may change your mind when you have heard this.'

'Harry, I cannot imagine anything that would make me change my mind. You should trust me, you really should.'

He took a breath. 'I am resigning from the Army.'

'What—but why?' She struggled to take it in. 'I thought you loved being a soldier. And now you have laid the Badajoz demons to rest—'

'That is exactly the point. In my dream, there was a part where the woman told me I have "another calling". I've known since I woke up on the battlefield what it is.' He gripped her hands again. 'I am meant to be your husband. *That* is my calling. I am no longer a soldier. That ended at Waterloo. I am glad I played my part, but that part of my life is done. I am at peace with all of it.'

She nodded her head slowly. *Yes.* She understood.

'So, will you mourn not being a soldier's wife? You have the stomach for it—not too many gently bred ladies could do what you did and brave the battlefield.'

'I *had* to do it. I had no choice in the matter. I was

never going to leave it to chance whether you were found or not.'

He nodded grimly. 'Now I have recovered it would be easy to forget the danger I was in. It was your voice that called me back. Who knows what might have happened if you had not come?'

She reached out and stroked his face. 'I am just grateful to have you back with me. And I care not whether you are a soldier, or follow some other profession. Being together is all that matters.'

He was insistent. 'People will no longer speak of Captain Fanton, but instead you will have to settle for plain The Honourable Harry Fanton. I do hope he is enough for you.'

This time, she did not reply with words, but pulled him towards her and offered the reassurance of a passionate kiss.

Chapter Twenty-Five

'Not far now.' Her mother had an air of suppressed excitement. Juliana had been aware of it for the past few days—ever since they had arrived back in London—but it seemed to be more pronounced this morning. She had been receiving messages and letters over the past few days that she would tell no one about, and now this mysterious outing!

Mama looked out of the carriage window and Juliana took the opportunity to glance across at Harry, who was seated opposite. He shrugged slightly; he had no idea either. Her gaze lingered. She was now accustomed to seeing him out of uniform and instead clad in the tailored coats and tight-fitting breeches that society favoured; they certainly showed his form to advantage. Catching the direction of her gaze, he returned her look with one full of promise. Juliana squirmed slightly in her seat.

Outside, the streets of London were familiar to

her, yet so different from Brussels. They had arrived on Saturday and everyone in the Fanton household had been delirious with happiness at Juliana and Harry's news.

'So, in the end, we are sisters!' laughed Charlotte, hugging Juliana tightly. Juliana's happiness was complete.

'Here we are!' The carriage stopped outside a non-descript building in Coleman Street—the sort of place where a lawyer or banker might have his offices. They all alighted from the Fanton carriage and Harry directed Joseph to walk the horses while they went inside.

Sure enough, the legend outside the door pronounced it to be the place of business of Messrs Mason, Mason and Lowen, Solicitors. Mama had insisted that Juliana and Harry accompany her today. It made a little more sense now. Perhaps she wanted them to advise her on a matter of business.

'Good morning!' A cheerful clerk welcomed them and took them directly through to an inner chamber. 'Mr Mason the Younger is expecting you.'

The younger Mr Mason turned out to be a soberly clad gentleman in his late sixties, with white hair, a lined, amiable face and an air of elderly distraction. He was small and slight, and looked vaguely familiar. Juliana, with a humorous look at Harry, assumed the elder Mr Mason was no longer active in the business. The lawyer welcomed them stiffly and bade them take a seat.

'What on earth are *they* doing here?'

Juliana turned towards the voice. There, in all her vulgar glory, was Mrs Wakely. She wore a garish satin gown in an unbecoming shade of puce, topped with a straw hat crowned with three large feathers and a still life of improbable fruit. Her lips and cheeks were rouged and her mouth was open in an expression of outrage.

Her husband sat beside her, as thin and weasel-like as ever, his quizzing glass raised to study them, as if trying to verify that his eyes were not deceiving him.

'Yes, indeed—this is a private meeting! We did not invite these people and they have no right to be here!' He was white with anger.

Juliana did not know quite what to make of it. Taking her cue from her mama, who had taken a seat seemingly unperturbed, Juliana also sat down. Harry pulled a chair up and sat beside her.

The Younger Mr Mason seated himself in a large leather chair behind his desk. Taking a set of eye-glasses from his pocket, he balanced them on his nose, then carefully slid a set of papers towards him.

Juliana watched him, fascinated. Seemingly satisfied, he raised his head and addressed them all. 'Thank you for attending. I have invited you here today to settle the matter of the disposal of the estate of Clarence Milford, Baron Cowlam, including the house and lands in Surrey known as Glenbrook Hall, as well as assets valued at eighty thousand pounds and an income of approximately six thousand pounds per year.'

Juliana's jaw dropped. What? *Milford?* Lord Cowlam was a Milford?

Suddenly it all made sense. Her grandfather's cryptic comments. Her father, John Milford, must have been related to the Baron! Did that mean Mama was entitled to something? But—her thoughts faltered. Her parents had never married, so there could be no legal claim on anything. She stole a glance at her mama, who looked composed.

The lawyer continued. 'There was one known claimant, Mrs Wakely, but there was also information that the Baron's son had eloped in his youth, with a general's daughter, and sired a child.'

Juliana and Harry exchanged glances. Mama remained expressionless.

'On April the twelfth this year I received a letter from a Mrs Campbell, who is the housekeeper at Glenbrook Hall.'

There were gasps from the Wakelys. 'Mrs Campbell!' spluttered Mrs Wakely. 'If she has betrayed us, she shall be our housekeeper no longer.'

The lawyer continued, inexorably. 'She raised the question that the rumours of John Milford fathering a child might be true and that that child might be Miss Milford.' He nodded at Juliana.

Mama spoke up. 'My daughter is now Mrs Fanton.'

Mr Mason looked at Harry keenly. 'A recent event, I take it?'

'We were married in Brussels last week,' confirmed Harry. Juliana felt a distinct tingle as he said the words and threw him an impish look. It was still such a thrill to know they were actually married!

'Hrrmmph!' opined the lawyer, dismissing this news as being of no consequence. 'Following discreet enquiries, I was able to establish that Mrs Milford was likely the daughter of General Hunter.'

Harry and Juliana exchanged glances—*the bank*! The younger Mr Mason must have also paid the informant for details of General Hunter's financial affairs!

The lawyer continued, his voice sure and calm. 'I therefore contacted Mrs Milford—'

'She is not entitled to use that name!' snarled Mr Wakely. 'Why, she was nothing more than Jack Milford's ladybird!'

Harry was out of his seat and leaning into Mr Wakely's face in an instant. 'You will keep a civil tongue in your head, or you will answer to me!' he enunciated menacingly. Wakely shrank back. 'Now—apologise to Mrs Milford!'

Sullenly, Mr Wakely mumbled an insincere apology. Mama serenely waved a hand, as if the Wakelys barely intruded on her consciousness.

Quite as if the interruption had not occurred, the lawyer continued. 'I contacted Mrs Milford, who informed me that John Milford, known as Jack, only son of Lord Cowlam, was indeed the father of her child—' he indicated Juliana '—Mrs Fanton.'

Mr Wakely intervened. 'We are willing to accept this possibility, given that...er... Mrs Fanton looks extremely like her—like John Milford. However, that means nothing, since she was simply his byblow— Er... I mean she was his base-born sideslip, as it were.'

Juliana closed her eyes in anguish. *The shame!* Harry stirred beside her and she felt her hand enveloped in his large, reassuring one. She squeezed his hand gratefully. She knew he did not care that she was illegitimate, but it was still hurtful to be described using such distressing language.

'So you acknowledge that Mrs Fanton is John Milford's natural daughter?' The lawyer looked intently at Mr Wakely, whose eyes narrowed.

'We acknowledge nothing! Hush, my love.' Mrs Wakely subsided. 'However, we are generous people.' He sent a sickly smile in Juliana's direction. 'We would be willing to gift a small sum on Mrs Fanton—say, a thousand pounds—as a full settlement against any claims she might make against the estate.'

Juliana was outraged. 'I thank you, but I have no need of a gift from you!' How dared he!

'I then considered,' uttered the lawyer, evenly, 'the question of a marriage between John Milford and Mrs Milford.'

'Stop calling her that!' muttered Mrs Wakely, unable to hold her tongue.

He continued as if she had not spoken. 'With Mrs Campbell, I visited Mrs Milford in the Fanton town house on the twenty-fourth of April. With Mrs Campbell's assistance, I confirmed her identity as Elizabeth Hunter—the woman who was believed to have eloped with John Milford in 1793.'

Juliana tightened her grip on Harry's hand. *Poor Mama!*

'Mrs Milford confirmed that, although John Milford had attempted to arrange a church wedding before leaving England, this had proved impossible.

They therefore travelled to Brussels, where he again attempted to marry Mrs Milford.'

Juliana sat up straighter. She had not known this!

'Mrs Milford informed me that, due to the actions of the French Republic in banning church weddings by non-juror priests, the couple had had to settle for a civil wedding in the Town Hall at Brussels.'

Juliana's mother turned to her. 'John always said we would be married properly, in a church, when he returned. But he died before we could organise it. I never felt truly married, because we had not made our vows before God.'

The lawyer continued, smoothly. 'That's as may be. But I am concerned about matters of law, not matters of religious faith.'

Harry, quick to the mark, saw the logic. 'So are you saying the marriage was legally valid?'

The lawyer nodded. 'I am, if it can be proved that such a marriage took place.'

Harry looked as astounded as Juliana felt.

The Wakelys exploded in an inarticulate protest, the gist of which was that a heathen foreign marriage could not possibly be held to be a true legal marriage and it was all a hum, and a plot to steal their inheritance. Mr Mason quieted them by raising a hand and enunciating clearly, 'That is the law. You may seek the counsel of a hundred lawyers and they will all say the same. But—' he eyed Mrs Milford keenly '—I have not yet had proof that this marriage took place.'

Mama opened her reticule and withdrew three documents, which she silently handed to the lawyer.

The room was silent as he perused their contents. Juliana, her mind whirling, could barely take it in.

'That is a copy of the marriage entry in the municipal register, as well as two certificates of authentication,' stated Mama. 'I travelled to Brussels before the battle in order to get these documents.' Her voice was soft, but determined. 'Not for myself, you understand. For my daughter.' She turned to Juliana. 'I could not tell you before, until I had the proof. My love, you are not illegitimate. The papers prove it. I wish we had been able to marry in a church, but it was not to be. Until Mr Mason explained the validity of a *legal* marriage—even if it did not take place in a church—I had no idea there was no stain on either of our reputations. However, until I had this proof, I could not challenge those who doubted me—including my own father.' She smiled mischievously. 'I shall look forward to telling him about this!'

Juliana shook her head slowly. So much was now clear. Mama's behaviour, her sudden transformation from timid mouse to fearless avenger, her insistence that they travel back to Brussels on the eve of war...

'What does this mean, eh?' Mr Wakely looked grey. Juliana almost felt sorry for him.

Mr Mason was unperturbed. 'As I made clear from the beginning of this process, there was no guarantee Mrs Wakely would turn out to be the true heir. Indeed, I specifically cautioned you both against living on the expectation. You have been provided with a home and a generous allowance for almost a year.' He glanced down at the documents relating to the Milfords' marriage. 'If these documents are authentic—which, on first reading, they seem to be—then Mrs Fanton, John Milford's daughter, will be confirmed as the heir.'

Mrs Wakely made a high-pitched keening noise. Mr Mason cleared his throat, then continued, a little more loudly. 'Mrs Fanton might choose to be generous and gift a small sum on Mrs Wakely—say, a thousand pounds?'

Epilogue

With a sigh, Juliana relaxed against Harry. She could feel the warmth of his chest against her back, skin on warm skin, and now his arms were closing around her, cuddling her securely. She adjusted the soft blanket that covered them both, then rested her arms over his. He nuzzled her hair, then planted a gentle kiss on the top of her head.

Juliana smiled. She had never known such happiness was possible.

They had just left their rumpled bed and moved this *chaise-longue* to the window bay of their bedroom at Glenbrook Hall, as the low window would allow them an unfettered view of the stars on this clear autumn night. They had blown out the candles and the only light now was the starlight gleaming through the window.

They had retired hours ago, as was their habit. As master and mistress, they were free to keep their own hours, and as newlyweds still, no one could be surprised at it. This was their pattern when they could—retire early, then spend hours awake, enjoying each other's company.

They had both settled into their new life at Glenbrook Hall as if it had been meant for them—which Harry insisted it was. Mrs Campbell and the estate steward both adored their new mistress and master.

'And why should they not,' asked Juliana, 'when we have replaced the Wakelys?'

Harry was no longer troubled by visions of Badajoz, and his demeanour since Waterloo was markedly different. Gone was the shallow flirt—he barely noticed young ladies now and was unfailingly and indiscriminately polite to females of all ages and dispositions. His mischievous character remained intact, however, and he mercilessly teased his bride as they both went about the business of adapting to their new and unexpected roles—Gentleman Farmer and Lady of Glenbrook.

Juliana had taken up fencing again and was becoming ever more proficient under Harry's tutelage. She was completely unafraid and resolved to become an expert fencer. He drove her as if she was under his command as Captain, and she responded with determination and dedication.

Harry had not taken up embroidery.

Tonight, her husband was in a tender mood. As Juliana gazed at the skies, he murmured in her ear all the love that was in him. Moved, she turned to face him and they kissed, long and slow.

'Harry!' She sighed. 'It seems incredible still that we are here together, man and wife, and that you can say such things to me!'

He was tracing with his finger a small cluster of freckles on her arm. Briefly, he leaned forward and kissed them, each freckle in turn. 'A constellation,' he murmured, 'just as beautiful as those above us.'

'You really do love me, don't you?' she said stupidly. It was evident in every word and gesture, and her heart swelled with it.

For answer, he gestured at the glimmering stars outside—thousands of individual points of light creating a tapestry of wonder. 'You see these stars. How long have they shone in the heavens?'

She shook her head. 'I don't know.'

'And how long will they shine into the future?'

'I don't know. A long, long time.'

He looked intently into her eyes, his glittering darkly in the starlight. 'I will still love you when they are gone.'

And as she leaned forward to kiss him, Juliana knew. She had found her home.

* * * * *

LET'S TALK

Romance

For exclusive extracts, competitions
and special offers, find us online:

f facebook.com/millsandboon

⊙ @millsandboonuk

𝕏 @millsandboon

Or get in touch on 0844 844 1351*

For all the latest titles coming soon,
visit millsandboon.co.uk/nextmonth

Want even more
ROMANCE?

Join our bookclub today!

Visit millsandbook.co.uk/Bookclub and save on brand new books.

MILLS & BOON